Blessings

Blessings

A NOVEL

Anna Quindlen

RANDOM HOUSE

NEW YORK

Grateful acknowledgment is made to Simon and Schuster, Inc., for
permission to reprint "There Will Be Stars" from *The Collected Poems of
Sara Teasdale*. Copyright © 1926 by The Macmillan Company.
Copyright renewed 1954 by Mamie T. Wheless. Reprinted by
permission of Simon and Schuster, Inc.

Library of Congress Cataloging-in-Publication Data
Quindlen, Anna.
Blessings : a novel / Anna Quindlen
p. cm.
ISBN 0-375-50223-8 (alk. paper)
1. Foundlings—Fiction. 2. Administration of estates—Fiction.
3. Women landowners—Fiction. I. Title.
PS3567.U336 B59 2002
813'.54—dc21   2002024802

Random House website address: www.atrandom.com

Printed in the United States of America on acid-free paper

24689753

FIRST EDITION

Book design by Carole Lowenstein

For Christopher Krovatin, the dreamer.
Who taught me to laugh constantly, love unconditionally,
and live without fear.

There will be stars over the place forever;
Though the house we loved and the street we loved are lost,
Every time the earth circles her orbit
On the night the autumn equinox is crossed,
Two stars we knew, poised on the peak of midnight
Will reach their zenith; stillness will be deep;
There will be stars over the place forever,
There will be stars forever, while we sleep.

—SARA TEASDALE

Blessings

I n the early hours of June 24 a car pulled into a long macadam drive on Rolling Hills Road in the town of Mount Mason. The driver cut the engine, so that as the car rolled down the drive and into the oval turnaround between the back of the big white clapboard house and the garage, it made only a soft swishing sound, like the whisper of summer rain those first few moments after the dirty gray storm clouds open.

There were deer in the fields that surrounded the house, cropping the rye grass with their spotted fawns at their flanks. But the fields stretched so far from the drive on either side, and the deer kept so close to the tree line, that the does did not even raise their divot heads from the ground as the car slid past, although one or two stopped chewing, and the smallest of the babies edged toward their mothers, stepping delicately sideways, en pointe on their small hooves.

"I don't feel that good," said the young woman in the passenger seat, her hair veiling her face.

The moonlight slipping at an oblique angle through the windows and the windshield of the car picked out what there was of her to be seen: a suggestion of the whites of her eyes between the curtains of her hair, the beads of sweat on her arched upper lip, the silver chain around her neck, the chipped maroon polish on her nails—a jigsaw puzzle of a girl, half the pieces not visible. She was turned away from the driver, turned toward the door as though she were a prisoner in the car and, at any moment, might pull the door handle and tumble out. The fingers of one hand played with her full bottom lip as she stared at the black shadows of the trees on the rough silver of the lawns, silhouettes cut from construction paper. At the edge of the drive, halfway down it, was a small sign, black on white. BLESSINGS, it said.

Blessings was one of those few places that visitors always found, on their return, even more pleasing than the pleasant memories they had of it. The house sat, big and white, low and sprawling, in a valley of overgrown fields, its terrace gardens spilling white hydrangeas, blue bee balm, and bushy patches of catnip and lavender onto a flagstone patio that ran its length. The land surrounding it was flat and rich for a long ways, to the end of the drive, and then the stony mountains rose around as though to protect it, a great God-sized berm spiky with pine trees.

The house had a squat and stolid quality, as though it had lain down to rest in the valley and grown middle-aged. Ill-advised additions had been made, according to the fashion of the times: a den paneled in rustic pine, a long screened porch, some dormers scattered above the horizontal roof line like eyes peering down the drive. The weeping willows at one end of the pond dipped low, but the cedars at the other were too tall and rangy for grace, and there had been sporadic talk of cutting them down almost from the day they were planted. The gardens were of the most conventional sort, hollyhocks in the back, day lilies in the center, alyssum along the borders. Wild rhododendrons grew in the shade wherever a stream sprang from the ground to spill down the hillside and into the big pond, a lake almost, that lay along one side of the house. None of it amounted to much on its own.

But taken altogether it was something almost perfect, the sort of place that, from the road, which was how these two had first seen it, promised plenty without pretense, ease without arrogance. From the road Blessings looked like a place where people would sit on the terrace at dusk, sip a drink and exult in the night breeze over the mountain, pull a light cardigan around their shoulders, and go to bed content. At one time or another, in fact all of these things had been true, but not for some time.

In the fashion of the young, the two in the car, peering down the drive some months before, had convinced themselves that appearance was reality. For the girl, it was the awnings that had finally convinced her, faded green and gold stripes over each window, like proud flags of this little nation-state, where it had been arranged that the sun would never fade the upholstery. That, and a small boat to one side of the pond, in which it was not only possible but indubitable that children could sit safely, row handily, put out a fishing line. In the light from a thumbnail moon the boat, upended on the grass, shone as though a smaller moon had dropped down to earth. The girl saw the sign by the side of the drive in the car's headlights as a benediction, not as a sign of ownership, the proud name of an old family at the end of its bloodline.

The pond made the car's driver nervous. It was shiny bright as a mirror, every star, every constellation, even the path of planes, reflecting back within its dark water and seemingly magnified by the pitch black of the night and the stillness of its surface. Frogs called from its banks, and as the car rolled silently into the circular driveway turnaround a fish jumped and left circles on the surface of the water. At the same moment the car tripped the automatic light at the corner of the house's long porch, and it lit up the drive and the water and the bats that flew crazy eights in search of mosquitoes. The light caught the car itself squarely, so that the two people in the front seat, a boy and girl, each poised between the raw uncertain beauty of adolescence and the duller settled contours of adulthood, were illuminated momentarily as though by the flash from a camera. Their light hair shone, enough alike that at first glance they could have passed for siblings.

"Oh, shit," said the driver, stepping down hard on the brake, so that the car bucked.

"Don't do that," cried the girl. Her hand touched a cardboard box on the backseat, then her own forehead, then dropped to her lap. "I'd kill for a cigarette," she murmured.

"Right," whispered the boy harshly. "So you could have an asthma attack right here and wake everybody up."

"That's not why I'm not smoking," the girl muttered.

"Let's just get this over with," he said.

The car glided to the corner of the big garage, with its five bays. There was a narrow door on one side of the oblong building, and three flagstone steps leading to it. The boy had oiled the doors of the car that morning, with a foresight and industry and stealth the girl had not expected of him. They had both surprised each other and themselves in the last two days, he with his hardness and his determination, she with her weakness and her grief. Anyone familiar with the love affairs between men and women could have told them that theirs would soon be over.

As he slid out and opened the back door there was almost no sound, only the sort of clicks and snaps that could have been a moth hitting a screen or a raccoon stepping on a stick in the woods that stretched behind the garage and into the black of the mountains and the night. The girl was huddled against the door on her side now, all folded in upon herself like an old woman, or like a child who'd fallen asleep on a long journey; she heard the sounds of him as though they were musical notes, each distinct and clear, and her shoulders moved slightly beneath her shirt, and her hands were jammed between her knees. She felt as though they were somehow alone in the world, almost as though the house and its surroundings were a kind of island, floating in a deep sea of ordinary life through which the two of them would have to swim back to shore by driving back up the drive.

She thought this feeling was because of the boy, and the box, and the night, and the ache in her slack belly and her bruised groin, and the pain in her chest that might have been the beginning of an asthma attack. But she was only the latest in a long line of people who had felt that Blessings was somehow a place apart. In the moonlight the high points of it, the faint luster of the slate roof of the house, the shed on the knoll where the gardener had always kept his tools, the small white boathouse at one end of the pond: all of them were set in high sepia relief like the photograph hung carelessly now on the short wall of the library, the one of

Edwin Blessing, who bought the place when it was just another old farm and lavished money on it in the years when he had money to spend. The people from Mount Mason who worked there, washing up at the parties in the old days, fixing frozen pipes for the old lady in the years after the parties ended: they all said it was like going somewhere out of this world, the quiet, the clean smells, the rooms and rooms full of polished furniture and toile draperies, which they only glimpsed through half-open doorways. Above all the pond, the gardens, the land. The real world tried to intrude from time to time upon Blessings, but usually the real world failed.

Even Lydia Blessing, the last of the Blessings, had once said as a girl that when she left the city and went out to the house for the holidays she felt as though she were in the kind of snow globe that all the girls in her class at the Bertram School were given one Christmas, the Christmas before the crash, when she had just turned seven. She felt that God was holding her in his hand, look- ing through the orb of glass at the blue spruce by the barn, the path around the pond, the pillars on the front porch, the swampy bog in the far field where the turtles lay their eggs and the cat- tails rose. It was hard to believe that God could concern himself with anyone in the city, with all of them hidden in the hives of their apartment buildings and narrow limestone houses. But at the country place she stood on the great lawn between the house and the road and raised her face up to the lambent blue and felt certain that the air was transparent down to the patch of ground on which she stood, and that she was watched, and watched closely and well.

"I don't know where you come up with these things," her mother had said, working on a large piece of floral gros point in the failing light of the living room fire. But her father had smoothed his hair and said, "I get your point, Lyds, my love." That had been the year when he was drawing up plans for the apple or- chard, when he could be heard at every dinner party at their house in the city referring to "our old farm," his light high drawl rising up the circular stairwell like pipe smoke.

"Why do you think Papa is so nice and Mama is so mean?" she had asked her brother, Sunny, once, when they were in the boat in the center of the pond, where you could say secrets and no one would hear.

"That is a question for the ages," Sunny had said. Confucius, they called him at school when they studied the religions of antiquity with the chaplain in the third form.

The only way Lydia Blessing could remember the child she had once been was to look at photo albums, and even then she seemed strange to herself, incredible that the seeds of her old age had been germinating within that pink inflated flesh. When she used the mirror every day to fix her silver hair in one of the three pinned-up styles she used, when she rubbed cold cream briskly on the fine skin that had been shirred around the eyes and lips for decades, she was occasionally incredulous, not about the fact that she had gotten old, but about the notion that she had ever been young. There was no longer any thought of snow globes, or the hand of God. The gros point had been made into a pillow; it sat on the chair in the back guest bedroom, the one she had used for house parties only if the house was very full. Every time she saw it, which was very seldom now, she remembered that her mother had complained about the price of having it made up. Those were the sorts of things she remembered nowadays.

And Sunny. She remembered Sunny always, as though he would come walking up the rise from the barn, his cornsilk-colored straw hat in his hand. Sometimes she dreamed about him on nights like this, and he was always young and happy.

A fresh breeze blew across the mountains and dipped down into the valley, and the willows on the banks of the pond, where the muskrats made tunnels between the fingers of the roots. The boy took the cardboard box from the backseat and carried it to the flagstone steps that led upstairs to the second floor of the garage. He stumbled and almost fell as another trout leaped from the black water and fell back with the sound of a slap. He caught himself, and never looked at what he was carrying, even when he put it down and stepped back to turn away. "Drink Coke," it said on the box in red letters.

"Not the garage," the girl hissed frantically, leaning across the seat and almost out the car door as he opened it. "You're supposed to leave it at the house. The house! Not the garage!"

"Somebody'll find it," the boy mumbled, his resolve gone now.

"You can't leave it at the garage," she said, her voice trembling, but he had already started to turn the car slowly.

There was a world around them that they never even noticed as they drove back down the drive, the girl weeping, the boy wiping his hand on the leg of his shorts. The moths wheeled and dipped mindlessly around the lights that were always left on on the porch, the lights that had lit the house every evening from nightfall until sunup since the day the Blessings had first moved in. The possums were faint gray ghosts stumbling in their ungainly way behind the garage, their pink tails trailing them like afterthoughts. A male bear, heavy with skunk cabbage, loped across the dark field, but the two people in the car did not see him as they stared ahead. And once again a trout jumped and fell, and as it did the car turned onto Rolling Hills Road, and the headlights jumped to life and lit the surrounding woods as though they were searching for something. Before the circles from the big fish had disappeared on the surface of the water, any trace of the car and the couple was gone as well, and the house and the land around it was as it had been before, apart, unchanged. Except for the box on the steps.

The girl wiped her eyes with a tissue and put gloss on her lips with the end of her little finger from a plastic pot she took from her purse.

"You want to stop and get something to eat?" the boy said.

"I'm not hungry," she said.

"It'll be all right," he said. "The house had those automatic-light things. I couldn't go too close or I would have woken somebody up."

"I guess."

"I can't believe I did that," he said, his voice low.

The girl looked back at Blessings through a stand of birches, white and slender shadows at the edge of the black lawn. "I want to go home," she finally said.

"School home or home home?"

"Home home," she said.

Maybe it was the last purring of the car engine, or the faint shriek of the nesting bird that one of the barn cats leaped for, clawed, caught, and then lost, that caused Lydia Blessing to turn fretfully in the big cherry bed that had once belonged to her parents. She'd heard her father's voice for a moment, that voice strangely high-pitched for such a big man, so that he'd sung tenor parts in the St. Stephen's choir. Elegant Ed, they'd called him at school. The prettiest penmanship at Princeton, he liked to say, looking down at his copperplate cursive. Lyds my love, he called her. The sound of voices in the night was commonplace to her now, more so, even, than in the old days, when there really had been voices, arguments from the guest bedrooms, conversations from the stragglers on the patio, whispers from someone sneaking into the dark waters of the pond long after the house was closed up.

Lydia Blessing pulled the openwork blanket about her shoulders and fell back to sleep as the box on the garage doorstep shuddered, shimmied, and finally was still.

The first light of dawn, the color of lemonade, was coming over the Blue Mountains when Skip Cuddy opened his eyes and turned toward the window. He couldn't remember at first where he was, just knew by the fragile fog of the summer light that it was early, that his alarm clock would sleep longer than he had. That was all right. For his whole life, as far back as his mind could wander, he'd woken up early, easy, as though morning held a nice surprise, which had never been dimly true.

Still, he'd never, ever woken up entirely sure where he was. Joe and Debbie's trailer, where he'd slept on the pullout couch in the living room, beer bottles and played-out butts on the end tables on either side of his pillow, half of them smeared red-black from Debbie's lipstick. The county jail, top bunk, with the sprayed concrete ceiling only a foot from his face and the sounds of people hawking and snoring and farting in their sleep. Even his room in the back of his aunt and uncle's house just off Front Street in Mount Mason, where the maple tree outside had grown so big that the room was dark day and night. Almost four years he'd lived in that room, after his father moved south, and four years he'd woken befuddled and adrift. He thought that maybe he'd known where he was when he'd lived in his parents' house, before his mother died, when he was little. But he couldn't remember. He couldn't remember anything except that his bed had a quilt with a cowboy on it, riding a horse that was trying to throw the cowboy off. And that his mother hung her stockings to dry over the taps in the tub. And that his father had a strange little stand-up thing in the bedroom that he hung his shirt and pants on overnight. First the pants, then the shirt. Shoes at the bottom. It wasn't a whole lot to remember. His whole childhood seemed to have gone up in smoke with the little Cape Cod where he grew up.

Skip's pants were lying on the floor at the foot of the bed. He tried to get two days of wearing out of a pair of pants, since he wasn't allowed to use the washer and dryer in the big house, and there wasn't one in the rooms over the garage. Blessings garage had bays for five cars and a small but complete machine shop in the back, but no washer and dryer. Old Mr. Blessing had had big ideas when he bought the place in 1926 and hired Mr. Foster to run it. He'd had the carpenters build an apartment over the garage, not too big but big enough for Foster to move his family in, so that the caretaker was always around to see that the stone walls stayed straight, the paths stayed mowed, the roofs stayed sound, always around to fix the leaks and the cracks that came with a house with eight bedrooms and ten baths. After that first Foster got arthritis in his hands and gave in to his wife's nagging about being closer to town, a second Foster, the first's middle son, took over. His name was Tom, but everyone at Blessings just called him Foster, as they had his father. "Just like a plantation," Sunny Blessing had murmured once. That Foster liked to work on cars and his wife cooked for Mrs. Blessing, meals that were always described as good plain food, which meant meatloaf, stew, and homemade pie. The couple had had three boys, and Edwin Blessing had died happy, thinking there would always be Fosters to keep the grass trim and the paint fresh. But those three grew up and got jobs in town and later buried their parents and carted some of their stuff away and gave the rest to the Goodwill or just abandoned it in the garage apartment.

Now Skip cooked with Mrs. Foster's pots and pans, which the sons had left behind. When he cooked, which wasn't often. Canned soup, mostly, that he ate in front of the little television he'd put in the living room at the end of the hallway, on an old steamer trunk that actually had hotel stickers on it. If he put his soup bowl dead center, at his right hand was a big blue-and-white sticker that said "Stateroom number," then an *18* that someone had written in in black ink.

He put on his pants and ate a doughnut that had gone hard around the edges from a box on the kitchen counter. He wanted to get outside, to trim the hedges and weed around the plants in the vegetable garden he'd started behind the barn, to cut some more of the winter's firewood into just the right length, long enough to stretch from one brass andiron to another in the living room fireplace, or the dining room fireplace, or the library fireplace, or the fireplaces in the bedrooms. He'd discovered that nothing made him feel better than a nice neat stack of wood.

He'd had the job at Blessings for a month and he liked almost everything about it. He had the inchoate and overwhelming love of the land that a boy has when he lives in the country but in a house in town, barely two arms' length from the houses on either side. He had the love of the land that a boy has when he rides his bike through forest and fields, past streams and lakes, goes hunting and fishing, and then returns every night to a forty-by-eighty lot on a street where you can hear the guy next door fight with his wife through your wall as clear as if he were sitting on your sofa.

Geography was destiny in Mount Mason. The kids with a little money, whose parents were teachers or contractors or accountants, lived in the neat suburbs that had grown up just outside of town after World War II. The designated dirtbags, who had transitory or seasonal jobs, plowing snow or cleaning houses, lived in one of two places: in the sagging old frame houses ranged around the center of the shabby downtown, or way out on the country roads, in trailers at the end of gravel tracks, with old cars scattered around the patches of dirt and grass like lawn ornaments, and Christmas lights that never came down. Skip had moved from one to the other, from way out to downtown, during the course of his Mount Mason boyhood. Then somehow he'd landed at Blessings, the most beautiful place in town.

He'd never had a job he'd liked before. The drive-through window at Burger King. The night-shift cleaning at the mall, mainly popcorn cemented to the floor of the multiplex with congealing soda and blots of ice cream, or tissues you didn't even want to look at, much less touch. Laundry at the county jail, better than doing push-ups all day next to the bunks, but it was hell on the hands, cracks in your fingers that burned all the time, so that if you picked up a fry with salt on it your skin sang for an hour after.

He went down the stairs that led from the apartment down the side of the garage and out onto the driveway. There were no cars in the garage except for the old lady's black Cadillac, ten years old with barely five thousand miles on it. But there was the riding mower, the tractor, the old red truck. "Jesus Christ," Joe had said when he helped Skip move his four boxes of stuff in. "It looks like the antique farm show at the county fair. Except for the mower, man. That's a nice mower."

"Don't get any ideas," Skip said.

"Fuck you, man. I go reminding you of your mistakes?"

"Don't go talking around town, either," Skip had said. He thought about how his uncle always said there were two types of people, leaders and followers. Joe had always been a follower, from the time he started following Chris around in first grade. Chris had called him Snotty then because of Joe's allergies. Joe still sniffed all the time, and he still told Chris anything he thought would pique his interest. Of the four of them who had been hanging out together since they were kids, Chris was the one who qualified as a leader, Skip knew that for certain and for always.

"How much you getting paid for this job?" Joe said. "Jesus, you stepped in shit with this one."

"It's about time," Skip had said.

He hadn't had Joe back to the place since, and he hadn't even seen Ed, or Chris. Especially Chris. The old lady had lousy locks on the door, for all that there was a security system. It would be like meat to a dog for Chris. It was like he couldn't help himself, even when they were little and there wasn't a whole lot any of them wanted anyway, besides Butterfingers and Blow Pops. They'd go into the Newberry's on Main Street for loose-leaf paper just before Labor Day, quarters from their parents rattling around in their jeans, and when they got to the bench at the bus stop Chris would unload his pockets, and there it would be, his senseless booty: a bottle of cologne, a paper of hairpins, a box of playing cards, plastic earrings, breath mints, baby aspirin.

"Drive us over to the Quik-Stop, man," he'd said to Skip a year ago Memorial Day weekend, Joe walking behind him, and the next thing Skip knew, he was doing 364 days in county jail and grateful for the deal, because it meant he wouldn't go to the state prison at Wissahonick. Chris had slid on that old ski mask. That's how Skip knew, when they pulled into the lot and Chris pulled that mask out of the bag. He'd stolen the mask, too, one day when they'd been in a sporting goods store buying a mitt so they could play in the McGuire's Tavern summer league. "Don't even think about driving away," Chris had said in the lot at the Quik-Stop, with that sudden cold violence to his voice that made people step back from him. So Skip just sat outside, sweating and swearing and thinking about what a chump he was, and the surveillance camera read his license plate as plain as the lottery number at the bottom of your TV screen on Tuesday nights. But Skip didn't give Chris up, or Joe either, even when the sheriff's office offered him a walk. He just didn't think it was right. It was only because he didn't have any priors that he'd gotten a deal that kept him in county. He'd been let out in just under ten months for good behavior.

He sharpened the clippers on the whetstone, and filled the bird feeder, and watched the watery early morning light get warmer, less pastel. He washed his hands at the deep soapstone sink. Both Mrs. Fosters had done the family laundry there, hung it way back on the line hidden behind the garage while their husbands were mending the furnace or dredging the viscous end of the pond. The old lady didn't want anyone driving up and seeing laundry flapping in the breeze. Skip took his laundry to the Wash-N-Dry in town. He washed his hands again.

"Ah, hell, let's get it over with," he said, the same thing, in the same tone of voice, that his uncle had said as he took off his belt when he was going to whip Skip's butt in the basement.

"I'm washing my hands of you," his uncle had said when Skip got busted for the Quik-Stop holdup.

Skip went around to the side of the big house, to the basement door that gave out onto the drive. "This way," Nadine, the house-keeper, had said to him, her mouth drawn up tight when she'd had to tell him what to do, and, more important, what not to do. Don't use the front door. Don't use the back door. Come up through the basement. Wipe your feet on the mat. Don't make any noise. Don't wake up Miz Blessing. That's how she said it, Miz, like one of those old movies and Nadine was the mammy. Or maybe it was just that weird way Nadine talked, as though she were wearing a retainer like the one Skip had worn to pull his snaggled front teeth into line, the one he'd lost and his father said there was no money to replace. Nadine's name had been some-thing else once, and her language something else, too, that she still talked to herself, under her breath, when she was angry, which was often. But that had been when she still lived in Korea, before she came over with their little girl to marry Mr. Foster's nephew Craig, who got her the job at Blessings.

"First grind beans," Nadine had said. "Not too small, not too big. Just right. Consistency of cornmeal." The old lady must have said that to Nadine. In a million years Nadine never would have thought to say that herself: "consistency of cornmeal." The words themselves sounded more like "con me" in Nadine's mouth. Skip didn't think he'd ever actually seen cornmeal. When Nadine said "consistency," it sounded like someone whistling with a toothpick in her teeth.

He thought he must be getting the hang of it. A cupful of black beans, shiny as onyx beads, sealed in brown bags with the name of someplace in New York City stamped in black on them. The growl of the little motor in the grinder, the slow hiccuping of the old percolator behind him as he went back down the cellar stairs.

He never knew what happened after he left. He never knew if Mrs. Blessing came downstairs herself as soon as she heard the cellar door close to pour a cup of coffee, or if she stayed in bed, sleeping the long satisfied sleep Skip imagined was the birthright of people who owned as much land as the whole town was built on and just let the land lie there, sleeping, too. Maybe she waited until Nadine came in at eight-thirty. Maybe Nadine brought her breakfast and coffee on a tray, and Mrs. Blessing took a sip and lifted those pale blue eyes to the sky that was the same color, the way she did when she was aggravated, and said, "Too weak" or "Too strong." Maybe he was one bad pot of coffee away from sleeping back in Joe's combination living room–dining room–kitchen and listening to Debbie yell "Oh, JoeJoeJoeJoe" through the particleboard wall.

He loved the goddamned job but he hated making the coffee every morning, and he couldn't figure out why. Maybe it was because he didn't understand the point of it. He could understand cleaning the pumps in the frog ponds, or spraying the paper wasps that set up noisy housekeeping in the corner of the porch and the boathouse roofs. If he could just work like that, outside from morning until night, sweaty, sunburned, fixing the screens, mulching the plants, keeping the lawn as smooth and even and green as the felt on the pool table at McGuire's, his life would be perfect. He'd like somebody to sleep with, too, but he wasn't going to make any more mistakes. And a washing machine. Maybe he'd buy himself a washer, once he'd saved enough money.

The big barn cat was sitting smugly outside the basement door, a mole on the ground at its feet. The cat followed him across the circular driveway that separated the big house from the garage. At the center of the circle was a maple tree four stories high. Maybe today Skip would trim the lower branches and prune the holly that flanked the flagstone path to the apartment door, the one he never used, that came out by the side of the pond. He looked toward it and saw a cardboard box lying at the foot of the steps.

That was just the kind of thing the old lady would see from the upstairs back hallway window and give him hell about. Not give him hell directly, no, she'd tell Nadine, who would tell him, which would make him feel low, like a boy, like nobody, nothing. "Miz Blessing say . . ." Like he was too low for her to talk to directly. She talked to him directly only when she thought the task was too complicated to explain to Nadine, which probably made Nadine feel like nothing, too.

The cat bounded ahead, the mole dangling limply from the side of its mouth, and sniffed the corner of the box, and cried. Skip bent down to pick up the box and carried it to the tool bench in the garage. He could tell by the weight that there was something inside.

There were a couple of times in his life when he'd felt his mind slow down almost to a dead halt, when it seemed like his brain had to tell the rest of his body what was happening, slow, in words of one syllable, the way Mr. Keller had talked to them in American history when he was annoyed because too many of them had failed a test. When his father sat in the driveway, his head down on the steering wheel, just home from seeing his mother at the hospital, and Skip could see him out the window—that was one time. And when his uncle had come by to tell Skip that he was to move in with him and Aunt Betty, that his father's trip to Florida had turned into a life in Florida—that was another. "It's warm down here," his father had said on the phone, as though that explained everything.

After that he'd learned to recognize the feeling, like moving underwater in the river when the current sucked you down and you had to push with your hands and kick with your feet, working with all your strength just to stay still. The time he'd broken his leg falling off his bike and seen the bone poking like a birch branch through the rent in the skin. The moment when he'd seen Chris pull on that ski mask on his way into the Quik-Stop. The day after he got out of the county jail in April and went to Shelly's back door and saw her belly jutting out beneath the T-shirt and the half-sheepish, half-truculent look on her face. Counting out the months he'd spent in jail in his head, trying to make ten months come out somehow to less than nine, turning around and walking without saying anything, Shelly calling to him, "It's not like we were that serious, Skipper." Which he guessed meant that she'd been screwing around even before he went to jail.

Skip felt that feeling when he opened the cardboard box and looked inside. "A baby," he said, as though if he spoke it he'd believe it. He was an only child, the last healthy thing his mother had managed before she faltered and faded into a life of vague physical complaints that ended with the big finale of breast cancer. He'd been one of the few kids at the high school who didn't have a first or second cousin in his class, one of the few who wasn't from the kind of big Mount Mason family that meant you had to be real careful about who you felt up in the basement at a party. He knew a lot more about machinery than he did about babies, but even he could tell that the baby in the box was more or less newborn. Its maroon skin was streaked with a motley mask of dried blood and mucus, and its small fist pushed into its face as though it were trying to shield itself from the glare of even a half-lit garage.

"*Eh-eh-eh,*" it was wheezing, its tiny, ugly baked apple of a face contorted by fear or frustration or hunger or something else that Skip couldn't understand. The baby's body was wrapped tight in an old flannel shirt, the sleeves wound round and tied beneath the chin. Swaddling clothes, Skip thought to himself. He'd never been able to figure out exactly what that meant. Swaddling clothes. It was hot outside, and there was a sheen of sweat on the skull, crystalline drops in the pale, colorless down that covered the baby's head. The cat licked the down with its rough tongue. "Go away," Skip said, knocking the animal off the bench. "Get. Get."

Skip wiped his hands on his jeans and slid them under the baby, lifting it out of the box. There was a wet spot on the cardboard where the baby's butt had been, and another about even with its mouth. Its head wobbled as he lifted it onto his shoulder the way he'd seen people do easily and effortlessly so many times. It was a lot harder than it looked; he wasn't sure exactly where to put his hands. The small head bounced forward, then back. The wheezing went on, then a bark of a cough.

"Oh, man," he said as he started up the inside stairs to the apartment above the garage, the light weight somehow heavy against his shoulder. "What the hell am I supposed to do with this?" He didn't know why, but halfway up he turned around and went back for the box.

L ydia Blessing ate breakfast each morning in the summer
   months at a small drop-leaf table in one corner of the long
   porch overlooking the pond. In the winter the table went
into a corner of the library, since the long porch was too cold after
the first frost came to Mount Mason. Both locations had the ad-
vantage of allowing her to look out over a substantial swathe of
her substantial property. Her father had begun the tradition, and
more often than not, sometime during the meal, he would say
happily, "Lord of all he surveys." Her mother ate upstairs on a tray
in bed.

Lydia had continued because she liked to think of herself as a
person who honored tradition, and because from this vantage
point she could usually keep a close eye on anyone working on the
property. She could see her new caretaker on the rider mower in
the back field. He was hunched forward over the seat and the
steering wheel looking, as her father would have said, as though he
had the weight of the world on his shoulders. She wondered why
his posture was suddenly so poor. She was of the school that believed that the spine was a reflection of character, and that only the
weak stooped. She had not noticed this young man's poor posture
when she had hired him, nor for the first month he had worked
for her, but for the last few days he had gone about his tasks
with the rounded shoulders of an old man. She narrowed her eyes
thoughtfully. A bad sign, for a young person to be so bowled over
by the summer heat when it was only the first day of July.

"Now today the coffee is too strong," Mrs. Blessing said, looking at the front page of the newspaper. "Yesterday it wasn't strong enough."

"Not my fault," said Nadine, clearing the breakfast dishes from the small table onto a silver tray with the monogram of Mrs. Blessing's mother at its center. Lydia had had half a grapefruit, a bowl of All-Bran with strawberries on top, and two cups of coffee, black. Bananas, she always said, had a tendency to bind her. Nadine hated it when she talked like that. "Keep herself to herself, the old wrinkled lady," she said to her husband, Craig.

"That's a nice way to talk," Craig had said.

"You never mind," said Nadine.

Mrs. Blessing wiped her mouth with a napkin that had her monogram on it in white, thread so very much the color of the linen upon which it had been placed that it was easier to feel the letters, as though they were in Braille, than it was to read them. This, too, drove Nadine nuts. The fabric and the floss had faded in tandem, so that both now were a pale ecru, the color of age. Mrs. Blessing herself was the same shade. So was the face of the watch her parents had given her for her graduation from Bertram's. The white dial had become ivory, then the palest café au lait, the black letters brownish, then coffee-colored. The gold band had acquired a matte finish. It had had to be mended only six months after she had gotten it, when she had caught it on the edge of a rented gilt chair at her deb party, then again in 1946, when it had exploded from her wrist on the tennis court as she served, and sometime in the early 1960s, when one of Jess's sons had carelessly trod on it on the dock while she was swimming the length of the pond.

Each time it had been returned to the jeweler on Madison Avenue from whom her father had bought it. She wound it every night before bed. For her seventieth birthday her daughter, Meredith, had given her a gold watch with a brown leather strap. "I don't see how you can even read the dial of your old one," Meredith had said. "This one never needs winding," she added. The watch had been in its box in a drawer for a dozen years, next to several boxes of stockings from the old B. Altman's store, closed now. "I don't know why I even bother to buy her things," Meredith had said to her husband the next time she visited.

At the Bertram School they had learned that old was always better than new, that the past was always nicer than the present, that white was always more elegant than any other shade except for black, which was inappropriate for girls under age twenty-one. She'd graduated from Bertram's when she was seventeen, in 1937, but there were long afternoons now, when she dozed off in the wing chair next to the fireplace in the living room, when Bertram's seemed more real than the news in the paper she'd read that morning. The long linoleum hallways, the smell of starch in their uniform blouses, Miss Bertram's lace-up shoes black against the red Turkish carpet in the head's office when a girl was called in for insolence or bad temper or lack of charity or insufficient effort.

The sins of the past seemed so venial in light of what she now read each morning in the *Times* that Nadine fetched from the newsstand in Mount Mason, stories about girls who had sex for money and got sick and died because of it, who killed their friends and their parents and themselves. There had not been truly bad girls at Bertram's, or at least not bad in ways that mattered or were openly discussed. There was in each class one girl who was clever and slightly profane and who had what Miss Bertram referred to as "errant ways." It was always understood among them that these girls would come to a bad end, but Lydia Blessing had noticed that it somehow always happened that those girls did very well for themselves. The girl with the errant ways in Lydia's class, Priscilla North, had become an ambassador to one of the smaller European countries after her husband died, and was often asked back to the school to talk about the new American woman.

Lydia Blessing had become outspoken only as she'd grown older, coming late to the realization that saying what she truly thought provided a certain satisfaction and had no material effect on how people treated her. As a girl she had been hugely obedient, especially when compared to her brother, Sunny. If she slammed the door of the house on East Seventy-seventh Street, she was sentenced to quiet reading in the library for half an hour. If she pushed one of the visiting children down on the lawn tennis court beside the boathouse, she was forbidden bathing in the pond for the rest of the day. She wore white all summer long at the country house, dresses, never pants or shorts. Sunny wore shorts, and when he was older, white twill pants that yellowed as they were laundered, just as the face of her watch had.

Sunny was disobedient not so much in deed as in word. He once told one of their mother's friends that he had never seen a dress that so closely matched the upholstery. He had already left the room before the two women realized what a clever insult it had been, so clever that neither said a word to the other, although Sunny was whipped by his father and the woman never again came to the Blessing home. It had been especially insulting given Mrs. Blessing's taste in upholstery, which ran to dark brocades from the fabric business left to her by her father.

Sumner was his real name, but Lydia called him Sunny when she was a baby, and then everyone else did, too. The gardeners had called him Master Blessing, and her Miss Lydia. There had been three gardeners when she was a child: one for the trees and shrubs, one for the perennial borders, and the last, the youngest, for the vegetables. Foster had overseen them all. The first Foster, not the second one.

She sipped her coffee and looked from the window across the fields at the figure sitting hunched astride the riding mower. This new man must be made to sit up correctly. Mrs. Blessing thought of her own back as still straight. The faint hump was behind her, and so she did not notice it. She insisted her white blouses did not fit as they once had because tailoring, like everything else, had gone down in quality.

"I think he's settling in, this new man," she said. "Except for the coffee."

"Been in jail," said Nadine.

"So was Thomas More," Mrs. Blessing replied. She had set her lawyer to work, to find out if this was true and how serious the offense had been.

"Kill everyone with knives."

"Oh, for goodness sake, Nadine. You can tell by looking at him that he's not about to kill anyone. Except for that groundhog out by the asparagus patch. I need to speak to him about that."

Of course if Mrs. Blessing had known in the Wal-Mart lot that the young man was recently released from prison, as Nadine so vehemently insisted, she would have rolled up her window and gone on her way alone. But she was not about to back down now. Lydia Blessing did what she wanted: that was something upon which she had prided herself. Once she moved to Blessings for good she told it to herself and to others over and over again, so that after a time it was said to be true: Lydia Blessing does what she wants. One of Foster's nephews had set himself up in the apartment over the garage, as though it were his sinecure, the third generation of his family to do so, and two weeks later she had noticed from inside the sleeping porch that the garbage cans had been left at the roadside for a full day after the truck had come. She had even used the binoculars next to her bed to make certain that she was not being precipitous. Then she'd fired the man, and hired another, the man who plowed the driveway in winter. His coffee had been vile, and in his second month on the job he had left the door to the basement ajar, and a soiled work glove on the kitchen counter. She had looked at it for a long time, remembering when the grounds staff never went farther into the kitchen than the pantry, the kitchen staff never farther into the house than the dining room. There had been a succession of unsatisfactory men. It had never occurred to her that she was demanding.

There was something furtive about this new one in the last few days, but he worked hard, never cut corners, never complained. From time to time she would see him disappear into the garage, but she also saw him hosing off the boat just after dawn as she watched the pond and the fields and the faraway road with her binoculars. He seemed to work odd hours now, but there were no weeds around her tree peonies, and the bachelor buttons had been properly pinched, so that they were spreading a constellation of blue beneath the window of the small office where she attended to her correspondence on stationery stacked in boxes ten deep inside the storage closet, stationery that would surely survive her.

It was just luck that she had found him at the Wal-Mart. That morning she had told Nadine that the household expenses were exorbitant, that Nadine paid too much for paper towels and dish-washing detergent and light bulbs, that she was profligate with money that was not hers. Mrs. Blessing had put on her old driving jacket, the plaid one from the place Father liked so much in London, the one near Regent Street with all the guns and walking sticks, and walked slowly, her back straight, her head high, to the garage. The odor of mothballs and bath powder hung like a miasma in the still summer air of the car. The Cadillac had been dusty. It had been three weeks since she had taken it out, to go to the club for a drink with her lawyer. And she was between care-takers. The last one had brought a woman into the apartment one night and been fired by the end of the week. It paid to know what the staff was up to. Her mother had always said that.

Mount Mason had seemed dusty, too, dusty and out-of-date, aging the way that the cheap houses around the industrial park did, peeling, cracked, disintegrating instead of mellowing. So many of her landmarks had gone, the old limestone bank building chopped up into a travel agency, a beauty parlor, and a used-book store; the boxy red brick hardware store refaced with some horrid imitation stone and made over into a place that sold records. She had had to drive around the circle in the center of town twice, unsure of which way to turn for the commercial strip, and a car full of teenagers had honked at her and driven far too close to her back bumper. And then there had been the horrid noisy glare of the store, and the insistence of the other shoppers on pushing past her and screaming at their dirty children. But she had found light bulbs cheaper than the ones Nadine had found at the ShopRite, and paper towels, too, in a bargain twelve-pack. "Could you put that in my cart," she had said to one of the stock boys, with no hint of a question in the sentence. In a locked drawer in her dresser Mrs.

Blessing had a handmade leather case crammed with her mother's old, ugly, and rather showy jewelry: diamonds as big as almonds set in a piecrust of sapphires or emeralds, ropes of pearls that dropped to the waist with jeweled clasps. She owned nearly twelve hundred acres of the best land in the northeastern part of the state. But she was cheap the way the rich are often cheap, about small things that do not last. "Thrifty," she called it. "For pity's sake, Mother," said Meredith, who felt a faint throb each time she looked at the old watch on the ropy spotted wrist.

The Cadillac had died in the parking lot of the Wal-Mart. The engine rumbled disconsolately and then was silent, no matter how many times she turned the key. She had heard a peculiar sound from the car and suddenly realized that it was a man tapping on her window. He was thin and pale, his hair a kind of flat brown, tan really, all this way and that way over his forehead and his ears. He had small, closely set eyes and a big, wide, mobile mouth. There was a space between his front teeth. Alma, the cook at their house in the city, had once told the maids that this was a sign of licentiousness. "That's a mark on a girl, and all the men can see it," Alma had said, and she'd pushed her hips into the air, not knowing the little girl was lurking in the dim area just outside the pantry.

Mrs. Blessing had held her handbag close as she looked at the man outside her car window.

"You need a jump?" the young man had said loudly.

"Pardon me?"

"You need a jump? A jump? Do you— Sorry, do you want me to charge your battery from my battery? From my truck? It won't take but a minute."

"What would be the charge for that?"

He'd smiled then. It was a smile like Sunny's, just this side of a grimace, as though it were a social gesture and his heart wasn't in it. "Presentation!" Father had shouted at Sunny, hitting him between the shoulder blades. "Presence!"

The car had started instantly after he had attached the cables from a dented pickup truck to the Cadillac. She'd had a moment's panic when he'd pulled the jaws of the connectors from the two, afraid that the engine would sputter and stop again. Then she'd remembered herself and taken two dollars from her handbag and rolled down the window little more than an inch to slip them through.

"Nobody'd charge you for that," he'd said. "But you do need a tune-up. I don't know who services your car, but they're not taking good care of it."

She couldn't say why, except that she thought he was too dim to be duplicitous, but she'd had him follow her home along the roads that left Mount Mason for the mountains.

"What is your name?" she had said, seating him at the table in the kitchen as Nadine cleaned vegetables at the sink, making a good deal of noise, as though she were playing a concerto of disapproval written for colander, knives, pan lids, and faucet.

"Skip," he said. "Cuddy," as though his last name were an afterthought.

"Skip is not a name for a person. Skip is a dog's name. Skippy. I knew a boy named Quad once."

"What?"

"Quad."

"What?"

"You deaf?" shouted Nadine.

"Mind your own business," Mrs. Blessing called over the noise from the sink.

"I'm sorry, I thought you said Quad," Skip had said, pushing his hair back and fidgeting in his chair.

"I did. Quad Preston. Leland Preston the Fourth. Quad. Because of the Fourth. I refused to call him Quad. I don't care for most nicknames. What is your real name?"

He'd flushed, looked at his hands, which were cut and marked by the work in the prison laundry and the day job he had now, putting in fences. "Charles," he said.

"Charles, are you looking for work?" she'd asked.

"Oh. Oh." Nadine groaned and slashed at a head of broccoli with a carving knife.

Mrs. Blessing liked to think of herself as a good judge of people, and of horses, although the horses were long gone, sold when Meredith went away to college. The cosmos grew so well in the far field because that was the land on which the horses and, before them, the cows had grazed, when Father had liked the idea of the place as a farm and himself as a gentleman farmer. "You've got a good eye, Lyds," he said when they went to other farms to buy animals. He'd wanted to give the house a name when he first bought it, but before long everyone called it Blessings, and soon another name seemed beside the point.

She thought now she'd had a good eye for that young man. He was done with the grass in the fields and was clipping the yews around the pond spillway. Ed and Jeanne Chester had noticed an improvement in the property right away when they'd been out there the other night for drinks and dinner. "The place looks grand, Lydia," Ed had said, sipping his Manhattan. "Wonderful," Jeanne had added. "I've never seen the flowers looking finer."

"I have a new man," Mrs. Blessing had replied, and the two of them had nodded solemnly. Jeanne was the daughter of Mrs. Blessing's old friend Jess, with whom she had played tennis on the grass courts out back for so many Tuesday and Thursday mornings, filling the hours of their long aimless young lives. But Jess was dead now, like nearly all of Mrs. Blessing's friends, and her daughter had grown from a young girl into a middle-aged woman. She and Mrs. Blessing, once a generation apart, had somehow become contemporaries and secondhand friends of a sort. Still, Jeanne and Ed were always deferential.

"Where did you find him?" Ed asked, cocking his head to one side.

Nadine made a snorting noise as she passed around the cubed cheese and olives. Mrs. Blessing made Nadine stay late when she had dinner guests, although Nadine stubbornly refused to wear a uniform.

"Nadine doesn't countenance change," Ed said, with that twinkle that Mrs. Blessing had always found so irritating.

"Pick up like dog," Nadine said. "No references, no nothing."

"That's enough, Nadine," Mrs. Blessing had said.

Nadine did not like change, but, then, neither did Lydia Blessing. It had been many years since she had cared to travel outside of Mount Mason, more than thirty since she'd driven up Park Avenue, which had once been the Main Street of her life. She liked her routines now, her breakfast, her *Times,* her letters posted, a light lunch, a walk around the pond with her stick at her side, perhaps a surreptitious doze in one of the Adirondack chairs with a book facedown on her lap, an hour of talk shows on television, an hour of news, a bowl of soup, two drinks, and an early bed. She didn't sleep most of the night. She rested for the day ahead and thought about the days behind. It was a puzzle to her, how eagerly she'd rushed into life when she was eighteen or twenty, and in what a desultory fashion it had dragged out ever since. Even when she had been younger, thirty, forty years before, when there had been long house parties at Blessings and games of golf and swimming at midnight and dinners for twelve—even then, the days were so long, and the years somehow so short.

"Nadine," she called, sipping at her coffee. "Nadine. Tell Charles not to prune the hydrangeas. Or the rhodies. Not until fall. Nadine?"

She watched Nadine march across the drive, clenched fists at her side. "What a brave thing to do, hiring someone like that, Lydia," Ed had said, but Mrs. Blessing knew people, and she had recognized in the young man holding jumper cables in the Wal-Mart parking lot that delicate balance between efficiency and servility that had characterized the very best servants of her childhood and youth. The cook here at Blessings had had it, and the head gardener, and the man who had tended the cows and taught Miss Lydia and Master Blessing how to pull down on the soft udders and aim right into their open mouths, so that the milk was warm and sweet on their lips. The maids in the city house had somehow never had it, but perhaps that was because of the way Father had treated them, brushing against them sometimes in the hallway, when he thought no one was looking, using the serving spoon so that the upper part of his arm gently touched the curve of a breast beneath a white bib and gray cotton. How handsome he'd been, with his center-parted yellow hair and his mustache and his full bottom lip and bright blue eyes.

When Nadine spoke to the new man Mrs. Blessing saw him jump slightly, answering Nadine over his shoulder as though he did not want her to see his face. He moved oddly, as though he were stiff, or hurt, as though he'd thrown his back out and couldn't straighten up. Hard work never hurt anyone, Mrs. Blessing's father used to say as he walked with her around the place, swinging his stick, although he'd never worked hard a day in his life.

Nadine was walking back toward the house and the young man had resumed his raking. He'd learn, this one, Lydia Blessing thought. She had a feeling about him. She'd just have to remember to tell Nadine to remind him to straighten up. There was no point in having him throw his back out the very first month on the job.

He hadn't been this afraid since his first week in county jail, when he was convinced that any minute some big guy was going to jump him. Or as tired, for that matter. A deadbeat dad who worked with him in the laundry finally took pity on him. "You can get some sleep, junior," the man had said, stuffing sheets in the big top-loading machine. "The worst it gets in here is when somebody bodychecks somebody else during a basketball game."

"I don't play basketball," Skip had replied.

"There you go, then," the older man said.

The rider mower was going round and round in a clean monotonous motion that was putting him to sleep. The windows of the house glittered in the sunlight so that it was impossible to see if someone was watching him. He hadn't been this afraid since he sat in the parking lot at the Quik-Stop and watched Chris shout into the clerk's face through the smoggy glass of the window. And at least then he'd known what crime he was committing, waiting with the engine running for someone with a cash register's worth of dirty bills stuffed into a brown bag. He'd been afraid now for more than a week, but he wasn't certain exactly what he was guilty of. When he looked into the bottom drawer of an old bureau he'd lined with a blanket at the baby, looking closely for any sign of life, he wondered whether this was kidnapping, or theft, or some sort of accessory thing. Maybe it was a parole violation of some sort, harboring a minor child. Mainly he wondered how long he could trim and tend two hundred acres of land with his spine curled around a baby strapped to his chest and an old woman watching him from the window.

"She must think I'm the hunchback of Notre Dame," he said aloud without meaning to speak, and the small downy head stirred slightly. "Please please please please don't wake up," he whispered. "Please."

He'd had a dog once, in that way he'd had everything in his childhood, ordinary but a lot less lasting. It had been a beagle-mix puppy of some kind, with a sharp bark and long incisors and a tail that swept knickknacks off low surfaces. One evening it tore open a bag of garbage left at the curb, scattering tin cans and pieces of waxed paper across the lawn; the next it soiled the thin beige wall-to-wall that was the jewel of his mother's living room. "We gave him to a family with a farm, Son," his father had said when he got home from school. "The farm deal," Chris had said, curling his lip. "That's what they always tell you." Skip had heard his mother sighing on the telephone to her sister. "You don't realize the constant responsibility," she'd said. "Like the kind you have with a baby, where you can't do a single thing for yourself." It was the kind of thing she always said, as though he wouldn't hear, or wouldn't take it personally if he did.

Now he knew she was right. That first day the baby had slept with a release and abandon that made him conclude it was sick or, sometimes, when the light did not fall fully on the small slack body, actually dead. He'd checked to make sure it was breathing right around twilight and then left to go shopping at the Wal-Mart. He figured that was probably a crime, too, leaving an infant alone, but he knew from watching one of the bartender's girl-friends change their twins on the back table at McGuire's that he was going to need Pampers and something to put in a bottle.

He'd picked up skim milk because it seemed healthiest, and Pampers with a stay-dry lining in the newborn size, and some plastic bottles with balloons painted on the side, and a book on baby care, and a canvas sling that let you carry an infant strapped close to your chest, and any piece of clothing with ducks on it that he could find. He had slithered up to the registers with his head down and the bill of his John Deere hat pulled low in case any of the girls knew him from high school or hanging at the bar, trying to get in and out and back to the house in the pickup truck before the old lady noticed he was gone, or the mottled squirming thing in the box awoke. He spent $81.19 at the Wal-Mart, half of it on things it turned out he wouldn't need until later: baby food in jars, a cup that popped right back up when you tipped it over, a rattle.

When he'd pulled into the garage he'd listened and heard the baby screaming from above, tearing into it in short bursts like a car alarm. It was another reason to be glad that the garage was so far from the house, far enough so that maybe the old lady wouldn't hear. Before he'd gone out he'd taken the baby out of the bureau drawer and put it back in the box and put the box under his bed, just in case. The damp flushed face was covered with a sifting of gray dust, like what was on the Christmas ornaments when he was a boy and they took them out to decorate the tree, he and his dad, on their own. The cheeks and forehead looked swollen, almost bruised beneath the ruddy sheen of baby rage, and the eyes were slits. The gray silt shone like mica in the down that promised to become eyebrows.

"Okay," he had said, lifting the baby out of the box by the armpits, the flannel shirt coming unwrapped, the whole of the little body dangling, naked legs bowed like parentheses. "It's a girl!" he thought to himself as he looked down at the shrimp-pink body, thinking that maybe worry was making him punch-drunk and that maybe there was a different kind of crime involved in harboring a girl baby. He carried her into the kitchen and laid her wailing on the counter while he poured the milk into the baby bottle and turned on the radio. "Okay," he kept repeating. "Okay okay okay."

And, Jesus, the blessed weight of silence when he put the nipple in her mouth and she shut up, no sound but Patsy Cline singing "Crazy" on the country station. Skip knew he should put a diaper on her, but he was afraid to remove the flannel shirt entirely, afraid to move her little legs, afraid to wake her again, once she'd dropped off after eating, her head hanging heavy to one side of his cradling arm. When he'd had her naked on the counter he was afraid that she was having a seizure; her arms and legs splayed and shook convulsively, as though she were trying to grab at the air. But now the tremors were gone, and he wanted to keep it that way. He was afraid to put her down, too, so he sat in an old rocking chair and rocked her gently, urine seeping warmly into his pants. "Don't poop, baby," he whispered. "Don't poop." He was still murmuring when she turned her head and vomited so violently that the milk hit the wall and the window.

"Oh, shit," he'd said, and the crying began again.

He was amazed that he'd gotten through that first night: clean her up, put on the diaper, put on a shirt, put on the sling, pick up the book, read about formula, curse himself out, drive down the highway to a convenience store and buy enough cans of the stuff to feed a dozen babies. When the sun began to come up over the pond he was cleaning sour milk off the windowpanes with the baby in the sling and a new day stretched before him during which he was expected to rake the flower beds and clean the pond spillway and ride the mower.

"I can't keep doing this," he said to himself, but somehow he did.

He'd been doing it for ten days. A full day of work, most of it done with the baby on his chest, a wet spot of perspiration and drool always now faintly cool in the center of his sternum. Sometimes, after she ate, she would sleep so deeply that he felt safe leaving her upstairs while he sprinted around, caulking windows, spraying the tomato plants. He went back again to the Wal-Mart, this time to buy a monitor he saw on television, so that he could hear what was happening above the garage when he was outside. He learned how to slump on the tractor, hunch his shoulders to make a valley for the small rounds of head and bottom. When he saw the glint of Mrs. Blessing's binoculars, he turned his back. He thought he knew what Mrs. Blessing would say about this. He didn't know her well yet, but the first thing he'd noticed about her were those small sharp lines radiating from around her mouth, the lines a woman got when she'd been pursing her lips in disapproval for years at the wayward ways of the world. And he realized she would figure out what he already had: that someone had left this baby here not for him, the sad-sack caretaker who didn't even have a checking account, but for her, the richest woman in Mount Mason.

"She say radio too loud at night," Nadine called across the pond to him.

"Tell her I'm sorry and it won't happen again," he called back.

The radio was to cover the sound of crying, and the crying was for no reason he could fathom. Sometimes the baby seemed to have gas, and she would lift her knees to her chest, groan and fart and groan again, then scream, then drop off for twenty minutes, then wake with a start in his arms and scream some more. He rocked her and rocked her and turned the pages of the baby book and looked for an explanation and fed her and rocked again. "You've just been given the most miraculous gift imaginable!" the baby book said. Skip thought colic was a possibility. Or maybe she was just pissed off that her mother had ditched her at Blessings and hadn't even had the brains to leave her at the big house. The fibrous stump of the umbilical cord, brown with dried blood, had been clamped off near the rounded belly with a blue enamel butterfly hair clip, the kind he'd seen the high school girls wearing at the mall.

In the mornings she always stopped crying, as though the thin light at the window mollified her. Sometimes she seemed to stare right through him, her eyes a dark clear blue, a small bubble of a blister forming at the center of her upper lip. Her legs and arms moved in strange calisthenics as he cleaned her with a warm cloth.

"Okay," he said. "It's okay. I'm gonna take care of you. It'll be okay. Okay?"

But by the end of the workday he was ready to drop, so tired that one day he drove back to the pasture behind the barn and slept in the back of the truck in the midday sun, waking to find his clothes soaked through with sweat and half his face sunburned to an angry purple-red. Some days he was so tired that the percussion of the pistons in the rider mower would begin to put him to sleep, and he'd start awake and look back at the slightly wavy trail that came with cutting the lawn half-conscious.

Even when he did sleep it was hardly like sleep at all, more like slipping in and out of daydreams, like the sleep was as thin as the cotton sheets that were all he used in bed at night because it was so damn hot in the apartment over the garage. He had two fans. Mrs. Blessing had said something about it to Nadine, two fans, lots of electricity. What did she care, with all her money? He couldn't tell her that one fan pushed the hot air over him, and the other over the deep bottom drawer to the old dresser that was filled with a wadded-up satin bedspread he'd found in the cupboard, and the baby he'd found in a box.

"What is it you want?" he'd said in an angry whisper one night just after four in the morning. "What the hell is your problem?" It was as if, unformed as she was, she could read the rough anger beneath the words. The incessant crying turned to choppy wails and she began to scream until she was gasping for breath, her face as brightly colored as his sunburn. He wanted to shake her. Instead he took her into a room at the back of the apartment that had one small window facing toward the fields; in it there was only a daybed and he laid her on it, closed the door, and walked up and down the hallway. "I can't do this," he whispered to himself. "I can't. I just can't." After ten minutes he went back in and lifted her to his shoulder. "I can't do this," he said. Her face was wet against his neck. "This is nuts," he muttered. "This is really crazy." Four A.M. and the darkness had a quality of inexorability and menace as though it would never lift, as though, without anyone noticing it, the dawn of the day before had been the beginning of the last light ever in the history of the world. He finally felt the baby go limp as a half-spilled sack of flour just as he looked out the bathroom window and saw a line of blue-gray appear around the edge of the pond, signaling dawn.

He could not have said when it was exactly that he decided to keep her, or why. It made no sense. He'd never thought much about having children, and having one now would cause considerable trouble, as he'd already learned. But he knew that there were things that seemed lunatic to the world that you decided to do anyhow. That was what his father must have felt, working as a long-distance trucker, seeing less and less of his son, meeting a woman who was waiting tables at the restaurant in the Quality Inn near Tampa, finding out once again how it felt to roll over in bed and find the sheets no longer cold, deciding to stay in Florida although he had a house and a son a thousand miles north.

Or maybe it was the damn dog he kept thinking about. Over the years whenever they'd passed a farm in his uncle's truck he'd stared out the window at the barns and the fields and the long gravel drives and looked for an old beagle basking in the sun. He just wished there'd been something permanent about his life, something he could look at or hold or keep in his dresser drawer that spoke of years of cereal breakfasts, after-school milk, homework at the kitchen table, family trips to the county fair, or just those moments before sleep when the ceiling of your room was as familiar as your face in the mirror.

There was no premium in it for him. He was certain there'd be trouble if anyone found out, and he was certain that sooner or later Mrs. Blessing or Nadine or someone would hear a noise in the night or see the dome of the head peeking from the neck of his shirt.

But a couple of days in, he'd realized that, no matter how often and how haphazardly he put his index finger in her creased little palm, she would surround it with her fingers like a greeting. "Your baby will hold tight to your hand!" the book burbled, and without realizing it he'd fixed on that one word, the word *your*. Or maybe it wasn't that at all. Maybe it was when he was raking out the old branches underneath the stand of birch trees along the fence that bordered Rolling Hills Road and was surprised by a small sound, like the one the deer made when they were startled, and realized that she had sneezed.

"Bless you," he murmured, and when he knocked off at the end of the day he looked up "colds" in the book's index.

Maybe he didn't really have a choice, like so many people who wound up with children haphazardly, accidentally. When he thought of what else he could do, he could imagine only various cold and cruelly lit rooms that smelled of disinfectant. The hospital in Mount Mason, where he'd had his leg set when he was fourteen and his burns treated when the deep-fat fryer at Burger King spit back at his scrawny bicep just before closing one night, leaving a magenta blot. The police station, that looked like an elementary school and smelled like one, too, Lysol and fried food and cigarettes, where he'd sat on a bench with his hands cuffed behind him after the robbery. The courthouse, that had been refurbished in the sixties, so that it was still a grand limestone hulk without but inside a maze of particle-board paneling and checkerboard linoleum and gray metal desks.

He wasn't taking anybody to any of those places, those places of impermanence and phony concern. He might as well drop this baby down a well and listen for the splash. He knew those people. They'd piss away a couple of years, passing around paper, looking for a mother who just wanted to be left in peace. The little girl would be three years old and still living in some lousy foster home with people who spent the money the state sent on Camel Lights and a satellite dish.

He bought some disposable cameras, and he took her picture, sleeping, waking, even screaming. Her angry maroon color had faded, by the beginning of the second week, to an almost ghostly white with a faint mottling of pink, like the flowers on the magnolia trees along the drive. Her umbilical cord fell off, scaring the hell out of him until he saw the small neat navel in its place, and he took the barrette that had been clipped to the cord, and the cardboard box, and the flannel shirt, and put them all together on the top shelf of the closet in the back room. He put the cameras next to them. He was constructing a history for her the way he wished someone had constructed one for him.

And as though she knew all this, on the tenth day she rested. He lined the bottles up in the refrigerator, put her down, and fell asleep himself, expecting to wake to crying in an hour or two. And instead she slept until three, woke and ate, went back to sleep, complained just before dawn, drank down a bottle scarcely waking, and went back to sleep again, her small mouth pursed, her fingers splayed, until around nine o'clock. So he had time to go up the basement steps, make the coffee for Mrs. Blessing, clear fallen branches from the drive, and water the vegetables and the zinnias before she woke demanding more. In the afternoon he rode the tractor far from the house and took her from the sling to lay her on a towel beneath leggy elm trees waving in the wind. A breeze blew and her eyes widened and he swore that she smiled vacantly at the sky. The book said that she wouldn't smile for weeks, but he knew what he'd seen. "Whoa," he said, kneeling beside her. Solemnly she blinked, closed her eyes, and tightened her fist around his finger. As far as Skip was concerned, that was that. She was his.

Often in the middle of the night Lydia Blessing had wakened to the sound of a baby's cries. Over the years she had learned to identify the sources: sometimes something as pedestrian as the wail of a cat in heat; occasionally the high thin call of the coyote, which had snuck back into this part of the Northeast from the West a decade before.

The first few months after she had discovered she was pregnant, when the new wedding band, while slender, felt like some unexpected weal on her finger, the cries had seemed to be the spectral calls of the child within. That was after she had moved her things from her parents' house in the city to Blessings for what she had vaguely thought of as a wartime interlude, Benny's letters on transparent airmail paper arriving in the old rural-route mailbox.

And then Meredith had been born, and the cries had been real, yet somehow as foreign as their imaginary counterparts. Slowly she would struggle through the veil of her dreams to the momentarily sinister forms of the lamp, the dresser, the highboy, and the desk ranged around her bedroom, and for a moment she would wonder whose baby that was, crying. Her legs would struggle with the sheets, the blankets, and then there would come the even *tap tap tap* of the footsteps of the baby nurse that her mother had hired and sent out from the city, a thin woman with cropped hair and a faint middle-European accent who played solitaire in the kitchen in her off-hours. Lydia Blessing could remember, in those early weeks, thinking she would not be able to go back to sleep, hearing the tick of the mantel clock, feeling the soreness where she'd been stitched straight up the middle after the Caesarian birth. And then she would waken again to the bright clear light of full day through the branches of the maple outside the bedroom window. She never slept that deep sleep now, and her bedroom in the dark was as familiar as the dimpled face of the moon over the pond.

In the last two weeks the cries had come again, more plaintive and more demanding even than those she had heard when there was truly a baby in the house. Sometimes she thought she was dreaming of those days, sixty years ago now, when Meredith had cried and been comforted, in some fashion, by that foreign woman, who carried the small flannel-wrapped bundle under her arm like a loaf of fractious bread. Sometimes she would start awake, then realize she was hearing the sound of a radio faintly from the garage apartment. She had told Nadine to put a stop to that.

Tonight she could hear nothing but the steady timpani of thunder rolling in from the northeast. She went to the window and peered out into the darkness, but the storm clouds had muted a half-moon. Most of the time she could see one corner of the barn roof from the sleeping porch off her bedroom, one green-shingled curve and one of the lightning rods, a horse in full canter in copper faded to a dull brown. She had put the horse atop the rod herself, held around her waist by her father at the top of a long, long ladder held steady by two of the men who had built the barn. "Must everything be a show?" her mother had said in the dining room that morning when her father had suggested it. Ethel Blessing had not even come down to watch. She had stayed on the long front porch, in a rocking chair, while everyone, the servants, the workmen, the gardeners, had come to see Lydia lift the glowing copper horse into place. She remembered that it had been warm in her hands. Sunny had been at Benny Carton's house in Rhode Island that day, she remembered. It was her only disappointment.

Her father had built the barn in the summer of 1930, when there were no jobs in Mount Mason. The father and an uncle of one of the girls in Lydia's class at Bertram's had killed themselves after the stock market crash, and two of the girls in her class had gone elsewhere even though Miss Bertram had offered them scholarships. But Lydia's mother had never believed in the stock market, or even banks for that matter, and somehow all of the money from the business she had inherited from her father, which had once been called Simpson's Dry Goods but was now called Simpson's Fine Textiles, was safe. They moved not long after the crash from a narrow house on Seventy-seventh Street near Lexington Avenue to the larger house on Seventy-fourth Street near the park, a house that was sold at a considerable loss by a man who had had to be hospitalized at Flower Fifth Avenue Hospital just before the Christmas holidays after he realized that all his capital was gone.

The people in Mount Mason had been glad of the work, and the barn had gone up fast, the wall supports and roof struts laid out flat in the middle of the big grass gully next to the swamp that Edwin Blessing had decided upon for its site. He had also decided that Sunny should work on the barn with the hired laborers from town. "Make a man of him," Mr. Blessing kept saying, as though even character could be contracted out. "Teach him the value of hard work." Sunny had been thirteen years old that summer. His hair grew pale as sunlight, and his skin golden. Lydia thought her brother was beautiful.

"I was so in love with him when we were children," Jess had told her one day when they were waiting to have lunch until Sunny's train came in, the children passing time playing Parcheesi in the library. "He was so dear." Lydia remembered that Sunny had not arrived for lunch that day, had come on the last evening train smelling of gin, a fresh cut at the corner of one eye. She had put him to bed in his usual room. "I'm a bad boy, Lydie," he'd muttered, belching loudly and then falling asleep as though he'd been given an anesthetic. Fifty years ago, that had been, and she could still see his tanned arm dangling from the single bed.

Her sheets were cool as she slid back between them, shining white as a night-light in the dark room. In the years that Blessings had been hers and hers alone, she had never had a colored sheet in the house. She intended to keep it that way. White towels, too.

She had not been down to the barn in many years. It was deserted now, empty of all but pigeons and mice and the odd foraging fox. There was a long steep slope down to it; the builder had said that was the disadvantage to the site, but Father had wanted it there, with a long back drive to the road and a deep pasture to one side. The wife of the farmer from whom he'd bought the cows wept in the doorway as they were driven into a truck with open slatted sides, and Lydia, who was in the old Lincoln with her father, had thought that the farmer's wife must know each cow individually, and was sad to have them leave. Bessie. Brownie. Calico the calf. Perhaps she was saying good-bye in her mind. Years later Lydia had told the story at a dinner party, described the woman in the pink flowered apron holding open the screen door with her hip, wiping her eyes with the hem of the apron, watching the black and white cattle lumbering up the ramp, her husband prodding them with a sharpened broomstick. And Jess had left before coffee and dessert, and next morning had called Lydia and told her in that choked and breathy voice she used when she was angry that the reason the woman was crying was that the sale of the cows was the only thing that had forestalled foreclosure on a farm that had been in her family since before the Civil War. Jess had known because her father was the president of the bank that held the mortgage.

"I had no way of knowing that, for pity's sake," Lydia had said.

"That's forever your problem," Jess had said. "You ought to have known. There are always these things that you ought to know and yet somehow you don't. Open your eyes, Lydia. You are not the center of the universe."

Those were the two people who had been the center of her universe: Jess and Sunny. Both of them gone now. And the people she had thought she'd loved were gone, too, her father, who had built Blessings and then lost it to his wife and daughter, and Frank Askew, still handsome and sleepy-eyed in his obituary photograph in the *Times* fifteen years ago, still married to Ella, still on the hospital board and the Bedford town council. Both men had sung to her. "Let me call you sweetheart, I'm in love with you," her father would sing in his clear tenor as he danced her around the drawing room of the house in the city. "Night and day, you are the one," Frank had sung one night at a deb ball for one of his daughters at the club. There had been a breakfast afterward at the Askew apartment on Park Avenue, and he'd locked the door to one of the maid's rooms and made love to her on the single bed, and all the time she had been able to hear Ella Askew down the hall, with her distinctive voice, loud and bright as dinner chimes, tell a long story about difficulties with the tent for her sister's lawn wedding. "Beautiful," Frank kept whispering. "Beautiful." She was shamed by it all, flushed bright as a peach, but perhaps that had been the pleasure, too. At age twenty her body had seemed to have a mind of its own, to open of its own accord, as automatic as a heartbeat. It was hard to imagine now.

Once she had said to Jess, when they had finished a bottle of wine out on the terrace during the long lunches they had had, the children grown and the men gone, when they were back to what they'd been as girls, "I'm sixty years old and I've never seen a man completely naked."

"Oh, Lyds," Jess had said. "Oh, dear." And then, "Well, it's not all it's cracked up to be." They'd laughed till they cried. Just cried.

Jess had come back to her then, for a few years. She had not meant to leave Lydia alone: she had simply done that most perfidious of things, made a happy marriage, with a good man who loved her and did everything he could possibly think of, from emerald earrings to keeping the children quiet on Saturday mornings, to show her that he did. They had both been married at the beginning of the war, she and Jess, and they had both been widowed during it. But Jess had made another life: two sons, three daughters, and Roger. And Lydia never had. Her life was a life in sepia and black-and-white with deckled edges, framed in silver, mounted in scrapbooks. It had been a former life even years ago.

There was a clammy stillness to the warm summer air, as though the atmosphere were exhaling slowly. An enormous moth danced on the window screen by the head of her bed, determined to get to the faint light filtering up from the hallway lamp downstairs or to die trying. His wings made a sound like a deck of cards being shuffled, and his feet clicked against the wire mesh. For a moment she thought she had dropped off to sleep, heard in her dreams the sound of those old trucks climbing the rise from the drive and then heading down to where the barn was being built, their gears straining with a deep rumble. Then she remembered that it was the Fourth of July, and that there would be fireworks in Mount Mason. That was how she had first met Jess, when her father had taken her to the big field behind the train tracks to watch the holiday fireworks. "The bombs bursting in air," he'd roared, his car lurching along the dirt roads. Jess's father had invited her to share his daughter's blanket, and he and Ed Blessing had shared a bottle. "You should have come, Sunny," she'd said next morning. "I met a nice girl."

"Whose daughter was that?" her mother had demanded, but her father had mouthed the words *bank president* and then it had been all right. But after that they had always had their own fireworks, and Lydia had done the same once the house was hers. One Fourth there had been thirty people staying at the house, sleeping on the patio divans, doubling up in the bedrooms, and they'd had starbursts and Roman candles at midnight, and then strawberry shortcake and champagne, sitting on quilts spread around the front lawn. She remembered that Jess had not liked the people who came from the city. She thought they drank too much, and one of the women, she thought it was Penny Lind, had tried to sit on Roger's lap.

There was another boom, and then another, and a series of them, in waves, and she couldn't parse out which were fireworks and which the storm building overhead. There was the silken sound of wind pushing the tree branches aside, and her room was lit silver with a strike of lightning nearby. The rain came with another gust of wind and a faint groaning sound from the old house, and the thunder again, sure of itself this time, filling the air. She hoped the Fosters were checking to make sure the barn doors were closed. Then she remembered that the Fosters were gone. There had been Fosters in Mount Mason for years and years. There had been Blessings for Lydia's lifetime, and soon there would be none.

"Don't say anything to Mother and Father," Sunny had said when he came up from the barn that first day he was supposed to be working, holding his right arm with his left one, a scratch across his cheek. She had been sitting on the grass by the frog pond, holding some new barn kittens in her lap, and in the slanting sun she could see the pale down on his face where his beard was coming in. He got through dinner, eating left-handed without anyone noticing, and somehow he made it through the night, although in the morning he looked as if he hadn't slept at all. Lydia wondered how he'd gotten on his dungarees and the frayed white shirt from his old school uniform that he wore to work on the barn.

"Mr. Blessing, sir, this arm's broken," the foreman had said, jerking his head toward Sunny when her father had gone down to stand around and talk about the progress of his barn. Mr. Foster drove them to the little hospital in Mount Mason, and she held Sunny's hand while the doctor set his arm. He'd cried out twice, turned white, then red, tiny beads of perspiration like pearls along his forehead. Then he'd fallen against her. "I need some salts in here," the doctor had yelled to a nurse while Lydia held Sunny's slack dead weight.

"That boy is a disappointment," her father had said after they put him on the train to Newport to stay with Benny Carton. When he came home Sunny said he'd learned to sail with just one arm.

The rain was strong now, like the sound of gravel falling on the old slate roof. A gust blew a handful of drops through the screen and onto her pillow. Mrs. Blessing struggled slowly to her feet and brought down the sash. Her left arm was aching where she supposed she'd slept on it. She began to drift off again when a clap of thunder like an explosion settled over the house. They'd used dynamite to blow open the earth, to pour the cement foundation for the barn. She remembered being deaf and dazzled afterward, as though all her senses had been rattled by the sound. The thunder was like that, and on its heels another jab of lightning, so bright this time that for a moment it outdid the outdoor lights. Then the light outside her window, and the ones by the front door and front walk, went out. She realized, looking from her pillow into a black night deep as a well, that the lights in the hallway and kitchen had gone out, too. She was irritated, and then, when she smelled burning, afraid.

The alarm for the house went off with a shrill scream, and she pressed her hands to her temples. When she could bear the sound no longer she stepped into her house slippers and felt her way down the stairs as though she were a blind woman, her white gown rippling like a sail in a high wind, driven by the gusts coming in through the bedroom windows, the hallway windows, and finally, when she had touched each step tentatively on the way down, the windows downstairs. The alarm would not turn off. Her foot slid on a patch of rainwater in the hallway and she started to fall, then caught the knob of a closet door. Feeling along the walls, she sank into the wing chair in the living room and lifted the phone. There was no sound. The burning smell was stronger.

"Damn," she said aloud in the empty house, with no one to hear, with the ringing and the thunder and the percussion of the heavy rain drowning out the word.

From inside the closet she took out her raincoat and then tied a scarf around her hair. On the dining room table there was a bell that she used to call Nadine sometimes, and she took it to the back door and swung it frantically, the rain blowing into her face. The small silvery sound was nothing to the din. There were no lights on in the garage apartment, and no sign of life. In the kitchen drawer there was a large flashlight. She swung the beam around the room, then stamped one foot in rage and frustration. The sound of the alarm was intolerable, like having a tooth drilled.

By the time she got to the stairs leading up to the garage apartment her slippers were soaked through. The rain was sluicing down the drive in great sheets, and during one long lightning strike she could see the pond roiled by the wind and a big limb from the willow tree lying on the lawn. "Charles!" she cried up the narrow stairway. "Charles!" There was a faint echo. She was appalled by the notion of finding him sleeping. It was not that she felt she was intruding on his privacy, more that he was intruding on hers by forcing her to come up to his living quarters and ask for help when he should already be providing it as a matter of course. Even here the screeching of the alarm was loud.

She shone the flashlight around the apartment kitchen and frowned as she saw how untidy it was, with cans and saucepans ranged around the counter. She edged her way down the hall. "Charles?" she called again. The door to the biggest bedroom was closed, and she knocked, then knocked again. When she opened it she could see that the bed was made. There were two fans in the window, and both of them had blown water onto the wood floor before the power outage shut them down. Beneath one of the windows was a bureau drawer, and as she shone the flashlight into it she moved closer to peer inside. There was a baby sleeping on its side, a rolled towel behind its back to keep it propped in position. There was a faint luminescent freckling on one cheek, the mark of raindrops that had blown in but not waked it.

Mrs. Blessing stood there until her legs threatened to give out. The hem of her nightgown dripped onto the floor. For just a moment she wondered whether she was having a particularly strange dream. Finally she found her way to the living room and sat down in a shabby chair by the window. She shone the flashlight on the old-fashioned striped material, and remembered that the chair had once been in her father's study, to one side of the fireplace there. It seemed the only bit of sanity in the wild cacophonous night, and she clutched its arms. After a few minutes she went back to check, but the child was still there, sleeping peacefully while the alarm screamed on. She had read about the eye of a storm, about how it was the only still place in wild weather. This appeared to be it.

If anyone had asked Skip where he'd least like to be on July fourth in a thunderstorm, the answer would have been easy: McGuire's. But there he was, nursing a beer in a greasy mug, watching one of Ed's younger brothers play a pinball machine with so much body English that it looked like he was going to slam Batman-a-rama through the back wall of the bar.

"Yo, dude," yelled the bartender over the noise of some country song, "ease up on the machine."

Skip looked at his watch. He figured he had roughly an hour before the baby would wake up. She'd seemed to settle in the last two days, eating, sleeping, eating, sleeping, with one pissed-off hour right around the end of the workday, as the sun was dropping down from the sky. He had to walk her then, back and forth, but when she finally dropped off there was a sweet quality of submission to her small body. She burped, spit up on his shirt, then went slack and silent. He realized that there was a point to that ungainly empty area between the human shoulder and chin: it was the perfect place to rest an infant.

Nadine's daughter had told Nadine, who had told him in her particular furious fashion, that some girl named Debbie had a letter for him from his father. That was the only thing that would bring him to McGuire's now, although once he'd practically lived there. He looked around at the guys nursing their beers and playing pool and wondered for the first time in his life who the hell was taking care of their kids. Women, probably—wives or girlfriends or even their mothers, when the wives and the girlfriends went out or cut out. Skip figured he must be crazy, the only full-time single father in Mount Mason.

He tapped his foot impatiently on the bar rail. He knew from living in their trailer those first few months after he got out of the county jail that Debbie cut hair during the day, and worked from ten to two at McGuire's four nights a week. She might as well work there, Joe had said, since she'd be there anyway, and she could give him free beer. McGuire's was what they all had instead of a social life, a tavern on the corner of Front and Route 211 that was long and narrow, with a pool table and a dartboard in the back room. Skip's father and uncle used to drink there, and Joe's father, and Ed's, too. Chris had never had a father that anyone remembered, although Chris's mother had been known to sit at the bar at McGuire's until closing time. It set her apart when they were kids. Women went to McGuire's when they were single, and then when they were married they went to baby showers or Tupperware parties or Weight Watchers or over to see their mother or their mother-in-law.

McGuire's was owned by a family named Jackson now, and they'd gone through a period, about ten years back, when they'd had somebody paint, in gold letters edged in black, "Bar and Restaurant" on the plate-glass window. And there were menus, and fancy coffees with booze in them, Irish and Neapolitan and whatever. It hadn't been completely successful. Now occasionally someone would order a burger and fries, or those nachos that everyone had on the menu because you just popped them in the microwave. Most of the food consumed at McGuire's consisted of the peanuts on the bar. Lots of the food consumed at McGuire's got thrown up in the parking lot. Skip remembered the year after he graduated high school, when he was working the Burger King job, kneeling on the asphalt at least once a week, one time in snow so deep that he'd lost the feeling in his knees. If he ever went back to that life he thought he just might as well shoot himself and get it over with. He remembered some mornings, when he was living with his aunt and uncle, coming into the kitchen and seeing his uncle having a beer at eleven A.M. "Breakfast of champions," his uncle had said, hoisting the can in the air.

"You want another beer, Skipper?" the bartender said.

"Nah," he said. "I'm driving."

The bartender shrugged. "Been watching too many public-service announcements," he said.

"Goddamnit!" yelled Ed's little brother, banging his fist on the side of the pinball machine.

He'd never had a letter from his father. Postcards, about twice a year, always with a picture of palm trees or a beach. When he'd been in the county jail his father had taken a detour, after picking up a load of machine parts in Connecticut, and come to see him unexpectedly. The two of them sat at a long table that was bolted to the floor, and his father bought him soda and a Ring Ding out of the vending machine. "The important thing is that you learn something from this," his father kept saying, and Skip kept nodding, thinking, yeah, I've learned never to drive a getaway car. But he didn't say anything. Actually, neither of them said much. His father said that Linda, who was the woman he was living with, was working as a hostess now, which was easier on her back and feet, and that the two of them had gotten a double-wide trailer that looked just like a house and came with the curtains already hung and the wallpaper already on the walls. Skip said that he was getting out in four and a half months. They hadn't really had a lot to talk about.

He wondered what was in the letter his father had sent him. He wondered if Debbie was always late to work, or just tonight, to torture him.

He didn't even hear Chris come up beside him until he felt the iron arm around his neck. Chris smelled of beer and pot smoke, and he had a bruise on his face that looked fresh. His freckled face had that puffy creased look that had come with sleeping in, drunk, when they were younger, but that just became the way you looked if you slept in, drunk, for enough years. He had a tattoo on his upper arm, the Tasmanian Devil. He'd gotten it one night at a place at the beach in Virginia when the four of them were all to-gether, sleeping in one room at a Motel 6. Skip had gotten sun-burned and he hurt all over, and when the tattoo artist had put the first needle in, to put a lightning bolt on the back of his hand, he'd seen black stars in his peripheral vision, and come to on a cot in the back with an egg coming up on the side of his head. "I'm not doing that, dude," the tattoo guy said flatly. "I got a policy."

The Tasmanian Devil arched his round belly as Chris picked up his beer. "Where you been, Skippy?" he said. "How come I never see you anymore?"

"You need me to drive you again?" Skip said.

"Don't be a wiseass, man. You know I never wanted to fuck you up."

Skip knew that in some twisted way that was true. He and Chris had been friends since first grade. He'd always stuck by Chris, even in fourth grade, when Chris got the ski jacket from Santa Claus, the really good one with the fleece lining, wore it to school, all proud, and then caught Robert Bentemenn, whose father was a lawyer and a magistrate and something-or-other with the chamber of commerce, staring at it.

"That's my old jacket that my mom gave away to the Salvation Army," Robert'd said, and Chris was on him, *bam bam bam*. Half the class jumping on Chris's back couldn't stop his arm from going up and down, up and down. The jacket went into the Dumpster behind Newberry's, once Chris found Bentemenn's name written inside the pocket in indelible marker, and Chris had to go to counseling, and the counselor told his mom he had poor impulse control. Memorial Day weekend last year his impulse had been to hold up the Quik-Stop, and Skip had been stupid enough to be driving. Chris hadn't really meant any harm, but that hadn't made ten months running laundry through an industrial mangle any easier to take for Skip.

"How's life in the Magic Kingdom?" said Chris, and Skip shrugged. "They need any part-time help out there, 'cause I just got laid off from my sheetrocking job?"

Skip shrugged again. It froze him, to think of Chris anywhere near Blessings, or the baby. He looked at his watch. Debbie was almost half an hour late. A girl named Mary Beth down the bar waved at him. "Hey, Skip," she said. "What's new with you?"

"I need a job, and I need pussy," Chris murmured in his ear.

"Ah, man," said Skip, putting down his beer on the bar with a thud. "Don't talk like that. You're too old for that kind of talk. That's low. That's just low, man."

"Fuck you, man. You're pussy-whipped by that old woman. You never come to the bar, you're never at Ed's. You missed the demo derby. What the hell is it with that place? When I was a kid my aunt Patty used to pass around the food there at parties and she'd come home saying, ooh, the silverware, the flowers, the fucking lake. I bet you don't fish in that lake, my man, because she'll cut your heart out. Jimmy's old man went out there once, and he pulled a twenty-two-inch brown trout out of that lake at six in the morning, and there she was, standing on the front porch. She wanted him to weigh that goddamned trout and she told him she wanted him to pay for it by the pound. By the fucking pound!"

"What'd he do?" Skip said.

"He paid her six bucks for the goddamned fish. Which reminds me, I'm going to come out there someday and fish in that pond. I hear there are still some big browns in there. And it's not like she'll ever notice. We'll go fishing, and then you can either quit, or we'll get you fired. You got to get out of there, man. You even smell like a girl. You smell like suntan lotion or something. What are you doing, basking on the diving board?"

It was the baby wipes, and the baby powder. Skip was thinking about how to explain away the smell when Debbie blew through the swinging door from the back room, but not before Chris narrowed his eyes and looked at Skip like he was seeing him through smoke. "Yeah, yeah, yeah," said Debbie, knowing she was late, pulling the letter from the back pocket of her jeans.

Two minutes and he was out in the parking lot, the rain so heavy that he couldn't make out his truck right away. He turned on the interior light and ripped open the envelope like it mattered, like the old man really had something to say to him after all these years. He was amazed by the faint pulse of hope he felt in his own throat. On lined paper like the kind he used in school his father had written: "Son, We thought you would like to know that you have a baby brother. His name is Lance he eats good but doesn't sleep all that much. Maybe you can come see him soon when he's sleeping better. Take care of yourself and have a drink on me. Your father."

A ten-dollar bill fluttered from inside the letter to the floor of the truck. Skip leaned over and picked it up, then let it fall again. He started up the engine and peeled out from the parking lot onto the flooded road, his back end fishtailing. He wondered whether his father's wife had the same baby books he had, and whether she'd found out yet that the newborn diapers were too small for most babies and cut into the soft skin of their upper thighs. He'd be goddamned if he'd tell her, or send a card. Lance Cuddy. What the hell kind of name was Lance? A soap opera name, was what.

Lights came up on him suddenly out of the wall of water, a car heading his way, and both of them slowed down, afraid that the wind and the rain might just blow them headlong into each other. He was lucky with the lightning. It zigzagged toward the earth a minute later, when he was edging over the bridge over the big creek, and in the strange silver light he could see that someone had already blown out the guardrail on one side, so that there was a drop of ten feet or so to the creek bed. He went across at maybe five miles an hour, praying for his old bald tires not to slide on the bridge grid. He couldn't afford to have an accident, not with the baby at home sleeping steadily toward her next bottle.

There was a car up ahead on one side of the road, its front end an accordion pleated around the engine block, and he pulled up behind it, his brights on, and ran to the driver's side to see if anyone was hurt. But the car was empty, empty with the emptiness of an abandoned house, and as he got back into the truck, soaked and shivering, he realized that he was at the Boatwright house, where cars were ranged around the drive and the lawn the way some people planted petunias. The Boatwright women all looked as though they'd been inflated with a bicycle pump and encased in stretch fabrics; the Boatwright men were short and wiry and always carried shotguns and cigarettes; Boatwright kids had gray skin and bad haircuts. In grade school there had been Boatwright twins in their class, girls with big round arms and raggedy bangs. For a nickel they'd show their privates behind the athletic-field bleachers.

As he crawled through the valley, the water running across the road in rills of mud and gravel, Skip realized that it was less than a mile from the Boatwrights to Blessings. And for a moment he was afraid that his wet engine would stall and he would be caught in the Boatwright world forever, the way a lot of the guys he knew had been, since Boatwright girls would sleep with anyone, and sleeping with a Boatwright girl just about guaranteed a pregnancy. For one terrible moment he imagined that his baby was a Boatwright. But he knew it couldn't be true. She was too plump, too pink, her nose and chin too distinct. Besides, there was no such thing as an unwanted child among the Boatwrights, just as there was no such thing as a wanted one. Babies just happened.

"Lance Cuddy," he said to himself. "Lance goddamn Cuddy."

He almost missed the turnoff into the driveway, as many times as he'd taken it, would have missed it if the birch trees had not made a ghostly show just before the fence curved in. At first he thought it was because of the rain, which was impenetrable, nearly as deep as the night, dark gray on black. But as he came down the long drive and around the big circle, the back of the house on one side of him and the front of the garage on the other, no lights came on to illuminate the truck, and from inside the house he could hear a high thin screaming sound. He threw the truck into park and ran up the back steps to the big house, and then realized that what he was hearing was the sound of the alarm. He knocked and knocked at the back door, cursing Nadine, who had refused to give him the alarm code, or even show him how it worked. "You don't need," she'd said, looking at him as though he had one hand on the strap to her purse.

Upstairs in the apartment over the garage the rain made a hard heavy noise on the roof. There were no lights there, either, not even the red glow of the clock on the stove in the kitchen. He felt his way to the drawer by the refrigerator and took out the flashlight. Outside the kitchen window, that looked back over the fields and then the long tangle of forest, he could see nothing but the rain. His work boots sounded of wet as he squeaked down the worn wooden hallway floor.

Like the birches that had been beacons on the road, there were two small columns of white in the living room, two candles burning on the old steamer trunk. Slowly he swung the the flashlight up, and saw Mrs. Blessing sitting on the sagging chair, holding a light-colored raincoat to her throat, two feet of wet white cotton hanging from beneath its folds. A scarf with some pattern of flowers was tied over her hair.

"Jesus Christ," Skip breathed. "You scared the hell out of me."

"Don't speak to me about being frightened," Mrs. Blessing said. "I've been here all alone, no electricity, no power, no light, for who knows how long. And that hideous alarm sound."

"Did you call the alarm people?"

"The phone's gone, too, everything's down, and then there's a terrible smell of burning and I don't know where it's coming from. And I had no idea where you had gone."

"How did you get in?" Skip said.

"I have a key, of course. What sort of a question is that?"

He was catching his breath now, his heart trying to slow down from the drive, the bridge, the alarm, and above all from the sight of Mrs. Blessing in the small room. He felt funny, shining the flashlight right at her like that, illuminating all the lines in her face and the fear in the set of her mouth and the wild glare in her light eyes.

"You have to do something," she said.

"I will."

"Right this minute. The entire house could be burned to the ground while you fiddle about."

"Not in this rain it won't."

There was no smell of fire in the apartment, only the smell of rain and mothballs, maybe from Mrs. Blessing's raincoat, and the smell of powder and the sweet smell of baby wipes, that Chris had scented with his nose for secrets and weakness. Skip shone the flashlight onto the face of his watch. It was twenty minutes until twelve.

"You needn't worry," Mrs. Blessing said sharply. "I'll stay here with the child while you see about the alarm and the fire."

"What?" Skip said.

"You can imagine my surprise," she said, her mouth pursed, "to come in here looking for help and discover that, behind my back, without permission, you had your child living here."

Of course. She'd come over and made a circuit of the place. She owned it, after all, and she owned him, too, in her way. Skip felt his shoulders slump, as though his body knew the sad pathetic ending to this latest brief episode in his life before his mind did. It was like when the sheriff's car had been waiting behind his truck at McGuire's the night after the Quik-Stop robbery; his whole body had gone slack, his eyes sad, in the moment before he had known to say to himself, well, that's it, then. Chris'd be pleased, he thought, when he heard Skip got fired from Blessings. "Welcome back," he'd say, standing at the bar at McGuire's. Lose the job, lose the baby. He guessed he'd wind up leaving her in the hallway at the courthouse for the social workers after all. His stomach turned, the beer gone sour.

"I was surprised by her, too," he said finally in a tired voice, pointing the beam of the flashlight down at the floor. The room was quiet and the rain slowing, so that the individual raindrops fell on the roof like the sound of a child hammering on one key of a piano, one low note again and again. From their pattern he could tell that the storm was moving, and that by daybreak the air would be clear. He went down the hall to the hook where he hung the big slicker one of the Fosters had left behind.

"Charles," she called querulously after him, and he stiffened. "What is this baby's name?"

"She doesn't have a name yet," he said.

"That's preposterous. Where's her mother?"

"She doesn't have a mother either."

"It's impossible to imagine how someone could do everything that is needed around here and take care of an infant as well," she said.

"I would never have hired a man with a small child," she said.

"Babies are very unpredictable," she said.

Mostly he said nothing. He looked down at the Aubusson rug in the small study and rubbed at a paint spot on his brown work pants. This was the room where Lydia Blessing did what she thought of as business, where she told the carpenter the estimate was too high, complained to Nadine's husband that the heat in the car was still insufficient, paid bills and wondered aloud why everything cost so much. Her father had done business here as well, with the decanter at his elbow.

"Are you absolutely certain?" she said. "Just placed on the steps like that, in a box? Wasn't there any sort of identification, or some sort of note?"

"It's not the kind of thing you'd make a mistake about, ma'am," he said.

"It's very difficult to believe that someone would just abandon an infant in the middle of nowhere like that," she said, straightening a stray envelope in one cubby.

"It is the ideal place for you to have the baby," her mother had said sixty years before.

She put her hand to her forehead. There it was again, the echo, the minuet of words spoken in the present with those from the past. It had gotten worse since she had seen the baby in the yellow glare of the flashlight, sleeping with a fist pressed to its pursed lips. Her mother had been right, of course. In the middle of nowhere had seemed a good place to raise a child during that first year of the war. There were always rumors that bombings would begin in New York just as they had in London, and the social life of the city was constrained, partly in deference to the war, partly because there were no men around.

Of course the young Lydia had thought it was a temporary measure, and that Blessings would once again become a country retreat when the war was over and real life began. In her mind's eye she could see the apartment she and Benny would have, the brocade sofa against the long wall of the living room, the barrel end tables, the painting of a sailing schooner over the mantel. Benny would go downtown to his father's firm, which would someday be his firm, and Lydia would play cards with girls she had once gone to Bertram's with, and their children would go to Bertram's, too, or the Thomas Makepeace Vester School for Boys, which was where Benny and Sunny had gone before they had gone away to boarding school. Sunny would come to dinner and make them both laugh, and the children would love him, perhaps as well as, if not better than, they loved their mother and father. It was as though it all really existed; it was all there, all true, as though, as their upper-school science teacher had said, Professor Einstein had indeed shown that all time took place simultaneously, only in different locations.

In the middle of the night, as Meredith had been mollified by the rubber nipple and the thick yeasty-smelling formula, as the soft sounds of the outside slipped into the silence of the house, Mrs. Blessing had imagined that in an apartment on Park Avenue an older, wiser Lydia was going over the menu for a dinner party and telling a roomful of overexcited children to go see Nanny, please, and go to the park to play. It was only the moments alone with Benny she could not imagine, what she would say, what he would say, how he would touch her, what it would feel like, whether it would always feel cool and hesitant and smooth when he kissed her.

"This is all right, isn't it, Lydie?" he'd whispered at the municipal building after they were married. "This will be good."

"A child should have two parents," she said to Skip Cuddy, folding her hands firmly in her lap and looking out over the pond. Still he was silent.

Lydia Blessing had known Benny Carton almost her entire life. She had been five when he and Sunny became friends at Vester. "You have a sister," Benny had breathed the first time his nanny brought him to the house, and he had reached out a hand to touch a blue ribbon tied around her hair.

"You have two brothers," Sunny said.

"It's not the same," Benny said. "Is she good?"

"I like her," Sunny had said. That was what she remembered, how happy she had been. "Sunny likes me, Mama," she had said that night at dinner after he'd been sent from the table for making his napkin into a hand puppet and refusing to make the hand puppet be quiet.

"Well, he ought to, oughtn't he?" her mother had said.

It was odd, how important those things were to children. She wondered what she had said casually to Meredith that she had never given a thought and that Meredith could remember like a motto on a sampler. Well, he ought to, oughtn't he? As though Sunny's liking was no more momentous than a napkin on the lap, or a fish knife with Dover sole. But it was Sunny's matter-of-fact "I like her" that she would never forget. He and Benny had always been together after that day, although now Benny lay beneath a white stone cross in a small cemetery by the sea in Newport and Sunny's ashes had been scattered over the pond, a breeze blowing them up and over, into the air and then into the green water eddying around the little boat.

She closed her eyes at the memory. Skip was still standing silent, and she wanted to make him say something. "I am far too old to have even collateral responsibility for an infant," she said loudly in the small dark-paneled room as he picked at the spot on his pants.

"I don't like that guy one little bit," Benny had said when he cut in on her and an older boy from Vester at a club dance. She remembered that, too. And that his hand at the small of her back had perspired, so that when they went onto the terrace that looked out over the children's zoo she felt a cold place there. "I don't like the way he behaves," Benny had said when they were outside, holding their cigarettes conspicuously, both of them experimental smokers. "I'd rather not be more specific than that." He had leaned over the ornamented limestone balcony, his head tilted to one side. "Listen," he said. "Can you hear the monkeys?" She thought she could, a faint hooting sound, like the disapproving crowd at a sporting event if you were outside the stadium. Benny smiled. "You can hear them from my gran's apartment. When I was little I thought they were talking. I used to think I could hear whole conversations in monkey talk."

"What were they saying?"

"Not much. They say a lot of the same things we do, really. Weather. Gossip."

"That's dull," Lydia had said. Even when she was younger, sweeter, more tractable, less deadened by life, she had been what the teachers called blunt.

Benny had laughed. He was not much taller than she was, and the way his hair arched back at each corner of his forehead foretold his future baldness. He had black eyes and long lashes, a small thin dash of a mouth bracketed by dimples, like a punctuation mark. That's what she had said on the balcony, and he had laughed again.

"You're the only girl in the world I like," he'd said, and he'd said it again the day they were married. He was still a little drunk that morning from the night before, and he sucked on peppermints so the clerk wouldn't notice, although they overlooked a lot in the city hall chapel in those days, especially if the groom was in uniform. Three days later he was sent south to a base in Georgia, and then quickly overseas to Europe. His letters suggested cryptically that his facility with languages would keep him out of harm's way. Her mother sent Lydia to the country to do the same for her, or so she said.

"It's been sixty years since there's been a baby in this house," Lydia Blessing said.

She had gotten the telegram telling her Benny was dead on the day that Meredith took her first step, lurching from the ottoman to the end table in the den. Benny's father sent a car to bring her to the memorial service at St. Stephen's, and afterward he took her into the library of the big apartment on Fifth Avenue and asked if Meredith could come to them in Newport for a month of every summer. All three of the Carton boys were dead, one of scarlet fever, another in the war two weeks before his brother. Only Benny had had time to marry. "Please say yes," Mrs. Carton had murmured in the foyer. "Or more often if you'd like."

"It's a good opportunity for Meredith," Ethel Blessing had said when her parents came out to the house for the weekend.

"Cherchez l'argent," Lydia had said bitterly, but Ethel Blessing, who had not gone to Bertram's, like so many of Lydia's friends' mothers had, but instead had been taught at home by a nanny who spoke bad French with a German accent, said only, "They have a lovely home. They are nice people." As though the two were one and the same, eighteen rooms equaling excellent character.

Lydia had stayed on in the country house for a while, thinking it was easier to have this interlude, with Mrs. Foster cooking and the baby nurse taking care of Meredith. It was difficult for her to imagine how she would manage to greet Frank Askew when she got back to the city, how she could affect the even uninterested gaze and the cool polite platitudes a girl was expected to use when she spoke to the fathers of her friends. It was difficult to imagine meeting his wife and daughters in Central Park with Meredith and watching their eyes light on the small face with swiftly veiled recognition. It made it easier when she remembered that the nannies usually took the children to the park, that in their heavy prams, in their embroidered caps, the babies all looked the same, as if they could be anyone's.

She spent hazy summer mornings walking around the pond, weeping, thinking about finding a place to live in New York and when it would be decent for her to return. She wept for her husband, not because she had not married him for love, but because had he lived she would have had to pretend she had until enough time had passed for them to settle into the passive give-and-take of the not unfriendly society pair. Each afternoon she took her baby with her in the boat, rowing from one end of the pond to another, while the nurse stood on the high ground by the dock, frowning down at her muddy shoes.

The boat still lay by the pond, shining white. She remembered that Charles had painted it the week before, and remembering, she had a picture in her mind of him, stoop-shouldered and furtive, and understood that he had been carrying the child with him everywhere for days.

"I can't imagine what sort of a person would abandon a child in this fashion," she said.

Two months before Benny died she had received the longest of his letters. It was clear from the scribbling on the envelope and a variety of official stamps that it had gone badly astray after it was mailed. His handwriting was difficult to read, the left-handed scrawl of a haphazard student. She had waited until she was seven months pregnant to write to him about the baby. They had spent three nights in a small hotel on Gramercy Park, and on none of them had he been able to make love to her in the usual way. His ways were Benny ways, she supposed at the time, gentle, tentative, generous, a little boyish, as though they were in the back closet at dancing class. The sight of his handwriting on the letter had made her fearful, but there was nothing to fear.

"Dear Lydie," he had scrawled, "I am really happy about the baby. I hope it will be a girl, and that she will look exactly like you. The happiest thought I have here is that someday I will come home and you will be there and the baby will be there and it will be like a regular ordinary family and all this will be like a bad dream. When I keep that in my mind I am all right. Love, Benny (your husband)."

It was as though with the parenthetical expression he was trying to convince, or remind, himself. And her. He had always loved babies, Benny had. He was the sort of boy who would help a pair of toddlers build with blocks at a birthday party while the other older boys were ripping up the drawing room and throwing cake. He was the sort of man who would have spent endless hours pushing a child on the swings in Central Park. She had been able to see him in her mind, singing nonsense songs, pushing a pram through the park paths while the nanny clucked disapproval. "Mr. Carton, sir," she would say. "Mr. Carton! That's my job."

That stayed with her for years, that sketch drawn in a few simple sentences, that idea of a parallel life that might have been hers, with Benny in a chesterfield chair, losing his hair little by little, and Meredith growing every day more like her mother, or even like Benny, instead of more like Frank Askew.

A week after she'd learned that Benny was dead an enormous box had arrived from the stationers on Madison Avenue, and when she opened it she found box after box of ecru-colored cards. "Mrs. J. Bennet Carton" was engraved at the top of each one in faint script the color of coffee with cream. "Blessings, Mount Mason." There was stationery enough to last for years.

It had been a winter day, snow thick upon the roof and trees, and in the silence broken only by the sound of logs spitting sap from the living room fireplace Lydia had looked at the cards and understood then, as surely as if they were legal documents. Her mother had decided that Lydia was to live in exile at Blessings, never again to sleep lulled by the sounds of cars struggling by in the morass of the streets of the East Side of Manhattan. She knew. Lydia did not know how, but her mother knew. The sin Lydia Blessing thought she'd hidden so neatly was known to some and had to be kept secret from all the rest. She threw one of the boxes of stationery into the fire, then another, until the flames reached out with blue-and-orange claws, burned Lydia's right hand, blistered and blackened the paint of the mantelpiece.

"I'm happy you've made up your mind to stay," Mrs. Foster said when Lydia told her she would remain at Blessings for a while. "The city is no place to bring up a child."

Lydia's younger self had punished her mother by exiling her, too, at least in effigy, by banishing all the customs and ceremonies that Ethel Blessing had held so dear at Blessings. Since she had never thought of herself as anyone but Lydia Blessing, she ordered her own stationery with her own name on it in a fit of defiance that surprised even her when the cards and envelopes finally arrived. Just as she had burned some of the cards her mother had sent and put the rest away in the garage attic, so she buried the formalities that had defined the lives of her mother and her mother's friends.

For a time life at Blessings was irregular: sandwiches slapped together by other young widows who came for the weekend and ate at odd hours, swimming in their underwear with men who played at being interested in women. White circles from drink glasses on bedside tables, a martini shaker always in the bar refrigerator, the faint creak of bedroom doors opening and closing in the middle of the night.

But the customs of slight degeneracy had become customs nonetheless, and after a time the swims became tedious, and sometimes dangerous for the guests who were really drunk, and everyone began to want better meals. And before she knew it Lydia's life, too, had become a series of small ceremonies. The house parties became one or two long-married couples staying the weekend, and the gossip was about their children and their children's friends instead of one another. There was tennis in the morning, croquet in the late afternoon, and Sunday brunch of Bloody Marys and omelets filled with herbs from the garden (in summer) or cheese from the farmer who raised goats down the road (in winter). During the week she played golf every Wednesday, followed by a swim, and tennis with her best friend, Jess.

"This is my birthday wish," Jess had said when she was turning thirty, a month after Lydia had done so. "I want you to meet someone nice and marry again and have three more children who will play with my children, and when we're old we'll sit by your pond and talk about old times and watch our grandchildren swim the way we swam."

But none of it had turned out as Jess had wanted. Her children had come by with their mother to swim in the pond with Meredith, but there had been no husband for Lydia, and so no more children, and it had become clear over time that there would be no grandchildren, either. Jess had not gotten old, she had gotten sick. Lydia had spent hours sitting next to her bed and holding her hand, and Jessie had cried, "Goddamnit, I feel gypped." And Lydia had felt gypped, too.

She did not care to play golf or tennis after that, and soon she could no longer swing a club, what with the arthritis in her hands and shoulders, and the weekends with houseguests had given way to the occasional visit from Meredith and her husband, the occasional lunch with her lawyer, the occasional dinner with Jess's daughter Jeanne and her husband, Ed. One set of rituals had given way to another as summer gave way to fall, not through choice but through inevitable custom. Sometimes she thought of Benny in his leather chair, reading the papers, losing his hair, but more often she thought of him as a boy listening to the monkeys talk, his head to one side, trying to figure out what the monkeys were saying. She thought of him and Meredith, rowing across the pond, laughing.

She sighed. Thinking of the monkeys had made her sad, and her voice soft. "Charles," she said. "Now that I am aware of this peculiar chain of events, at the very least you could bring her outside. Keeping her perpetually indoors can't be healthy."

And finally he spoke, perhaps because the frost had melted from her voice. "I can't be out with her, ma'am," he said. "If Nadine sees her, she'll tell Mr. Foster, and he'll tell some of the guys he works with, and they'll tell their wives, and then people will say I stole her, or she belongs to some girl in town that I was, I guess you'd say, fooling around with, and then there'll be all these rumors, and they'll send somebody official to see me, and there'll be this whole big mess, and who knows what might happen."

"Oh, nonsense. Who cares about one baby?" And all the voices of the past came back to remind her in a great chorus—Frank, her mother, Benny, her father, even Meredith—that one baby could change everything.

"You don't really understand the way things are around here."

"Nonsense! I've lived in Mount Mason since long before you were born."

"No, ma'am. You live at Blessings. That's totally different." He looked toward the kitchen. "Like here's an example. You bought the kitchen table from Harrison's furniture store around fifteen years ago. You got it on sale. I think maybe it was about two hundred dollars. Is that right?"

Mrs. Blessing nodded grudgingly.

"See, my dad is a long-distance trucker, but sometimes to make extra money he used to do deliveries around town. He delivered this table. And Mr. Harrison told him you bought the cheapest piece in the showroom. And my dad told all his friends at the bar that you didn't tip him, and when he asked for a drink of water you sent him to the pump."

Mrs. Blessing's lips were pressed tightly together. "What does that have to do with what we are discussing, Charles?"

"Everybody knows everything about everybody around here. And one of the things they know is that your family is better off than anyone else in the valley. So let's say some girl has a baby and she figures she has zero money or no good place to live or whatever. Maybe she's one of those big fat girls you hear about on the news who gets pregnant and no one even figures it out, just thinks it's too many Quarter Pounders or something. She might think if she has the baby in the bathroom and then leaves it here it will have this great life."

Tennis in the morning, croquet in the afternoon. A housekeeper, a pond, a rumored pile of money. She realized he must be right. Still she said, "Charles, I am eighty years old. My daughter, who never had children of her own, is now sixty. No reasonable person could imagine this family could care for a child."

"People think all kinds of things about this place. But then someone who thought they'd give a baby to rich people is at the

Wal-Mart or the drugstore and hears that I'm walking around with this baby, and now instead of the baby getting to live at Blessings the baby gets to live over the garage, which maybe isn't any better than where the mother was living herself."

"I beg your pardon. The Fosters found that a perfectly fine place to raise three children. They never complained."

"No, ma'am. I bet they didn't."

She should have called him in and fired him. That was what she had intended when she had had Nadine fetch him from the wood-shed. She did not know why she hadn't. It was so difficult to find decent help. And the baby had slept all the time she had waited for him during that terrible storm, while he reset the alarm and checked that the smoldering corner of the barn roof was not going to spread with the heavy July rain.

"I've been working with her in a front pack for two weeks now," Skip said, talking fast. "It doesn't work all the time, but it works most of the time. And I've got her on a pretty good sched-ule now. I have to keep her a secret for now. And this is a really good place to do that."

Mrs. Blessing sat up straight. "I have to give this some thought," she said. "In the meantime, the split-rail fencing on the south side of the drive appears to be leaning. Is there anything we can do short of replacing the fence?"

There was that crooked smile again. "I already ordered some steel supports to hammer in behind the uprights," he said. "I'll tie them together and we'll get at least another couple of years out of that section."

"And the child?"

"I'll put her in the front pack."

"You could leave her over here from time to time. There is a back bedroom with a cradle."

"I can't take the chance with Nadine," he said. "Besides, she should really stay at my place. She's my baby."

"A child needs a name, Charles."

"I'm working on it," he said. "I figure most people get nine months to figure that out. Besides, until now I wasn't sure I could still keep her. I just couldn't stand to name her if I couldn't keep her."

Later, as Mrs. Blessing ate her dinner at the table by the window, the sun melting orange into the pond, she remembered there was a bear somewhere upstairs, sitting on an old chair in a back bedroom that was used for children who came to visit, although none had come in years. It had been Benny's bear when he was small. Its fur was rubbed thin on the stomach and pate, and it was stuffed with something that made it hard and not huggable. Five-year-old Meredith had been clutching it one morning after she'd been driven all night in the Cartons' big car from Newport. Mrs. Foster had made her a cup of cocoa and some muffins. Sunny had been there, too, staying in his old room, and he had heard the car arrive and had come downstairs in a big plaid bathrobe, his golden hair every which way.

"Was my daddy a good daddy?" Meredith had asked Lydia, and Mrs. Foster had paused just a moment as she spooned fresh whipped cream into the cocoa.

Lydia had been trying to think of what to say when Sunny dropped down next to the little girl and put his face up close to hers. "Benny Carton was the best daddy in the whole wide world," he said, and held her tight. Lydia had gone upstairs and wept. She did not know it, but that was what Meredith would always remember, that she had peeked into the bedroom and seen her stern and undemonstrative mother crying, and for the rest of her life, even when she was a grown woman, she would recall that moment and feel as though her childhood had held something sweet and deep. She had not known, of course, that Lydia Blessing wept for herself, and for her own lost life, and for something in Sunny's voice that she had never heard before. Lydia had not known it, either.

Slowly she rose from her desk chair, and went upstairs, down the hallway of closed bedroom doors, to find the bear.

N adine's daughter, Jennifer, walked across the lawn with the muscles in the front of her thighs rolling beneath the skin. She was built like a swimmer, which was what she'd been at Mount Mason High School. Her hair was black and hung halfway down her back in a loose ponytail. Skip tried not to look at her too long. At his feet the tangle of willow roots splayed into the pond, and two large-mouth bass fluttered their fins and seemed to stare up at him; back in the blackberry bramble behind him was a basket with the baby asleep inside. There hadn't been rain for two weeks, since the storm on the Fourth of July, and he could hear the grass crunching as Jennifer Foster walked. Skip tried to sniff himself without raising his arm. Not too bad, although he thought maybe the smell of diesel fuel from the chain saw was mixed with the smell of Desitin from the baby, who had some kind of rash. Maybe Jennifer Foster didn't know what Desitin smelled like. It actually smelled a little like diesel fuel.

"Hello," she said. "I'm sorry to bother you."

She had a funny way of talking, as though she were older than she was. She didn't bother to say her name, and he didn't bother to say his. Nobody in Mount Mason was ever introduced to anyone else. Skip knew that her father had been in some peacekeeping force in Korea and had married Nadine there and brought his wife and kid over when he could finally manage to get them out. Skip knew that Craig Foster didn't speak to most of his family because one of his uncles had said at a Memorial Day barbecue that Craig was sleeping with the enemy and most all of the other Fosters had sided with the uncle, who, they said, didn't mean any harm, and how come Nadine had to be such a bitch anyhow. Skip knew that Jennifer worked part-time at the hospital and went to nursing school at the community college, which surprised him a little, since she seemed like the kind of girl who could go to State, maybe even someplace better. Skip knew that she'd never had a serious boyfriend, and that that made the mothers of Mount Mason pretty happy because, as well mannered and pretty as she was, she still wasn't white. She was more or less tan. In every way she was the opposite of most of the other girls he knew in Mount Mason, who got out of high school, got pregnant, and got fat.

"Come right back!" Nadine called from the kitchen window, all the consonants flat in that funny way she had of talking, like a person who was deaf.

Jennifer Foster didn't roll her eyes exactly, but she raised her brows a little bit. She probably knew that Skip's mother was dead. She probably knew that in high school he'd lived in one of those listing frame houses with the narrow front porches on Front Street with his aunt and uncle instead of in one of the brick ranches tented over by trees out in the valley with parents, like she had. And she definitely knew, by the way she was smiling so nicely but with a little bit of an edge in her eyes, about the stretch in the county jail.

"She want you," Nadine shouted.

"First she sends me out here to give you some message about the barn. Then she yells at me to come back." Jennifer Foster shook her head, then looked up. "Isn't this a great tree? When I was a little girl I used to sit under it and read. If it rains you don't even get wet, unless it's pouring."

"You have to keep after it," Skip said, putting the pruners down in the wheelbarrow. "The branches get too long, and then some of them aren't really as strong as they need to be, and they can come down pretty hard if there's a storm, and take the healthy ones with them. She's sort of let them go. Mrs. Blessing, I mean."

Jennifer Foster smiled. "I know who *she* refers to around here," she said.

It was hard to believe, looking at her, that Jennifer Foster was Nadine and Craig Foster's daughter. Together the parents looked like a sight gag. Craig was a huge man with narrow shoulders, a high pale forehead, brown hair fading to gray, and a mustache that somehow made him look silly, almost as though it were fake. Nadine was something else. She had the small and sexless body of a young boy, her legs slightly bowed, her arms muscled and bowed, too. Her face was flat, with an ugly mysterious scar across one cheek, part cut, part burn. All the times he'd seen her, Skip had never seen her hair any way but pulled tightly back into a ponytail, had never seen her wear anything but jeans and a man's shirt. The only jewelry she wore was a digital watch that beeped every fifteen minutes and a wedding ring. "Be like beating your meat against a board," Chris had said once when they'd seen the Fosters in town together.

It was cruel even to picture Jennifer with the two of them. He couldn't understand how two people who looked like that had produced one who looked like this. "Mongrels, Skippy," Chris had said. "They make the best dogs." Chris always had a mean mouth on him. One night in McGuire's he'd bought Shelly a beer, when Skip had just started dating her, if you could call it dating, getting drunk with someone in a bar, going home with them, sleeping with them, then sleeping it off. And Chris said, "Shelly, your tits wouldn't be so big if you weren't so fat." Skip waited for Shelly to throw her beer in his face, which would have at least made Chris respect her. But instead she ran into the ladies' room and cried. Skip went home alone that night. Sometimes he wondered if it was Chris who had knocked Shelly up. Chris loved sleeping with girls he hated.

Nadine was marching across the driveway turnaround, carrying a red-and-white striped dish towel like a flag, or a weapon maybe, like she was going to flog them with it. "You deaf?" she said.

"I'm coming."

"She want to see you," Nadine said to Jennifer, and then she turned and looked at Skip, narrowing her eyes that were already slits in her small flat face. She had the gift, or in her case the curse, of making you see yourself as she saw you. Skip could imagine the circles of sweat on his gray T-shirt, the dirt that must be smudged on his face, the grease on his hands. "She want to see you, too. She say you go to garage, take things back there, straighten up, come see her."

"Why?"

"Don't ask me," Nadine said, waving the dish towel, heading back toward the house.

"I imagine you know who *she* is, too," Jennifer Foster said.

He sure did. He and she had become part of a conspiracy. The instructions Mrs. Blessing had given Nadine meant that she was watching with her little birding binoculars and knew he was out with the baby, that he should settle her in the apartment before he came over to the big house. Two days before, a woman delivering some slipcovers that had been cleaned had come from town unexpectedly while Skip was working on the fences with the baby in the basket at his feet, and he had been flabbergasted by the sight of Mrs. Blessing waving him away from the house from a second-story window, her flowered scarf a bright flag of caution in her hand. "Charles," she had said the night before, "if you must go to town you must leave her here with me. You can wait until Nadine has left for the day."

"What will you do if she wakes up hungry?" he said.

"For pity's sake, I've had a child of my own," she said, but something in her pinched face told him she was wondering the same thing.

He looked closely at all the windows facing the pond and then put the basket in the wheelbarrow. The baby was awake, staring at the sky and trying to cram her fist into her mouth. There was a star-shaped swirl of hair at the crown of her head of which he was oddly proud, and her pointed tongue moved between her lips as though she were tasting the air. She had a scratch down one cheek from her sharp little nails, and Skip knew that Mrs. Blessing would have something to say about that, although he'd just trimmed the nails himself, an operation that made him so nervous he'd had to start and stop a couple of times. Skip never knew how to put her down to sleep either. He had one book that said on the back so she wouldn't die of crib death, and another, that he'd gotten at a yard sale for a quarter, that said on the stomach so she wouldn't die inhaling her own vomit. He'd decided to alternate, although sometimes he forgot what he'd done the night, or the nap, before. Reading the books had made him wonder how anyone came out of infancy alive. Or fatherhood. They'd had one more bad night, when she wouldn't sleep and wouldn't eat and never wanted to be put down for even a minute. Her head lurched from side to side on her thin stem of a neck, and she stopped crying only to suck noisily on the shoulder of his shirt, then on his nose. Luckily it had been a Sunday and he hadn't missed any work, but he'd had to put her on the daybed in the back room again and walk away to get his bearings.

"Let her cry it out," Mrs. Blessing had said when he'd made the mistake of mentioning it the next day. "That was the belief when my daughter was small. Otherwise they'll be terribly spoiled."

Skip hadn't said anything. He thought everybody needed a little bit of spoiling, particularly when they were no bigger than a groundhog.

He looked down at her sleeping, and he filled up with the simple fact of her, that she was alive and breathing and getting bigger day by day with nothing and no one but Skip Cuddy to care for her. Sometimes she seemed as though she was trying hard to see him, although the books said she couldn't really focus her eyes yet. In the evening, he would take her outside for an hour or two, take her to the far end of the pond and lay her down on a blanket folded double so the damp earth wouldn't touch her romper. "Charles," Mrs. Blessing complained, "it's far too damp down there. Bring her up closer to the house." But sometimes he just wanted to have her all to himself. The bats would make loop-the-loops above them, and the birds would trill to one another, hidden away in the top branches of the darkened trees. He wished he could bring her out into the sunshine more instead of keeping her curled up in the chest carrier so much. The books said sunshine was good for newborns. His next day off he'd drive somewhere far away, a half hour or so, and find a park and push her around in the stroller. If anybody asked, he'd say he was her father. He'd actually practiced in front of the mirror. "I'm her father," he'd say. "Four weeks. Yeah, a girl. Oh, about ten pounds. Good baby, sure, really good baby." He'd looked pretty good until he remembered he was alone and felt like a moron.

When he'd given her a bottle, put her down on her side in her Portacrib, and put on a clean shirt, he knocked at Mrs. Blessing's back door. Nadine brought him to the living room. It reminded him of a class trip he'd gone on in sixth grade to George Washington's home at Mount Vernon.

There was a big oil portrait of a man over the stone fireplace, and some watercolors of flowers on the far wall. Mrs. Blessing was sitting in a wing chair between the fireplace and the window, her binoculars on the piecrust table next to her. A teacup was there, too, and a newspaper with a magnifying glass atop it. She was wearing what she usually wore, a white blouse and a long blue skirt. In the light from the window he could see her scalp through the thin waves of her silver hair. Jennifer was sitting at the piano. It looked like no one ever sat on the living room furniture, except for Mrs. Blessing.

"Nonsense," Mrs. Blessing was saying to Jennifer. Skip had noticed that it was one of her favorite words.

"Well, it's only my first year," Jennifer said. "At the end of next year maybe I'll have a better idea of what to do."

"You should be at a fine four-year college," Mrs. Blessing said. "One of the Seven Sisters, perhaps."

"People mind their business," Nadine muttered behind him, but loud enough so that the woman and the girl turned and saw him.

"Charles," said Mrs. Blessing. "This is Jennifer Foster. Nadine's daughter. I trust her implicitly." She laid a hand on Jennifer's shoulder, the white thrown into relief by the golden skin of the girl. The bones of Mrs. Blessing's hand were articulated, each one clear through the spotted skin, as though she were being whittled down by the constant pressure of the years. It was one of the first things Skip had noticed about her, that, and the fact that the only jewelry she wore was a wedding band. On the piecrust table was an old black-and-white studio photograph of a young woman in a white dress. He could see that as a girl Mrs. Blessing had not been girlish: straight nose and mouth, large eyes and forehead, nothing rounded or soft, as though she had been designed specifically to age gracefully.

"We know each other already," Jennifer said. "We knew each other at school. Except for the Charles part."

"It's Skip," Skip said, feeling the heat in his face.

"Charles, before it slips my mind," said Mrs. Blessing, "I am unhappy about what you're doing to that willow tree. There's no need for you to prune that. That tree has a particular shape. It's not like a maple, or an elm. The weight of a willow tree goes down, not up. I would like to look at that tree before you do any more work on it. My father planted those trees. They are not replaceable."

"Yes, ma'am. But you'd better look at it soon. Half the branches on that tree are dead wood. There's all this poison ivy vine that's wrapped itself around the dead branches, that you can't see from here with the binoculars. The woodpeckers are having a field day, and if we have a good-sized storm anytime soon, which we will have, since it's July, it just might take off the good wood with the rotten stuff. That's what happened during the July fourth storm. If it happens again, your father's whole tree'll wind up in the pond and I'll be pulling it out with chains and the tractor."

Skip could feel Jennifer Foster watching him. He loved that tree, too.

"That tree has done fine without you for sixty-odd years, Charles," Mrs. Blessing said.

"Yes, ma'am."

"And it will be fine for sixty more."

"No, ma'am, it won't. I called the county extension service and they said that by rights I should prune a third of the small limbs on that tree every year. And there's one more thing. There's a repair that needs to be made to the roof of the barn, right near the door to the hayloft. It's that place where the lightning hit during the storm. It has—"

Mrs. Blessing got to her feet. When she moved, her clothes gave off a sharp powdery scent, like the lavender in the beds by the boathouse. "Take care of it," she said, moving toward the piano and riffling through the sheet music on its stand.

"I think it's probably too big a job for me. Someone was shooting off a gun in there, maybe shooting pigeons or wood doves, and then the rain made—"

She did not stop or turn back toward him, and there was a certain grave dignity to the precision of her slow and labored movements. Skip suddenly realized, looking at her curved back, that when she was younger she must have been a tall woman, nearly as tall as he was.

"Have it taken care of," she said.

Jennifer Foster followed him outside and across the driveway turnaround. She stopped by her little blue car. A straw handbag was on the seat, and a pair of sunglasses. There was a stuffed panda on the dash wearing a little shirt that said "Number 1 Daughter!" Skip figured it had come from her father.

"It sounds as if you can cut back the willow tree," she said. "If she doesn't object outright, then it means she agrees. If she really objects, you'd know about it."

"You translating?"

"Yeah, I guess so," Jennifer said, smiling. "I've known her a long time. I remember I wanted to cut my hair in sixth grade. She said, 'I won't hear of it.' And when I said I was going to Mason County Community, you should have heard her."

"She wanted you to go to State?"

"She wanted me to go to Wellesley. Or Smith."

"Never heard of them," Skip said.

"Waiting!" Nadine screeched from the kitchen window.

"Sorry," Jennifer said. "I have to go back in and play the piano. She says it saves on tuning." She smiled again, and squinted up at him in the sun. "You should just fix the barn. You don't even have to ask her about the barn when there's a problem."

"How long have you known her?" Skip asked.

"For as long as I've been in Mount Mason," she replied. "She had my mother bring me over in the beginning to satisfy her curiosity, I think. And then she wanted to make sure that I wasn't being allowed to speak Korean at home. Americans should be American. That's what she always says. She obviously doesn't know my mother. My mother wouldn't let me speak Korean on the plane, much less in Mount Mason."

"So you think of her as like a grandmother?"

"Not exactly. It sounds weird, but I think we're friends. She started out wanting to arrange my life, the way she arranges everything around here, you know. She still tries to do some of that. But then I think she got to like me. She must like you."

"Why?"

"She lets you in the house. I'm not even sure the Fosters were ever allowed in the house, except to serve meals or lay the fires in the fireplace. She's funny that way. And since you've been here she's seemed livelier, I guess I'd say. More tuned in than she has been."

"I'm not sure she likes me. I think she thinks I do a good job."

"With her it comes to the same thing. You should just fix the roof. It'll be fine."

"The thing is, I can't do it myself. It'll take a professional roofer. You need special ladders and scaffolds. It's not a one-person job."

"Then you should hire a roofer. She'll complain, but she'll pay for it. She never goes down to the barn, but she likes it kept up. Her father had it built for the cows, and her daughter used to stable her horses there."

"It seems like a waste. Nobody uses it."

"She doesn't care. She just wants it kept up. Her brother died down there. There's a stone, right where there's that big clump of lilac bushes. When they're in bloom I always cut her a big bouquet. The first time I ever came in the living room was to put the vase on the table."

"I didn't know you were allowed to just bury people on your property."

"I'm not sure he's buried there. Anyhow, Mrs. Blessing is allowed to do whatever she pleases. My father says she can make straw into gold and water into wine. Like Grimms' fairy tales or the Bible."

"Do you really think that's true? Not the straw, but that she can do what she wants and get away with it?"

Jennifer Foster shrugged. "The point is, if she needs something done, she can find a way to get it done. And she wants you to find a way to get it done, too."

"I get that," he said. "I meant to say before, your car is idling low. I could tune it the next time you're here, if you want. If you want, I mean."

"Thanks," she said, in the voice girls like her always used for guys like him at school. "My father owns a garage, so he usually does it."

"Oh. Yeah. I knew that. Stupid."

"No, no. Thanks, really." There was a spear of silver from the porch window. "Don't look now, but she's watching us."

"Did you cut your hair in sixth grade?" he said.

"Are you kidding? Of course not."

With a faint sense of irritation Mrs. Blessing realized that someone had invented many things that made having a baby infinitely easier than when she'd had a baby herself. Instead of the ungainly pram with its big stiff wheels there was this sling contraption that allowed a person to carry an infant around everywhere, hands free. Instead of the papers of enormous safety pins with Bakelite heads of pink or blue, there were these tapes to hold the paper diapers fast, printed with little dancing characters of some kind. Even the bottles were different, the nipple squared off, the inside lined with plastic bags. It reinforced her feeling that the young women of today had it easier than she had.

On the other hand, she was rather proud of her pink KeepSafe baby monitor. Skip had handed it over with an air of resignation, the compromise between leaving the baby alone and letting her sleep in the big house when he was out and about. "You can hear every noise she makes," he had said. "But don't overreact. Sometimes she'll just make a little sound and then go back to sleep." Mrs. Blessing switched the monitor on. "I don't hear a thing," she said.

"Listen real carefully," he said.

She pressed the receiver to her ear. In response she could hear faintly the sound of shallow breathing, in and out, in and out.

"That's her," Skip had said proudly. Shyly he added, "Her name is Faith."

Mrs. Blessing pursed her lips. "I like it," he added. "It's not one of those made-up names that everybody has nowadays, like Summer or Whitney or whatever."

"There are children named Summer?"

He nodded. "There's a guy I know, his girlfriend had twins. Summer and Autumn."

"Dear Lord," Mrs. Blessing had said. It was the closest she ever came to profanity.

"What about Faith?"

"I'm sure it will do nicely," she said.

"It just came to me," he said.

He had had to go out as soon as Nadine pulled away, to try to get to the motor vehicle office before it closed, to register Mrs. Blessing's Cadillac. "She just got fed and changed," he had said through the screen door to the living room. "She should sleep until I get back. Can you hear her?"

Mrs. Blessing held the monitor to her ear. "Perfectly well," she said.

Ten minutes after he pulled out she heard a faint snort and convinced herself that it was her responsibility to check on the child. It was an effort for her to climb the steps to the apartment, and when she arrived at the top she was perspiring and her shoulder ached. She realized that the other sound she heard on the monitor was the sound of the fans going. Perhaps she should buy an air conditioner for the apartment. Then she snorted herself. Another indulgence for an indulged age. She remembered how the baby nurse had given Meredith cool sponge baths on July days like this one. The baby had splashed spastically, sneezing when the water got into her eyes. Lydia had been afraid always that her child would slip beneath the surface and drown.

This baby looked sturdier somehow. The deep pleat in the fat at her elbow made her arms look muscled. Her mouth moved in a sucking motion. She was in the small vinyl Portacrib Skip had unloaded from the truck, along with a swing and a car seat. "I always wondered who shopped at garage sales," he'd said. "Now I know. I got all this great stuff for ten bucks."

Mrs. Blessing liked economy, particularly in those who couldn't afford to be profligate. But something sad stirred within her at the sight of the baby, who was becoming quite pretty in that puffy pink baby fashion, in the slightly shabby, slightly faded pastel print of the folding crib, a crib some other child had used when it was new. She laid her hand, which always trembled slightly now, atop the head and felt her fingers mold themselves automatically to the small skull. It was her favorite part of an infant because it seemed strongest, not as vulnerable as the wobbly trunk or flailing arms. There was a small mobile of mice hanging, grinning, from colored umbrellas; when she took her hand away she knocked it, and the first three notes of "Twinkle Twinkle Little Star" were sharp in the quiet half-darkness. The baby stirred, moved her head to the side, and brought a fist to her slack mouth.

When Mrs. Blessing went back to the house she felt worn out, and as she breathed in concert with the breathing on the monitor she felt herself slip away and begin to doze. When the telephone rang she came awake, terrified, as though it were the security alarm again. But it was only Meredith, who made it a habit to call on Wednesdays just before dinner.

"How are you feeling, Mother?" she always said now, instead of a simple *hello*.

"I'm fine."

"Were you sleeping?"

"Of course not. Why in the world would I be sleeping? It isn't six yet."

"How are the flowers?"

"About as well as can be expected in this heat. This new man takes good care but the bugs have made a hash of the nasturtiums, and the lupines are terribly thin."

"I'm so sorry," Meredith said. "How is Nadine?"

"Don't get me started on Nadine. If it were possible to find decent help, she'd be in Mount Mason looking for a job."

"I'm so sorry," Meredith said again, by rote, her voice breathy with boredom and impatience.

Two women long past their prime, talking about nothing, Mrs.

Blessing thought, that's what she and her daughter had become. Mrs. Blessing wondered what Meredith would say if she told her about the baby in the box, and realized that she had no earthly idea, which seemed terrible. She should know her daughter better, and she knew that this must be at least partly her fault. The baby nurse, the nanny, the summers in Newport, the boarding schools. Meredith had made an early marriage and moved to the horse farm in Virginia, which she'd bought with the proceeds from the sale of the Carton grandparents' house. The result was that they did not know each other very well. Mother and daughter had always to become reacquainted, like people who met from time to time at the same parties.

When she was younger Meredith had tried to talk to her sometimes when they were riding together, after school, before dinner, playing twenty questions to try to measure her young self and puzzle out what she was made of. What was your favorite food when you were my age, Mother? How many girls were in your class at Bertram's? Tell me again about the time you and Uncle Sunny tobogganed onto the pond and broke through the ice. Tell me again about the party Nana and Papa had when you were coming out. Lydia Blessing had felt rather smug that at least she answered her daughter's questions, not like her own mother, who often just had said, "Curiosity killed the cat."

"How is your leg feeling?" Meredith said now.

When she had opened her eyes in the hospital two years ago she had been dreaming about that coming-out party. Or perhaps dreaming was not what it was called, when you had had a stroke. In the dream, she had been in the library of a club on Park Avenue; she was wearing a white faille dress that fell off her shoulders in big stiff pleats. The room was not very crowded; many of the guests her mother had invited had had other parties that evening, or at least that was what her mother had said. Across the room Lydia saw Frank Askew, whose daughter had been two years behind her at Bertram's. He had a mustache and a widow's peak. It had all been much as she remembered it, except that in the dream he had come across the room to talk to her, which hadn't happened until a drinks party several months later. And he had bent and kissed her neck, the mustache tickling, which had happened some weeks after the drinks party, in a stuffy back bedroom at the Askews' apartment that smelled of Shalimar and laundry soap and lemon wax. In the dream she had wanted to turn and walk away, and yet had been unable to do so, as she had been unable to do so in life all those years ago. She had been paralyzed, and aroused, too, as she had been in life. Except that when she had looked down at Frank's brilliantined red head, bent to the curve of her shoulder, she had seen above the low neckline of the white dress the blue veins, the ropy muscles, the semaphore of brown cast across the skin, and realized that it was her old and not her younger self that he was kissing in the dream.

Then everything had gone bright white, and she had opened her eyes and been still paralyzed, at least on one side, and still deeply stirred, although the feeling evaporated so quickly, in the glare of the hospital lights and the sudden attention of the nurses and Meredith's guttural weeping, that she could convince herself that it had been something else, some medical condition.

There had been no private room available, and she had had to share a room with a woman from north of Mount Mason who had had her gallbladder removed. "She goes on and on about her grandchildren until you want to scream," Mrs. Blessing had said, slurring her words slightly, since the stroke had been a minor one. She had not noticed the look on Meredith's face. After so many years of living alone, she had to remind herself that part of saying the right thing was reading the face of the person to whom you were speaking. It was no wonder that her own mother, who had tended to look down at her own rings whenever she talked, had so often gotten things wrong.

"Come visit next weekend," Mrs. Blessing said into the phone suddenly as the breathing on the baby monitor beside her rose and fell. She was certain as she said the words that she meant them as she never had before, and as certain that she would regret the offer

once it was made. There was only so much change in her routine
that she could manage at any given time. She looked down at the
monitor again.

"What's wrong?" Meredith said.

"Nothing's wrong. Need something be wrong for me to invite
you to come to the house? Never mind. Never mind. Don't put
yourself out."

"Mother, we'd love to come. But there's a customer coming to
look at that foal that was born last month. And an assessor. What
about the end of the month?"

"Well, I don't know," Mrs. Blessing said, as though she were
studying her calendar. It always lay open on her desk: white,
white, like the dress in her dream, the dress that covered her face
like a cloud when Frank had thrown up the skirt. White except for
here and there an appointment with the doctor, a note about a
dinner. There was Jess's birthday marked on July 18, Jess's birthday
but Jess now sixteen years dead. "I suppose that will have to do,"
she said to Meredith.

"I could try to reschedule the assessor—"

"No, no, the end of the month is fine. I suppose Nadine can get
some decent corn by then."

Through the window she could see the lawns spread gray-green
around the pond, the grass dry from lack of rain. Some small black
birds picked at the foot of the dock and at the grass around the
boat. For some reason that curve of bright white wood on the
lawn gave her the sort of quiet feeling of contentment that she
now found rather rare, and she realized that cupping the baby's
head for that brief moment had done the same. Those moments
had always come rarely to her, and almost always about small crea-
ture comforts, never in times of great emotion. It was a feeling of
peace accompanied by a kind of settling in her chest, her chest that
was usually taut and thrown forward so that, when young, her
breasts had been emphasized in a way men found suggestive and
yielding and was really just the opposite. As a child, a pair of new
shoes might bring the feeling on, and later a nice restaurant meal,

or the simple sight of a quartet of iced martini glasses atop a tray out on the patio. The sight of Sunny had given her that feeling, too, when he came home from prep school or out to the house in the country, those years he had visited her here. And when she was much younger she had had that feeling when her father entered the room.

Everyone had expected her to have it with Meredith. Such a beautiful baby, such a lovely child, such green eyes, tip-tilted like the accents in her French text at Bertram's, *accent aigu, accent grave.* Of course her hair had been red, like a flame atop the long pale candle of her face. Red as Ethel Blessing had probably feared it would be when she sent Lydia away to the country, red as Frank Askew's had been when he was a boy, although when Lydia had first met him his hair was faded to a rust color. Benny's mother had dredged up an aunt who had had auburn hair whenever anyone thoughtlessly mentioned it. Now that it no longer mattered, Meredith's hair was as silver as her own.

Sometimes when she was young Meredith had taken the boat out to the middle of the pond and sat with a book, an old straw hat of her grandfather's pulled low on her head. She had a lovely widow's peak, Meredith, clear and deep. She never wore hats now except for the black riding helmet, always wore her silver hair pulled straight back so that the widow's peak stood out on her forehead like an arrowhead.

"Lyds, my love," Edwin Blessing used to say, speaking in comfortably unoriginal aphorisms, "a gentleman wears a hat or he stays inside."

"You girls will wrinkle dreadfully in this sun," her mother had said, on those rare occasions, after Meredith was born, when she'd come to Blessings and watched Lydia and her friends dive off the dock.

Mrs. Blessing had told Nadine that her little girl could use the boat, too, the boat that sat there day after day upturned, abandoned, unused. But Nadine would not allow it. "No, no," she had grumbled. "Not right." Mrs. Blessing had been surprised to like

Nadine's child. Like so much else in the world in which she found herself marooned, she had disapproved of the girl in theory. Men like Craig Foster should marry women from Mount Mason who went to the same church and knew the same people, not Korean women they had met somehow when they were soldiers stationed overseas. Nadine could not even be considered a war bride; Craig had been in Korea long after there had been an American war there. But his foreign wife and his foreign daughter had come to seem to Mount Mason more foreign still because some immigration regulations meant they had not been able to join the husband and father until three years after Craig Foster had come home. Legends had grown up about them during that time, like the legends about the man who lived on the dead end by the high school and never left his house.

Mrs. Blessing had met Jennifer for the first time twelve years ago, when the child was six, when Nadine had been working for her for six months and the little girl had had to stay home from school with an ear infection. She had perched on a stool in the corner of the kitchen all day long, so quiet that Mrs. Blessing knew she was there only because from time to time she heard, on the air, like a treble counterpoint to the atonal music of Nadine's flat fractured English, a high lilt.

"I am very pleased to meet you, ma'am, and I am sorry that I have had to come with my mother today," the child had said when Mrs. Blessing came into the kitchen, under the pretense of asking for a change in the lunch menu.

She had been tickled by the stiff little speech of a sentence, and the oddly outdated clothes the girl wore, what Mrs. Blessing still thought of as appropriate clothes, a plaid skirt, a wool sweater, knee socks, laced shoes. She had not recognized the clothes as Meredith's castoffs, four decades old, preserved between tissue, silted with mothballs. Mrs. Blessing had asked Nadine to give the clothes to the Salvation Army when a new roof had had to be put on and the attic cleaned out as a result. "There's obviously no point in keeping them for Meredith," said Mrs. Blessing, who in some inchoate way disapproved of her daughter's childlessness. Nadine had picked out the hand-stitched monograms with a pair of scissors, ironed and ironed until the peaks and valleys where the stitches had lain were pressed out, and kept the clothes herself.

Meredith was talking about one of their horses. A pulled muscle, she said, visits from the vet. Mrs. Blessing was not listening. Now, at age eighty, the past so distant and yet so perfectly clear, like one of the dioramas in the natural history museum, her mind tended to drift. From the monitor she heard a series of thuds, and her heart beat fast until she realized it was the sound of footsteps going up the stairs of the apartment. It irritated her, that she had been so addled by sleep and the heat and the surprise of the phone and what her father had called woolgathering that she had not heard the truck return. Or perhaps he'd used the back drive, which came from the road around the barn. That was a sneaky sort of thing to do. On the monitor she heard the footsteps louder now, and a few notes of the mobile's music box again.

"What's that?" Meredith said.

"Nothing," Lydia said. "I believe Nadine's listening to the radio."

"She's there late today."

What was Meredith saying? That she had hired a new housekeeper herself because the one she'd had had not suited. "The apple doesn't fall far from the tree," Lydia could hear her father saying. She was growing tired of all these people speaking at once, the past, the present, perhaps even the future in the slow breathing of the baby. From the monitor she heard a voice whispering, "Hey, sweet pea. Hey, Faith. I'm home. I'm home." Softly Skip began to sing "Twinkle Twinkle Little Star." He didn't know all the words, and his voice was almost tuneless. For some reason she simply could not fathom, Lydia felt tears fill her eyes.

"I hope I haven't made a mistake," she said, interrupting Meredith, who was talking about a stallion in Middleburg who was available for stud.

"Pardon?" Meredith said.

"About this new man," said Lydia.

"Oh, Mother, you're never satisfied."

"I'm perfectly satisfied when things are done correctly."

"And does he do things correctly?"

"I suppose he does," Lydia said.

The thing that amazed him, when he listened to her old-fashioned locutions, the *shall*s instead of *will*s, when he looked at her living room, that would have been faintly shabby and purely ridiculous if it had been in one of those big development houses down the hill, was that you couldn't get loose from what you were born into. Everyone believed you could, in America, but it wasn't true. One moment you were a Boatwright baby, with a crusty nose and a diaper that should have been changed two game shows ago, and then you were a Boatwright girl, giving hand jobs in pickup trucks and carting around a baby of your own. You weren't ever a cheerleader, or a college girl, or one of the women who sat behind a desk at the First National Bank and said, "Can I help you?" and "Your mortgage approval should take approximately ten to fourteen working days." Just like if you were Robert Bentemenn, and you ran your Corolla into a tree and got popped with hash in your pocket. Instead of going to jail, like Skip or Joe would, you wound up in rehab in Arizona, then at Arizona State, which would lead to law school, which is what your lawyer dad planned in the first place. Robert Bentemenn was a moron, and once burned a girl with a cigarette just for the hell of it, but thin blond girls with sweaters tied around their shoulders who would freeze Skip if he smiled at them sat at their desks in high school and wrote "Mrs. Robert Bentemenn" on the covers of their spiral notebooks.

Maybe, he thought, in the truck on his way to the Mount

Mason Medical Center, that was why he wanted to keep Faith, and why he thought he should give her up, too. Her parents were going to make the difference between that sweater tied around her shoulders and some flimsy maternity T-shirt with an arrow pointing down at her belly at age sixteen. Maybe if he gave her to some nice cookies-and-milk woman and suit-and-tie man she'd wind up sleeping in a canopy bed in one of those mock Tudor houses that clean people with new money seemed to like so much.

Or maybe he could just make something of himself, and so make something of her. He wasn't sure how to do that. "Not college material," the counselor had said in high school, looking at his shop courses and his address. But Craig Foster had managed to edge into the middle of Mount Mason society with his auto body shop, managed to mingle at the Elks club with the plumbing contractors and the restaurant owners. Maybe Skip could do something like that, try working his way up in some business in which he could work with his hands. He'd become one of those people who could take his daughter on vacations, not to Europe the way the lawyers and doctors did, but at least to Florida somewhere. He could just imagine showing up at his father's new place, in a polo shirt and pressed slacks, handing his old man a business card: "Cuddy Sheetrocking" or "Cuddy Painting Contractors." He'd show off his little girl, talk about their new ranch house a couple of miles out of town: "Wall-to-wall carpeting all through the house, and a spa on the patio," he'd say. He'd always had a little bit of contempt for those kinds of guys, all clean clothes and briefcases and high blood pressure, ruddy and smelling of lemon aftershave. But he'd join their ranks if it would buy a sleepover for Faith in one of their daughters' pink gingham rooms.

At least she had a cradle now, a carved cherry cradle on shallow rockers that Mrs. Blessing had told him to come and take from a musty back bedroom in the big house. He had tickled himself with the thought of tying a string to his toe and looping its other end around the ornamental curves at the head of the little bed so that in the nighttime he could rock her without getting up. But she was such a good baby now, so orderly and cooperative in her habits, that the idea was more of a cartoon construct than anything he needed to consider. He felt stupid sometimes, how he liked to watch her, how he still flinched when she popped herself in the nose with her spastic fist, how her face went real still and her mouth opened as she watched the sunlight shoot down onto the floor next to her blanket, how she would smile like a spasm and it would go straight to his heart. He'd watched some doctor on his little TV and seen him make babies, little babies, just as small as Faith was, imitate the things he did, and though they were stupid things Skip did them every day, pushing out his tongue slowly, watching her do the same, over and over. He figured when she was six months old he would start to read books to her, and when she started to stand he would get her shoes. Shoes were a problem, too, though, like sleeping positions; some books said that they provided support for the feet, others that they were unnecessary and maybe uncomfortable. He'd have to think about that one a little more.

When she went down at nine, woke at two, slept until seven, sucked down a bottle, and went down again for two hours more, he could convince himself that the future might be that regular. First grade, junior high, a life with a place for everything and everything in its place. When she stayed up half the night and threw up all down the back of his only remaining clean T-shirt, he didn't know if he was going to make it, and he figured it must somehow be his fault. He'd always been a pretty tidy guy, for a guy, but the apartment had clothes and towels and cans and bottles all over the tables and counters, and just when he thought he was getting it cleaned up a diaper would explode out the sides and into the legs of one of those little suits with the snaps that he'd bought, and there'd be dirty sheets and shirts tied up in a case by the kitchen window to isolate the odor.

"Charles," Mrs. Blessing had called one evening. "Where are you taking those things?"

"I've got to go to the Laundromat," he said. "The monitor is on and she's asleep."

"Nonsense," Mrs. Blessing said with a frown. "There's a perfectly good washing machine in the basement. Just use the basement door."

He tried to look into Faith's eyes at times when all the things she needed seemed too much for one man, to fasten on her face and not just the endless tasks she seemed to generate. "Teaching you to ride a two-wheeler is going to be so cool," he said once. He thought about when he had learned. He had been nine years old and his friends found out he didn't know how to ride a bike. Chris had taught him to ride. Chris had run beside him, his arms shaking with the weight of the bike and Skip on it. It hadn't been easy to teach him, but Chris had kept at it all one weekend, and by Sunday afternoon he'd finally learned.

"I learned to ride a bike," he said that night to his father, who was watching football on TV.

"That's good." It didn't seem to occur to his dad that he was about four years late on the learning. But the next weekend his father brought home a pretty nice secondhand bike he'd gotten from a guy who sold things out of his garage. "You know, I never did learn to ride one of these things myself," his father said, watching Skip make jerky circles in the driveway.

"I'll teach you to swim in the pond," Skip said to Faith. "And to fish." She hooted in reply, arched her back, shuddered, then hooted again.

"Talk to your baby whenever the spirit moves you!" the book said. "He understands more than you can imagine."

"Faith," he said each night when he put her to bed, "you're safe." Sometimes he really believed this was true. He did a lot of the outside jobs at Blessings in the evenings now, after Nadine was gone, and he could take the baby with him while he vacuumed the pool, filled the bird feeders, cleaned the boathouse. She would lie on a blanket twisting her head from side to side, watching the play of light on the surface of a window, the pond, the slowly darkening edge of the western sky. Sometimes Mrs. Blessing would sit in one of the white wooden rockers on the front porch and he would leave Faith on a blanket on the lawn just past the walk, lying among the small umbrellas of pachysandra. "This child is going to roll over sooner than you think," Mrs. Blessing said once, and "Those nails are badly in need of a cutting," and "She has especially long fingers." But mostly she rocked and watched and looked sideways over the pond while he worked.

He looked at the old woman and the big house and the spreading pachysandra and the roses growing along the terrace and he thought that maybe it would all work out, that the little girl could grow up here. When the breeze was soft and the fish flipped in the air over the pond and dove back down into the green water again and Mrs. Blessing's tight disapproving mouth relaxed into something like a smile, he could convince himself that somehow no one would notice that, instead of a mother and a father and a birth certificate, this particular child had this young guy and this old woman and a cardboard box and a barrette that had once clamped her cord. As Mrs. Blessing said, who cared about one baby?

"Faith, you have a good deal," he'd whispered on one of those nights.

But that night when he heard Joe outside his window, calling, "Yo, dude—dude!" he knew that any little girl of his in this town would have a hard road to hoe, even if he found a way to explain her to people.

"Yo," Joe yelled, "yo," and Skip went downstairs because he couldn't let Joe come up with Faith slumped in the baby swing, listening to its tinny workings picking out the *Sesame Street* theme song while she tried to get her thumb into her mouth. Joe smelled like turpentine and tobacco.

"You painting again?" Skip said.

"Yo, man, you need a phone for emergencies."

"What's the emergency?"

A light went on in the back of the big house in what Skip thought was Mrs. Blessing's bathroom. She'd managed to come around about the baby, but he didn't think Joe was the sort she'd want visiting the place. For that matter, Skip didn't want him there either. "Come in the garage," he whispered. "What's up?"

"You got a beer upstairs?"

"You drove all the way out here to get a beer?"

"What kind of way is that to talk, man? You think I'm a moron, I'd drive all the way over here for a beer?"

Skip sighed. Talking to Joe was like driving a tractor through mud. He remembered when he was living in the trailer, how Joe had a big sign on one side of the steps that said BE WARE OF DOG. He remembered pointing at it, saying, "You want someone to be ware? What's that, ware?" He'd laughed. "It's not two words, man," he'd said, but Joe's eyes had stayed blank, not getting the joke. "I don't get you," Joe had said.

"Joe, just tell me what's up," Skip said softly in the big bay of the garage, his words echoing faintly. "What's going on? You need help with something?"

"No, man, it's Chris, all right? Chris busted up his motorcycle bad. I tried to call you this morning but I forgot your old number didn't work anymore and I woke up your aunt. She was pissed, man. She said to tell you to get your stuff out of her garage. She's still really mean, you know? Like she hasn't mellowed at all."

Skip grabbed Joe's arm to get him back on track. "Is Chris okay?"

"It looked really bad, man. He almost coded on the table." Joe watched a lot of hospital emergency room shows. He'd wanted to be an EMT but he'd had a felony conviction for a B and E when he was eighteen, and that took care of running the cherry lights on an ambulance. Another reason why Skip hadn't given him up on the Quik-Stop deal.

"But he's gonna make it?"

Joe shrugged. "Maybe permanent damage in one leg, man. He broke a lot of shit. A lot of shit. But the thing is, he really wants to see you. I think he saw the white light last night." Joe watched a lot of shows about miracles and mysteries, too. He was always peering at people in the mall to see if they looked like anyone on *America's Most Wanted*. "He really needs to make things right with you."

"Things are right with me," Skip said. Things are right with me, he thought. I never see Chris anymore. That's exactly right.

"Dude." Joe gripped his arm. "Go see him. Go tomorrow."

He went. He put the baby to bed early, at eight, which gave him an hour to drive over before visiting hours ended at nine. Mrs. Blessing turned on the baby monitor and placed it by the chair in the library, and Skip left a bottle in the kitchen refrigerator just in case. He'd wound the mobile before he came downstairs, but the tune was starting to slow already. "She won't wake up," he said as Mrs. Blessing cocked her head. "I'll be back soon." Not much time to visit, which was fine with him. There was a picture of Mrs. Blessing's father in the lobby of the hospital. He looked like an actor in a period film, a high stiff collar, a mustache, and a level look from beneath a thatch of thick light hair. He was holding a shovel the way a man does who has never used one. "Time flies," Mrs. Blessing had said he'd had carved on those benches out by the apple trees. When he'd given them ten thousand dollars in 1925, the Mount Mason infirmary had been in an old colonial house. Then it had become the Mount Mason Hospital in a collection of sullen brick buildings with too-small windows, and now it was the Mount Mason Medical Center, and looked like an airport for a smallish town. The lobby was called the Blessing Lobby in the hope that a testamentary bequest would follow the compliment. Skip would bet money against that one.

You just couldn't get away no matter how hard you tried, he thought when he walked into Chris's room. There was Ed, and Ed's little brother Sam, and Joe, and Debbie wearing her waitress uniform, going right from the hospital to McGuire's. Actually they were probably all going straight from the hospital to McGuire's. There was Shelly, at least twenty pounds heavier, in stretch exercise shorts and a big T-shirt that wasn't improving things one bit, holding a bald baby dressed in a diaper and a shirt that said "Little Dear" with a picture of a fawn on it. And there was Chris's mom in a slippery white polyester tunic, smelling of bleach and beer, sobbing into the shoulder of his shirt as she hurled herself at his chest: ". . . could have been killed . . . stand to lose him . . . happy you're here . . . my baby . . . my baby." Skip patted her lightly on the back, the way he burped Faith.

"What's up?" Chris whispered, squinting at him through blackened eyes.

Skip was shamed by his first thought: that if Chris had taken it a step further and bought the farm, Spencer's Funeral Home would have had a tough time making him look presentable for his mother. He had two cuts on his face closed with stitches, long train tracks along his forehead and one cheek. Both eyes had gone black and he had big fish lips. His leg was in a cast. Skip felt weary, looking at him.

"This is why they passed helmet laws, man," he said.

Chris nodded and looked at him. "Everybody wait in the hall," he said. "I got business with Skipper."

"I have to leave soon, honey," Chris's mom said. "I got late shift at the nursing home."

"Go to work, Ma. I'll see you tomorrow. Bring me some glazed doughnuts, okay, and some decent coffee from that place on Main Street. The rest of you I'll see tomorrow, whatever. Sit down, Skip. Man, I haven't seen you in a couple weeks. Ed says you hired his old man to put a roof on the old lady's barn."

Skip could hear everybody talking out in the hall. Chris's mom was sobbing, saying something about glazed doughnuts.

Skip nodded. "It's a strange roof, kind of like an upside-down boat or something. He said you can't work it with a scaffold, only ladders."

"I've seen it," Chris said. "I had to deliver chicken wire up there one day, before I got fired at the hardware store. That's some sweet piece of land."

"So," Skip said.

"So," Chris said, his fingers drumming on the top sheet. "I got such a jones for a cigarette I'm going mental."

"Don't look at me."

"Yeah, well, next time. Here's the deal, dude. I figure this was a wake-up call. Like I have to get my shit together. You're the only one who would get that. And part of the deal is, like they say in AA, to make things right with people you screwed up with."

"You're going to AA?"

Chris laughed. "Man, I said a wake-up call, not a brain transplant. No, remember, I went out with that girl Kris, she went to AA. Or NA or Al-Anon, whatever. She told me you're supposed to make it up with people you screwed. The whole time I was in the ambulance—oh man, wait, I need to tell you, one of the ambulance guys was that kid Shorty, remember, that we stuffed in the urinal that one time after gym? He looks at me lying in the road and I swear to God, he got a look on his face like, if I didn't have this other EMT here, I'd just let your ass bleed to death."

"Yeah, well, we kind of made a mistake with him. He was four feet tall until he was fifteen. Then all of a sudden he was six-three."

"And he lifts, man. He's got upper arms on him like iron." Chris lifted his own arm, then let it drop. "I'm gonna be so out of shape when they let me out of here. I'm gonna look like shit."

Skip tried to look at his watch without looking like he was looking. Chris saw him. He put out his hand. Skip could tell just by looking at what he'd done to himself that he'd put the bike into a skid and flipped onto his left side.

"The cops run a blood alcohol on you?" Skip asked.

Chris grabbed his hand, tight, and squeezed, and his eyes filled. He nodded and bit his lip. "The weirdest thing is, I was stone-cold sober. I got work bringing in hay at Jensen's farm, and because of the weather forecast they made us start really early and work all day. We were still mowing when the sun went down. Then Mrs. Jensen, she brings out this big picnic thing, like chicken and potato salad and big jugs of lemonade. They're Mormons or Moravians or something, I can't remember, but they don't drink, and some of the other guys are like, man, I want a beer. But she made biscuits, too, and cake, and I figured I'd go to McGuire's later, because all I could think was that I hadn't had a dinner like that in I don't know how long. Ed's mom used to make us pretty good dinners when we were kids, remember, but they won't even let me in the house now, his parents. And Joe's mom is like my mom, you know, she thinks it's a big deal if she puts frozen pizza in the microwave. I must have stayed there until ten, sitting in the field, feeding chicken to the cats, just chilling, you know, looking at the stars and shit. I just hit the curve too fast on the way home, and then there was a raccoon or something in the road, and the next thing I know I hear this noise and feel this hard feeling and I'm looking up at the sky and I can taste my teeth, isn't that weird? All I can remember at first is tasting my teeth, then seeing Shorty and thinking, oh, man, I am screwed."

"You're lucky to be alive, man."

"I know, I know. That's the point. If I'd checked out, I'd have felt really bad about the way I left things with you. I would have felt bad that I didn't say, you know, I'm really sorry, it was really whack, how that whole thing came down, how you took the weight for all of us." Skip shrugged. "Yeah, I know you're still pissed. But I just want you to understand that I get that, and I screwed up, and I'm sorry."

"Yeah, okay."

"Yeah, okay, that's enough of that shit. What's up with you? You give Ed's old man work after how he's treated you?"

He shrugged again. "He does good work," Skip said. "I got to go."

"Busy man," Chris said. "So, are we cool?"

"Sure. Sure. No problem."

"Jesus, I'd kill for a beer, man," Chris said.

"Get him a beer," Skip told Joe out in the hall. Shelly was looking at him, trying to pretend she wasn't, certain that he was going to yell at her in the hallway of the hospital, hoping he would so she could talk about it at McGuire's for the next month, a little drama in a boring life. Skip walked over and looked at the baby. It had whiteheads on its cheek and was sucking on a pacifier. Pacifier to cigarette to Budweiser, Skip thought, and sighed.

"About six months, right?" he said.

"Next week," she said.

"Yeah, well, you might want to lose the pacifier. Those things are really bad for the shape of their mouths," he murmured.

"Who asked your opinion?" Shelly said. She smelled sour, or maybe it was the baby, or both of them. He could tell by the smudges beneath her eyes that she was still wearing last night's makeup.

"When he starts walking you'll have to pin it to his shirt."

"Who the hell asked you?" Shelly said.

"I'd throw it away now," Skip said.

"Come out with us, man," Ed said. "Come have a beer."

"I'm not going anywhere he's going," Shelly said. "God. Who the hell does he think he is?"

"I'm going home," Skip said. "I got to go home."

He had pulled the truck around so that the cab threw a thick divot of shade on the ground, and he had placed Faith there, faceup, out of the late August sun. Her eyes seemed to follow the motion of the apple trees as the twisted branches moved slightly in the occasional breeze. Once or twice she smiled crookedly at nothing.

"How old did you say she is?" Mrs. Blessing said, looking down, leaning as lightly as she was able on the old gnarled stick with a silver lion's head that had been her father's as she lowered herself into a canvas folding chair. That had been her father's, too. He bought it at Abercrombie's just before the war, just before all the canvas was set aside for the army.

"Ten weeks, give or take a couple days," said Skip. "She should have gotten her shots. I don't know what to do about that. It says in the book that she should get her first shots at six weeks. I don't think I can afford to take her to a doctor."

"I may be able to manage that," Mrs. Blessing said. "I know a doctor who will come here."

"But then—"

"He's very discreet. Doctors tended to be so in my day. There wasn't all this talking about things, cancer and so on. I don't know about these younger doctors. I saw one for my arthritis and I didn't care for him a bit. Korean, I think he was, and spoke as though he had mush in his mouth."

"Like Nadine."

"I can understand Nadine perfectly well. This man couldn't say a consonant to save his soul. Dr. Benjamin will come out to examine her. He's a good plain speaker."

"I want to see him first. The books say you should interview the baby's pediatrician to make sure you like him. Or her."

"Beggars can't be choosers," she said tartly.

"I guess."

Mrs. Blessing herself had never really read books about child-rearing. There had been one that had been popular when Meredith was young, that said spanking was a sin and would break the spirit, but Mrs. Blessing had thought that was nonsense. She had let Nanny paddle Meredith whenever she was badly behaved, just as she herself had been paddled. It had not happened often in either case. Only Sunny had been disciplined by a parent: her father, by the barn, with a belt. It had happened three times.

"I ruined my good linen shorts with blood," was all Sunny said the second time, when he was thirteen.

She had not been back to the orchard in so many years. The last time she could remember being there, Jess had persuaded her to pick fruit for pies. But the apples had been pocked, stunted, deformed somehow, and she and Jess had been younger women then, their hair stippled dark and gray instead of silver. It had never occurred to her that decades would pass before she would go again this far back into her own land. When she had first come out to Blessings to have her baby her world had been confined to Mount Mason. Then slowly she had stopped going to town much, and her world had been confined to Blessings, then increasingly to the house, and in the house to her room, the living room, the study, and the den. The dining room had the downcast look of rooms no one used anymore. That long expanse of polished cherry with the twelve waiting chairs made her feel lonely, though she preferred to think of herself as someone who merely lived alone.

Skip placed Faith on Mrs. Blessing's lap, and she held the child tightly around the waist, encircling her with her arms. One fist closed reflexively over Mrs. Blessing's index finger, and just as reflexively she began to stroke the small hand with her thumb. The baby felt warm on the hot afternoon, but with a different sort of warmth, the warmth of life, the same warmth that slipped from the body when life was gone. Mrs. Blessing thought of Sunny and shuddered. Her head dropped and her lips touched the light down on the small round head, and one of the baby's hands came up and grabbed at her hair.

"No no no, Faithie," Skip said.

"It's all right, Charles. She's simply exploring." A jay flew by and Mrs. Blessing felt the baby turn with its trajectory, her eyes on it until it was gone.

The trees had aged as she had, slowly, inexorably, indubitably. She could remember them as they had been after Papa had first seen them come into flower and then fruit, sixty of them planted over five acres beside the creek. The project had proceeded in fits and starts, as most of them had, because her mother would pay, then not pay, then pay again. "I'll not have him spend my money, the son of a bitch. Not if he can't keep his hands to himself," her mother had muttered one evening years later in the nursing home when her dementia was far along. Edwin Blessing had put a bench at either end of the orchard so that he could come out and sit in the evenings. "I can hear the fruit ripen," he had said once. Carved in the high backs of the benches were the words "Tempus fugit."

"What do you think?" Skip said, looking around at the trees' misshapen limbs and broken branches.

"I am not a botanist," Mrs. Blessing said. Nadine's eyes had burned with anger when he had come into the kitchen, said that he wanted not only to see Mrs. Blessing but also to take her with him in the truck to look at the apple orchard, which he felt needed special attention, spraying, pruning, more than he could manage. "My truck can handle the back drive fine," he'd told her. "It goes right up into the middle of the trees. You won't even have to get out if you don't want to."

"Almost lunch," Nadine had muttered.

"Nonsense, Nadine, it's just past noon. I won't eat for an hour at least."

"Too old!" Nadine shouted suddenly.

"I beg your pardon," Mrs. Blessing said stiffly. "Charles, go to the umbrella stand by the front door and bring me the walking stick. Nadine, I hope it has been polished recently."

"Crazy," muttered Nadine. "Crazy people."

The worst moment had been climbing into the cab of the truck. She clutched the edge of the door, her foot raised. It was high, higher than she thought she could manage. She was almost defeated, not by her body but by her mind and her memory, which could see herself—no, feel herself—leaping into the passenger seat with one swift easy motion. She could feel the girl and the younger woman, and she wanted them suddenly, terribly, as she had not wanted them before. It was as though all the people she had once been were contained inside her failing flesh, the watchful child in buckled shoes, the young woman leaning back against unfamiliar pillows to open herself up to Frank Askew, the new mother amazed and terrified by the indelible product of those covert meetings, the older woman waiting for something unexpected to happen in a life set in stone so long ago. Sunny's sister, Jess's friend. Benny's wife. Perhaps it was the memory of all of them that helped her to place the hesitant foot firmly and pull herself, with a sound like a sigh, into place. Behind the seat was a long basket covered with a striped dishcloth, and when they had taken the road behind the garage Skip reached back and pulled the cloth away so she could see Faith, blinking, big-eyed.

"It seems to me that she has exceptionally long eyelashes," Mrs. Blessing said.

Skip smiled. "That's what I was thinking. But maybe they stop growing, and by the time her face is adult-sized they won't look so long. I keep thinking of all these things I don't know. It's weird that I wasted time learning algebra in high school and yet they didn't teach us one thing about children. And there were plenty of girls in the class, too, and a lot of them have babies now and they're just as ignorant as me. You said she ought to get out more, so I'm trying to get her out more. The book says she gets vitamin D from the sun. Now, see, they should have taught us that. No wonder so many kids in Mount Mason are all pale and sickly-looking, like they live under a rock. I really do want you to look at these trees, but I thought it might make a change, too, you know, to sit outside and just watch her play in the middle of the day."

"She's too young to play, surely," Mrs. Blessing said, looking into the basket.

"You'd be surprised how much fun she has just looking around. Right, Faith? Right, Faithie?"

"That is a pretty name," Mrs. Blessing said.

When she had come to Blessings to wait for her own baby to arrive she had found something called *The Mother's Encyclopedia* on the shelves near the back stairs. In the blue light of an early snowfall she had sat by the fire in the library and tried to read it. Mrs. Foster brought her tea and toast on a tray. "I pray every day for your young man," she had said.

The set of books with the red cloth covers and gilt letters on the spines had been as much a part of her girlhood as prams in the park and lavender sachet pillows in her underwear drawer. *D* for diaper rash; *O* for obedience and otitis media (ear infections). She had found only one section underlined in pencil; after meningitis and money came a chapter on "Mother's Job," and someone had drawn a heavy gray bracket around "Can Love Be Compelled?" and underlined the sentences "for the mother, poor girl, is frightened at herself for not wanting the baby; she feels that she is a criminal and no one else was ever like her; perhaps she has even wished that it might die, and here it is now, rosy and sweet, kicking its heels and making funny amiable noises at her."

She was certain her mother had underlined the passage. She remembered the night she and Sunny had snuck out and slept in the boat. There was still a small gash in its prow to mark where they'd drifted hard into the far bank in the dark and been jarred awake by the impact and the willow branches trailing like fingers over both their faces.

"She's so strict about everything," she had whispered to Sunny. "When I wanted to wear my amber beads to Lucy Warren's birthday luncheon, she told me the Warrens would think we were vulgar. The Warrens! Half the chairs in their house have the stuffing coming out."

"You know why," Sunny had said.

"Why?"

Sunny had drifted with his hand in the water. He was sitting on the bottom of the boat, his head resting on one of the seats, and Lydia could remember that he was smiling to himself, as though he was pleased about what he was about to tell her.

"It's because she's Jewish."

"Who?"

"Mother. Her parents were Jews."

"Don't be silly. She goes to St. Stephen's every Sunday with us. Nearly every Sunday she says 'Jerusalem' is her favorite hymn. Jerusalem, Jerusalem, Jerusalem."

"It's all for show, Lydie," Sunny had said. "Before her name was Simpson it was something else. That's why everything has to be just so. So it won't matter that she's Jewish. But it does."

"How do you know?"

"I listen to things," he said. "At the Cartons' one day Benny and I were eating in the kitchen and these people were having drinks out in the sunroom and one of the women said that Mother had married Father for position and Father had married Mother for money."

"I thought Papa was the one who had the money."

"That's what everyone is supposed to think."

How wise Sunny had been; how much he could see that she could not. She thought that that was why he was so melancholy and so amused in equal measure. He had fallen asleep in the boat long before she had, one hand resting on her leg as though to make sure she would not go over the side. The air was pale blue-gray when they both heard the sounds of screaming from inside the house.

"What's wrong? Why are they doing that?" she'd cried, her hair in her face, pulled loose from its ribbon.

"Because of us, I think," Sunny said.

She must have been almost eleven, because it was six months after the Lindbergh baby had been taken in 1932. Their nanny had found her bed empty, then Sunny's, had gotten hysterics and then fallen to the kitchen floor. The Fosters had run across the drive, Mrs. Foster still in her nightgown with Mr. Foster's work jacket over it, held closed with one hand. Papa had rung the dinner bell. He had looked ridiculous.

But Mama had not even come downstairs. "They'll turn up," she'd said. "What a fuss."

After that day Lydia Blessing could never see her mother in the same way again, and she was never sure whether it was because Ethel Blessing had stayed in bed, waiting for coffee, when everyone else was panicked at the thought that they were gone, or because she was Jewish. When her mother had hired the Cartons' decorator to make their new house look more or less exactly like the Cartons', when she had forbidden Lydia to wear red to parties or to lighten her hair with lemon, when she had sent her to Blessings and made it impossible for her to come back to New York again, Lydia had always wondered whether an Episcopalian mother would have behaved differently. Perhaps she would have acted just the same. After all, what was Ethel Blessing doing but a careful imitation of an Episcopalian mother? How her two children had foiled her in what was to be the crowning gesture of her difficult passage into social Protestantism. Two good marriages: that was all it would have taken to launder Ethel Blessing's origins forever.

Instead there was Sunny, living in a top-floor apartment in a house in Greenwich Village, writing jingles, smoking small black cigars. Instead there was Lydia, living in purdah amid the possums and the lumbering black bear, living in purdah with a redheaded child with a widow's peak like a brand on her broad white brow. How she had clung, Ethel Blessing, to that Carton in Meredith's name, to the polite fiction, politely accepted, of the love match, the soldier, the bereavement, the early labor, the country air. "You are a careless girl," she had said to Lydia on many occasions. "You take for granted your advantages. You don't know the value of a dollar. The world doesn't owe you a living." The old truisms had the rote sound of repetition, almost like mimicry, and it occurred to Lydia, long after her mother was dead, that perhaps they had first been said to the young Ethel Simpson—or Sietz, or Simpkis, or whatever her name had been—by her own father, whose fortune made from bolts of brocade had allowed his only child to deny her past.

She leaned closer to look at the baby lying on a blanket on the grass. They knew nothing about her, whether her mother was young or old, rich or poor. But Mrs. Blessing could see that this baby was beloved, and in the soft grass, with the breeze blowing the crippled limbs of the old apple trees, that seemed to be all that mattered. Skip knelt before Faith and cleaned and changed her, then cradled her in his arms. He still had a bit of that tentative godfather-at-the-font quality that men kept, although Mrs. Blessing had heard that so many more of them took care of their children now. She had to admit that she was surprised by the name he had chosen. She had been a bit put out when she was not consulted, but what he had decided on was in impeccable taste. She would not have objected to a grandchild by that name. The baby was holding her head up now, her eyes enormous, ranging around the trees and sky and over both their faces like a searchlight. She made small bird noises of pleasure, then spread her arms wide, bounced slightly in Skip's arms as though she were ready to fly, then seemed to think better of it and clung to his shoulder with her starfish hands. She was an eager, playful little thing, with a constant light in her eyes. Mrs. Blessing was certain that not all babies were that way. Even Jess had had one, Henry, who had been dull and disconsolate.

"Do you ever give any thought to the woman who must have left her here?" she said.

"All the time. I try not to, but I wonder about her all the time."

"She is her mother, after all."

"No, see, that's where I think you're wrong. Because I keep

thinking that that's not how you get to be the mother. You get to be the mother like this. You get to be the mother by changing her and giving her a bath and walking her around in the middle of the night and loving her and making her feel like everything's all right. That's how you get to be the mother. That's what being the mother is. That means I'm the mother, more or less."

"Well, then, have you considered that she may be better off with a man and a woman who want to adopt a child, who have a proper home and so forth?"

"She's mine," he said. "You can feel it, can't you? She's mine." Faith reared back and looked into Skip's eyes and crowed and reached for his face. "Do you want to hold her again?"

"In a minute," Mrs. Blessing said. "She looks quite pleased with herself at the moment."

"Oh, she is," Skip said, talking to the baby, rubbing her nose with his own. "She is pleased with herself. I am pleased with herself. We are pleased with each other. And that's the deal. That's the deal. That's the deal."

"People talk such nonsense to babies," Mrs. Blessing said. "I wonder why."

"Maybe we all ought to talk more nonsense more of the time." He lifted Faith over his head and swooped her back and forth, up and down, and she sucked in her breath.

Mrs. Blessing looked over the rows of twisted gray tree trunks. She and Sunny had eaten apples from these selfsame trees, Rome apples so full of juice that it ran down their chins and onto the Irish sweaters Nanny made them wear in autumn. "If you have these trees properly cared for, will they bear fruit again?" she asked.

"I'm pretty sure."

"How much will it cost?"

"A couple thousand. It won't be cheap."

"And you've found someone capable?"

He slung Faith over his shoulder. She lifted her domed head sharply, once, twice, three times, then let it fall to one side and sucked her fist.

"Barton's Nursery. He says his grandfather put these trees in in the first place. He says his grandfather used to tell a story about how your father memorized the leaves and the bark and the flowers, so that he could walk from tree to tree and know whether it was Winesap or Yellow Delicious or Rome."

"He made us do the same," Mrs. Blessing said. "He said the trees would be here bearing fruit when he was only a memory in the minds of those who loved him. That's why he had 'Tempus fugit' carved into these benches. Time flies. My father had a very extravagant turn of phrase and mind."

"He was right, though."

Mrs. Blessing shook her head. "Since you have come to work for me I have managed to do a great many things I never expected to do." The baby made a grunting noise, then a funny whistle, then a grunt again. "Will you harvest the fruit?" she said.

"Yes, ma'am. Will you get her a doctor?"

"I will. But I think you must focus on the future, Charles, and how you will manage in the years to come. There must be something that can be done. Perhaps I will consult my attorney."

"Maybe," he said. "Maybe. Let me think about it. It's early still, isn't it? I mean, she can't even sit up yet."

One afternoon when the air was hot and thick as soup Skip heard music coming from the front of the house. He was driving back from the orchard, driving through dirty clouds of gnats with the long-handled pruning clippers and the Portacrib bouncing in the back of the pickup truck. Just after sunrise he had driven almost twenty miles to a twenty-four-hour Price Club in Bessemer to get diapers and formula. Women smiled at him in the bright white light of the aisles because he was wearing the baby in a front pack on his chest. It reminded him of the picture of the Sacred Heart of Jesus that Chris's mom had on the wall of her bedroom, his chest a glowing symbol of his absolute goodness. He imagined that all the women had dirtbag husbands who went out to the bar when the kid had a fever, or boyfriends who dropped a ten on the kitchen table for diapers. Last week in the paper there had been a story he almost skipped right over about single fathers, and then he realized that he was a single father. Holding a job, the story said, arranging play dates. He was nodding his head. The play dates part was pushing it, but he tried to imagine Faith going over to someone's house to build with blocks and sit in the inflatable pool. He didn't want her playing with Shelly's grubby son, or the kids that his other old friends might have, coming home covered in cherry Kool-Aid and saying, "What's *fuck* mean, Daddy?"

The guys from the trout hatchery had their truck parked at the base of the driveway and they were flinging fish into the pond from plastic sheetrock buckets. The sun struck pink fire off the sides of the rainbow trout as they twisted in the air and hit the surface of the water. The ones that were already in were jumping now as though they were trying to get back to where they came from, corkscrewing above the surface. Skip parked up the driveway by the steps to the front porch. The baby was asleep in the back of the truck underneath the little canopy of mosquito netting he'd bought. The Taylor brothers, who ran the hatchery, were no danger. They were so brain-dead that they wouldn't look twice at a baby. A hoe, a shovel, a chain saw, a baby in a basket. It was all the same to them. If Skip had had a corpse in the flatbed of the truck they would scarcely have noticed it, although if he'd had a new truck they would have been all over it. They spent most of their time sitting by the spillways shooting muskrats and snapping turtles before they could get to the fish. Smoking dope, too.

"Yo," Skip said to them.

"Get your rod out, man," said the older one, the one with the beard. "These suckers'd hit on baloney if it was on the surface there, they're so nuts."

The other one was closing up the back of the fish truck. He reached into his pocket for the invoice. "Give this to the boss, why don't you?" he said. "Tell her the herons won't go hungry no more."

"That's for sure," said his brother. "You find any fish floating with that spear mark in them, like a V shape?"

Skip nodded. He found four or five a week. Sitting in the chair by the living room window, giving Faith her first bottle of the day, listening to her suck with a gasping sound like she'd never been fed before, he could watch the big gray birds, tall and motionless at the edge of the water, until suddenly the curved bill plunged into the shallows and, with a movement of the throat not unlike an infant's, it swallowed the fish. Occasionally one missed and later that day Skip would pull a dull-eyed trout from the rotting leaves in the spillway.

There had been trout in Blessings pond since Ed Blessing had

had the hatchery first stock it in the hope that his son would take up fly casting. The boy hadn't, but every summer one hundred trout went into the pond, just like every fall the landscape gardener drove out from town and dug up the begonia tubers, wrapped them in cheesecloth, and put them in the basement.

"You stepped in shit with this job," said the younger Taylor brother, lighting a Newport and looking out over the pond, where the starlings were wheeling down to meet the fish leaping high, all of them chasing bugs.

"Yeah, I keep hearing that."

"I don't know that I'd want to work for her, though," said the other, looking back at the house and keeping his cigarette cupped in his hand.

"She's all right," Skip said. "Fair and all."

"Get your rod out," said one of the Taylors again as they hopped up into the truck.

The music started again. It sounded a little like what they had played on the loudspeakers on the football fields when they were graduating from the high school. Nadine was backing her car out of the driveway. She rolled down the window and leaned out toward him.

"You count fish?" she said. He never got what she was saying the first time. "You count fish!" she shouted.

"Yes, I did," he said. "Every one. One hundred even."

"You lie," she said, and peeled out. Nadine drove like she did everything else. Skip was glad his truck was nowhere near her. Whenever he cleared roadkill from the end of the drive, flattened frogs, turtles whose shells were broken mosaics, possums with their mouths half-opened to show their needle teeth, he wondered whether Nadine had run them over. On Fridays Nadine took two hours off to clean the Presbyterian church. She had vanity plates that Craig had gotten her for her car that said 4GSUS. Skip drove around to the front of the house to tell Mrs. Blessing about the apple trees, about how shoots were already beginning to grow from the freshly pruned limbs and even a leaf or two to emerge, soft and uncreased as one of her linen handkerchiefs. Faith stirred in the Portacrib, threw one arm over her head, and smacked her lips lazily. Skip was putting her on her back now. He wished the doctors would make up their minds about what position was least likely to cause crib death. He wondered if it was normal for parents to be as obsessed with their kid as he was. He'd be riding down the street, and he'd see one of those little pink bikes with silver streamers on the handlebars, and he'd file it away for later: pink bike, Christmas four years from now. Or he'd see some little girl in a lace top with her belly hanging out and pierced ears, and he'd think, no way. Maybe people with birth certificates in the dresser drawer could be more casual about those things.

Through the window he could see Jennifer Foster sitting at the piano playing, her face bent over the keys. Her hands rose and fell like pale birds balancing on a limb in the half-darkness that was always inside the house because of the trees and the deep striped awnings. He could see what would come next in the music, how the tempo or the mood would change, by the slight signals of her arms and head just a moment before. He stood for several minutes listening and watching, and then when she stopped playing he knocked softly on the screen door.

"Yes?" Mrs. Blessing called.

"It's me."

"Come in, Charles," she replied.

"I can't get used to the Charles thing," Jennifer said, smiling.

"Nicknames are pernicious," Mrs. Blessing said. "I was always grateful that your parents did not call you Jenny or Jen or one of those diminutive versions of Jennifer, which is a lovely name."

"I never really heard you play the piano," Skip said.

"I'm out of practice. The only place I play is here. It drives my mother crazy after all those years of piano lessons. Piano lessons, dance lessons, tap, jazz. You name it, I took it."

"My daughter, Meredith, took piano," Mrs. Blessing said. "She hated her lessons. Luckily one summer when she was with her grandparents in Newport she fell from a horse and broke two fingers and that was that. She was always injuring herself, riding so much. She was like my brother in that regard. Both of them were accident-prone." She looked at Jennifer. "Perhaps that's hereditary. Although I've never injured myself at all."

Skip wasn't sure why, but she looked different this morning, older, grayer, and yet less tense at the same time. Her hands lay open in her lap instead of tightly folded, and her mouth was looser, too. He wondered if it was the music. When he told her about the trees, he thought for just a moment that she was going to smile. He had thought from the beginning that there was something almost virginal about her, as though nothing had ever happened to her, as though her entire life had been listening to piano music in the living room and making sure the nasturtiums around the walk didn't have blight. All the women he'd known growing up, the ones with the suggestion of soft swaying skin beneath their dresses, or the ones like his aunt who were hard and wiry and lined, all of them had faces and bodies that spoke of hard work, childbirth, aging, heartaches. Maybe it was the way Mrs. Blessing's clothes were pressed, or her hair always pulled back in the same bun, that made her seem so different from those others. Today her manner seemed oddly youthful.

"I'm glad you're both in one place, and that Nadine has business elsewhere," she finally said. "Charles, I think you should tell Jennifer about what's been going on here."

"What?"

"I hate that word. The phrase is 'pardon me?' You know exactly what I mean. I think we should be prepared for any eventuality, including illness, for example, or discovery. By being in my employ you've made this my business, too, and I think you need some assistance in making certain that there won't be trouble in the years to come."

Jennifer was looking at Mrs. Blessing with a line between her eyebrows. It was the same line that Nadine had between hers, permanently, a kind of tattoo of ill humor.

"Jennifer is entirely trustworthy," Mrs. Blessing added. "I can tell you that from long experience. What will you do if the child is sick? What about school immunization records? She may know more than either of us does about how to proceed here."

"What child?" Jennifer said.

"He has a child," said Mrs. Blessing, the soft line of her mouth gone now, its narrow band of probity back in place.

"Hey, hey," cried Skip. "Wait a minute."

"Oh, God," said Jennifer Foster, looking away with disgust. "Not you, too. I am so tired of this. Doesn't anyone take having kids seriously anymore? I remember at home how angry all the women were about the American soldiers who had gotten them pregnant and then just left, but here it's exactly the same. Fathers who think it's a big deal to let someone use their last name on a birth certificate." The line between her brows deepened. "Oh, I know who it is. You knocked up that girl who used to work at the Red Lobster out on the pike. She was in my gym class freshman year. You can't even let her live here with you so you can see your own kid?"

Skip could feel the color rise in his face as the shame and anger bloomed in his chest. He walked out the screen door and went over to the truck bed. Faith was awake, staring at the leaves on the copper beech overhead with a sleepy smile. Her eyebrows were still light as dandelion fuzz, and her eyes had faded from navy to a lighter blue, more like the sky. Something about her peach-pink face, and the smile, and the way she was, the way she was such a good baby and scarcely cried and didn't get cradle cap or whiteheads or diaper rash or all the other disgusting things he imagined Shelly's baby got, made the shame disappear, and the anger rise in him along with the pride and love. He lifted her from the Portacrib and carried her into the house so that she was facing out, one hand around her chest, the other beneath her butt, with the kind of casual roughness he associated with a job a person knows how to do well.

"This is Faith," he said. "She's not mine. Or she's kind of mine. Whatever. I'm her father. I found her by the garage in June, and

I've been taking care of her ever since. You might be trustworthy, but you're too quick to judge people as far as I'm concerned."

"Oh, my God," Jennifer said, and reached out her hands like it was a cold night and Faith was a fire. "Oh, my God. You are so adorable. Look at you. Look at her. She's smiling right at me. Look at her eyes, how blue her eyes are. Come over here. Come here and see me, sweetheart." The baby made a noise, half-purr, half-growl, as Jennifer pushed forward on the piano bench and laid her down the length of her legs. Faith held on to Jennifer's fingers with her fists.

"So you see the difficulty," said Mrs. Blessing. "She needs her immunizations, and soon, as I recall. I'm confident that I can persuade Dr. Benjamin that she's some relation and that he will do it."

"Dr. Benjamin doesn't practice anymore." Jennifer looked down and pitched her voice higher. "No, he doesn't, does he, sweetie. He doesn't take care of babies anymore."

"He will do it for me. But what about the mother? What if some young girl suddenly decides that she's made a mistake? Although what counts as a mistake nowadays is beyond me. It seems there's nothing that counts against you young people. No one seems to care about the old rules."

"They just pretend they don't care about them," Skip said, reaching for Faith.

"Oh, let me hold her some more," Jennifer said. "Who is your mommy, sweetie?" She tilted her head to the side and the baby grabbed her hair and pulled until Jennifer's chin was bent low. It occurred to Skip that babies had a way of making people exactly what they were but more so. Faith had brought out the rectitude and responsibility in Mrs. Blessing, the warmth in Jennifer Foster, and the capability in him, so that she had made him think well of himself. And having a baby made all those people who were piss-poor humans more piss-poor than ever. "I can ask at the ER," Jennifer said, "but I think I would have heard if anyone had come in postpartum with no child. There's a girl on one of those big farms by the county line who's only fourteen and got pregnant, but she had her baby about three weeks ago and, from what I heard, her mother and grandmother went from calling her a whore to acting like she's the greatest thing since sliced bread as soon as she delivered. There's been a couple of girls I heard about who had babies without being married in the last couple of months, but that's no big deal these days. I guess I shouldn't talk. My parents didn't get married until I was five, when we came over here. But that was a different situation." Her head bent lower. "I need my hair back, sweetie," she sang to the baby.

"She has a really tight grip, right?" Skip said. "Strong."

"Does my mother know about this?" Jennifer asked.

Skip snorted. "Right," he said. "Nobody was supposed to know, not even you. But someone found out, and now that someone has taken it upon herself to tell other people."

"I have no intention of telling anyone except Jennifer," Mrs. Blessing said. "I suspect we may need her help."

"Well, don't tell my mother," said Jennifer. "She's strange about things, especially things like this. You can't be sure what she'll do. Actually, I know what she'd say. She'd say it's really yours and you just made this whole story up."

"I've still got the box they left her in," said Skip. "And the flannel shirt she was wrapped in."

"So you know of no one who might claim this child?" Mrs. Blessing said, putting her hand on Jennifer's arm.

"I don't know of anyone who's missing a baby, to tell the truth. I'll nose around a bit, though." Jennifer looked up at Skip. "I'm sorry I made you sound like a slime ball. Here's all these guys walking away from their own kids, and you're taking care of a baby that's not even yours."

"She's mine."

"Yeah, I get that. Can I play with her a little while longer?"

"She is a very good baby," Mrs. Blessing said. "I must admit it. She's no trouble at all."

Meredith was sawing away at her lamb chop. "Nadine told me that you had a lightning strike," she said. "And a blackout. That must have been sort of scary."

"Lightning is more dangerous than most people think," Meredith's husband, Eric, said.

Lydia scarcely listened to them. She watched Meredith's knife go back and forth like a violinist's bow. "Nadine," she called. "This meat is tough."

Sometimes, often, nearly all the time now, she felt as if she'd outlived her own life. Madame Guernaire's no longer made the cotton blouses she liked so much. The *Times* no longer ran engagement announcements, and they put divorces in the wedding announcements, as though anyone would want to be reminded on their wedding day that their previous marriage had ended in divorce. And four years ago she had gotten a card from the butcher on Third Avenue who had been sending her meat for fifty years announcing that he was retiring and closing his business. Even the butcher in Mount Mason, who had been hugely and publicly bitter about the meat sent to Blessings from New York—"No difference from what I stock, except that she's paying a premium, I can tell you that!"—was out of business now. Nadine had to buy meat at the Mount Mason supermarket. The chicken tasted like sponge. And not even like real sponge, the yellow misshapen kind that had once actually lain at the bottom of the ocean and that still could be sent to her, thank God, from the pharmacy on the corner of

Seventy-second Street and Lexington Avenue. The supermarket chicken tasted like that horrid manufactured sponge that Nadine used on the dishes.

"You can't get good asparagus this late in the summer," she said, picking up a spear with her fingers and then setting it down in disgust.

"Mother, you can get everything all the time now. You can get corn year-round. And tomatoes. Everything is shipped overnight from California or Florida."

"I don't call those things you can get in the supermarket tomatoes. I'm surprised you can, with the tomatoes we've always gotten here in the summer. Charles is taking good care of the vegetable garden. These are our own tomatoes and our own summer squash. I can't imagine why Nadine thought we ought to have asparagus in September."

Sometimes she thought that the world had lost its compass. Peaches were meant to be eaten in the summer, apples in the fall. Her mother had once seen a girl in dark shoes at a lawn party in June in Connecticut and turned away before she could be introduced. Miss Bertram had sent a senior home because she was wearing nail polish. It was clear nail polish, but nail polish nonetheless. Nail varnish, they called it then.

And sometimes now she wondered, improbably, whether the compass had been set askew to begin with. She looked at Faith sometimes, lying on the lawn in the growing dusk with a tent of mosquito netting around her and her Humpty Dumpty rattle in her hand, and wondered what all the old mores really meant. Lydia Blessing, who had been taught that illegitimacy was a curse and eavesdropping insidious, sometimes lay in bed with the baby monitor turned on on her bedside table and listened as though to chamber music to the faint sounds of the young man and the infant living happily together. Sometimes she forgot to turn it off as she fell asleep, and when the baby woke at three she woke, too, and heard the few irritated complaints and then the sound of Charles coming into the room. "Hungry again, huh?" he might croon.

"All right, all right, it's coming. Hold your little horses. Hold your little horses, you little honey. You little honey, you." It was the language of love, and it had shifted her made-up mind on its lifelong axis. What did it matter how you got to that moment, so long as you got there in time?

"You're looking well, Meredith," she said now, turning to her daughter, and she was faintly pained by the look of surprise on Meredith's face. What did it matter what had led up to that moment? Meredith suddenly looked pleased. "Thank you, Mother," she said, lifting a hand to her hair. "You, too."

"Oh, nonsense," Lydia said. "You haven't had surgery, have you?"

Meredith's smile fell a little. "No, Mother. No surgery."

"Good. I think all that is nonsense. Grow old, and learn to like it. Or live with it, at the very least." The three of them bent over their meals in silence. The lights in the dining room flickered.

"I'm glad you decided to have work done on the orchard," Meredith said. "I always loved it there when I was a child."

"Who says I'm doing work on the orchard?"

"Nadine did."

"Nadine should mind her business."

Lydia didn't like it when Meredith behaved as though the place were already hers. Lydia's father had hated that, too, had hated it when her mother had deeded Blessings over to Lydia five years after Meredith was born. It was after Lydia had had Mr. Foster, the second Mr. Foster, drive her to the city in the big Buick for Lucy Warren's wedding. It was the first big wedding after the war. "Oh, Lydia," Lucy had said when she'd seen her outside the church, "I never thought you'd come."

"But I sent you a card and said I would," she'd said.

"Well, my mother said you never would," Lucy had said, pushing aside her veil. Perhaps she'd imagined it, but Lydia thought that many of her old friends looked surprised when they saw her at the reception afterward, and one girl she'd scarcely known took her hands and told her how terribly terribly sorry she'd been about

Benny, and what a wonderful wonderful man he'd been, and how was the baby, was she well?

"She's scarcely a baby anymore," Lydia had said. "She's almost five."

She'd stopped afterward at her parents' house, but both of them were out, and she could not stay over because of Mr. Foster waiting in the car, his head swiveling as though New York were surrounding him on all sides and surreptitiously creeping forward to seize and eat him. Driving across the park, she'd realized that the city was like the pond at Blessings, that her life here had been a small splash, a series of concentric circles, and now the water was smooth again. She'd taken her gold compact out of her purse, the compact with her monogram that Mrs. Carton had given her for a wedding gift, and she'd looked at her own face in the mirror within the lid, touched her brow, her upper lip, to see that she was really there.

She'd been so tired when she got back to Blessings that day. Her garters had bitten into the flesh of her upper thighs and left red marks, and Meredith had come in while she was changing and tried to touch them, and she'd had to tell her that people needed their privacy when they were dressing and undressing. Now people changed clothes on the beach in front of strangers and thought nothing of it. People hired men to take care of their property, and somehow, out of the blue, infants turned up in their living quarters, needing to be held and fed and somehow cared for by these men who were supposed to be pruning the trees and keeping the creeping chrysanthemum from creeping.

But Faith was surprisingly easy to feed. Mrs. Blessing had done it twice now, once when Charles was out, once when he'd handed her the baby and the bottle. She had to hold her in her right arm now because her left ached so much of the time, and she worried that if the feeding went on too long the weight would be too much for her. But so far it had not. The baby sucked on the nipple with an avidity and a need that was somehow touching. Mrs. Blessing could not remember what it had been like to feed Meredith. The baby nurse had said she was inexperienced. The woman had rolled her *r*'s, so that *inexperience* sounded much more serious than it might have otherwise. She was German. Ethel Blessing always got the servants no one else wanted, the black cooks, the Irish girls with spaces between their front teeth, the German baby nurses during the war. It had occurred to Mrs. Blessing as she held the bottle while the child sucked noisily that perhaps she had never actually given Meredith a bottle.

She had been so young when Meredith was born. She'd been only nineteen years old when she'd gone to that drinks party she had dreamed of as an old woman in the hospital. Frank Askew had raised his glass from the other side of the room. He had given her that hard look that made her groin swim and her face turn red. She thought no one noticed. How stupid she'd been. How surprised everyone had been to see her, only five years later, at Lucy Warren's wedding, as though it had been arranged for the earth to swallow her up. Of course her mother had wanted her to stay hidden away at Blessings.

Six months after that first time, Frank had reached into the neck of her yellow voile dress and pulled her breast loose to kiss its upper curve, and she had felt her knees bend, and open. His mustache scratched her skin slightly, and then he drew back and stared down at the dark nipple, the swell of the skin, and his pelvis stopped pushing against hers as though he'd been struck by lightning.

"You need to go get looked at," he'd said, pulling the top of her dress up far higher than it was meant to be.

"Get looked at?"

"By a doctor."

She was so stupid then that she had needed a man to look at the swell of her breasts and feel the slight curve of her belly and tell her she was pregnant. "Eleven weeks," said the doctor in Westchester whom Frank sent her to see the next day. That night she went to Chez Nous, one of those clubs that had sprung up where girls who'd gone to college and come home again and men who were waiting to be shipped overseas went to have a good time before they got married, or had children, or surrendered to being grown-up. She'd had too much to drink, then insisted that everyone at her table go on the subway to a place she'd heard about downtown for breakfast. She was fast-talking and frantic that night, not like herself, and the New York she encountered was not her New York. It was an underground city in which strangers sat opposite one another on the train, eyes blank, shoulders touching anonymously. The New York she knew was the opposite of anonymous, in which all of them went to the same few schools and knew one another's parents and the servants knew everyone else's servants and everyone used the same apothecary and everyone's children wore the same broadcloth coat with a velvet collar and matching leggings from The Childe's Shoppe. It was, she was discovering, a small town in which things were secret, not because they were not known but because they were not spoken aloud.

The place she'd heard about turned out to be nothing more than an all-night luncheonette, but almost everyone there was someone they knew, except for one disgusted cab driver at the counter, eating sausages and making comments to the waitress about trust-fund babies and rich kids and uptown brats. Lydia threw up in the ladies' room, which smelled like disinfectant and had a sign that said, DON'T WASTE PAPER—THERE'S A WAR ON. When she came out Benny was at a table by himself near the window, wearing his new uniform. The sleeves were too long, the pants too short.

"Keep me company," he'd said. "Your brother stood me up."

He was drunk, too, and when he ordered fried eggs she thought she'd be sick again. She had toast with butter, and tea that she drank in little sips. Neither of them said much until Benny reached over and took her hand. "What's the matter, Lydie?" he said, and she started to cry. The only words that would come were "I need." "I need I need I need" between wet sobs and heaves and then another trip to the ladies'.

"What do you need, Lydie?" he said when she'd come back.

"I need help," she said softly.

"What kind of help?"

"I need someone to marry me."

There was a silence. Benny buttered his toast. The cab driver said, "You can't respect a person who doesn't work for a living." The waitress said, "Don't be so hard on people."

Benny said, "I'd marry you. I'd be happy to marry you."

Now Meredith said, "The landscaping is looking lovely, Mother."

Lydia's head came up slowly, like one of the water birds fishing around the pond that tried to pretend that they weren't there, that they were really a rock or a stick or a part of the dock. She hadn't been following the conversation. Her head hurt. "I need aspirin," she said.

"I'll get some," Meredith said. "Nadine? Can you bring two as-pirin and some fresh water? Are you all right, Mother?"

"Don't fuss, Meredith. It's only a headache."

"You have the healthiest pink dogwoods I've ever seen, Lydia," said Eric, whom she'd never grown to like, although to his credit he was always respectful and never slobbered much, unlike Jess's oldest son-in-law, the one who'd called Jess "Mama." Not Ed, who was married to Jeanne, but Brian, who'd been married to Marian, the one who died of cancer of the pancreas. That was how she remembered people now: heart, stroke, cancer of the pancreas. She swallowed the aspirin slowly.

Meredith looked so much like her father that anyone who saw the two of them together would have been amazed by the resem-blance. No one ever had seen the two of them together. When Meredith traveled to town as a child it was to go to the Radio City Music Hall Christmas show or the Plaza for tea with her grand-parents and then to come back to Mount Mason again. After Lucy Warren's wedding Mrs. Blessing had gone back herself only three other times. During her pregnancy, and then when the baby was small, she had sustained herself with the knowledge that before long the war would be over, and she would leave Mount Mason and go back to the city. Not leave for good, of course: Blessings would always be her second home, for weekends and holidays. But the city was where she belonged. When Benny's mother had first mentioned that long-ago aunt with the red hair and Mr. Carton had written the will that left Meredith everything, it had given her hope that everyone would be as publicly credulous as Benny's parents were, even the people who had been in the hallways when she and Frank Askew had emerged, never together, always one at a time, from certain unused rooms at certain apartments and clubs.

She had not counted on her mother. The week after Lucy Warren's wedding her parents had come for the weekend. While her father danced Meredith around the living room, singing, "Let me call you sweetheart," her mother had taken her out onto the porch and handed her the deed to the property. "Ethel Simpson Blessing to Lydia Blessing Carton." That was how the transference read. Her father had built the barn, added the porch, planted the trees around the pond, put up the fences, landscaped the terrace gardens, laid out the orchard. All of it had been owned by his wife.

"Ah, Lyds, my love," he'd sighed over dinner, his hands shaking as he lifted his coffee cup, the whites of his eyes gone yellow, "I miss this place terribly."

The past danced again with the present in her mind. Meredith was talking, using the flat of her hand to smooth back her hair. Lydia had named her after Benny's grandmother. The Cartons had liked that. They'd sent a monogrammed locket from Tiffany. Her mother had handed her the deed and said, "Now you'll always have a place to live."

Two months later her parents moved into a small apartment at a residential hotel on Fifth Avenue. Then there was no place for Lydia in New York, and no money for her to buy a place of her own. Her mother gave her an allowance to run Blessings, and her parents stayed at the house one weekend a month, and during the month in the summer when Meredith was in Newport. "I'd rather be here with the little girl," her father complained, but that was how Ethel Blessing arranged things.

Her father had seemed to get smaller and grayer, and afterward Lydia thought that maybe he'd been sick for years before he died. Or maybe he was just exhausted from the unacknowledged drama of his life. Sunny had betrayed him. He had gone into advertising and made a huge success of a slogan for a pen that read, "He's got the prettiest penmanship at Princeton—and he uses a Papermate!" When Sunny spoke of their father, when he came out to Blessings alone for the weekend, circling the pond with his head lowered and his cigarette trailing a plume of gray smoke, it was with amused contempt. On the patio one evening he had said, "Have you ever noticed that Father has never said anything of moment in his entire life?"

"You're so hard on him, Sunny," she had said.

"Ah, Lyds my love," Sunny had replied, imitating their father. "If only I were."

Their mother had given Sunny an allowance, too. Perhaps, Lydia had thought, she even put their father on an allowance. Maybe that accounted for the boxes. From time to time her father had sent Lydia a box at Blessings by mail, so that the postman had to send a boy to drive it out. "Simpson's Fine Textiles," it said on each of the boxes, and when she had opened the first one there was a bolt of heavy green brocade, the color of new leaves, and a note from her father on his personal stationery. "Put this away for a rainy day," it said. "Love and kisses, Papa." The boxes came two or three times a year, always with the same message, always with a bolt of fabric.

Beneath the fabric was money, lots of money, in big packages encircled with paper bands, like the money in kidnap scenes in movies. She estimated that the first box contained four thousand dollars, and then there was a second, and a third, and by the time her father died there were stacks of boxes in the garage attic, most of them unopened. It seemed dirty, that money, the green faded to gray, the paper soft from the hands that had touched it. To have money in her world had been to go to the right schools, live in a proper apartment, furnish it in the old style. It was not to have boxes of bills, like some old miser with a mattress full. They never spoke of it, she and her father, or her mother, either, or even Sunny. Sometimes she almost forgot it was there; sometimes she wondered whether the mice had gotten to it. By the time Meredith was starting school there was enough money over the garage to buy herself a place in the city. But for some reason she had had the guest rooms painted instead, and had stayed put.

"Do you want tea with your rice pudding?" Meredith asked.

"We'll have tea on the porch," Lydia said.

"Whatever you say, Mother."

"Those are beautiful delphiniums," Eric said heartily, pulling out her chair as she rose slowly.

"Staking," she said. "If you want delphiniums you must keep them staked." There were still some things of which she was absolutely certain.

S kip heard Jennifer Foster arrive before the roofers or Nadine did, while Mrs. Blessing's daughter and son-in-law were at the club playing golf. The idle on her car had been fixed; Skip could hear it as she pulled up and into one of the bays of the garage. When he put Faith in her arms the baby pushed back and stared her in the face. The books said Faith wouldn't have stranger anxiety until she was ten months old. Maybe by then she wouldn't consider Jennifer or Mrs. Blessing strangers.

"Good morning, pretty girl," Jennifer said in that high voice people always used for babies. "How are you? Did you sleep good last night?"

"She did," Skip said. "If I put her down at midnight now she goes straight through until six. I weighed her on the feed scale in the back of the garage and she's up to fourteen pounds, which I think is pretty big."

"Are you pretty big? Are you? You don't look so big to me." Jennifer looked up at him and smiled. "Mr. Mom," she said.

"That's me."

"You have my stuff?"

He closed the garage door over her little car and turned to watch her lope across the lawn with the sling across her chest and a backpack filled with bottles and diapers on her back. Jennifer had come the day before to say hello to Mrs. Blessing's daughter, whose name was Mrs. Fox. "Charles," Mrs. Blessing had called as Jennifer was leaving, and she came down the back steps slowly and carefully to join the two of them. "I told Jennifer there's too much activity here in the next day or two," she said quietly. "It might be useful for Faith to stay with her away from here."

"I can hear the rumors now," Skip said.

"I won't leave the property," Jennifer said. "I know how you feel about that. I can take her way back by the stream, where nobody comes. Otherwise, between Mr. and Mrs. Fox and the roofing crew, somebody's going to figure out she's here. Speaking of rumors, there aren't any. There was a girl at the hospital about six months ago who had a baby and gave it up for adoption, but these people came from Chicago and picked it up. Tracy at the pharmacy on Main Street says the girl's even gotten pictures from them since. One of the Boatwright girls had twins in June, but they were both boys and she has them both home in the trailer and complains to anyone who'll listen about how hard it is to have two. And some couple who live in the Foxwoods development had a baby girl near the end of June, but she was born with some terrible birth defects and died the next day."

"Oh, man," Skip said.

"So Faith fell from the sky, I guess, right down to Mr. Mom."

"Mr. Mom." That was what she called him now. He didn't kid himself that it meant more than a nice person being nice. Watching her disappear behind the line of tall cedars, her stride springy and sure, Skip thought that Faith would have a nice long day and he would merely have a long one, ripping shingles from an old roof on a clear blue morning with a full sun beating down.

There was one honest roofer in Mount Mason, the rest being beer-drinking thieves who took a couple of thousand dollars and slapped shingles haphazardly along the roofline. Luckily the one honest roofer was Ed's father, Jim. "Mr. Salzano," Skip had called him when he hired him, which maybe wasn't the best way to begin a professional relationship in which he was supposed to be the boss. But he needed the barn reroofed badly now. The lightning had hit the rod, that was for sure, but it had ricocheted onto the asphalt shingles and the wood beneath and feasted, delighted, on the dry wood and gummy roof cement for at least a few minutes before the rain had doused it. The rain that had poured in over the weeks since then was beginning to rot the timbers and the floor of the hayloft.

"There's not a whole lot of point in doing this unless we rip it down to the roofline and start over again," Jim Salzano had said when he came out to look at it the first time. "There's a lot of rot along the gutters. Nobody's done anything to this roof for maybe thirty years."

"Go ahead," Skip said.

"Big job."

"I'll get up there with you. Might as well."

"That'll help, then."

Mrs. Blessing's daughter came down to watch them work while she was visiting. She was a tall woman, too, in a big hat that kept the sun off her face. He had heard Mrs. Blessing calling from the house, demanding that she come back inside and get something on her head so she would not freckle. By the time she and her husband came back from playing golf and having lunch, old shingles were scattered in heaps around the grass, and a pile of them were on a big flatbed to be taken away. The two lightning rods lay on their sides. She nudged one with the toe of her shoe, then put out her hand to Skip. He could feel the calluses as he shook it.

"It's criminal, the way this building has been allowed to degenerate," she said.

"It's not used for anything."

"I know. If I had it down at our farm, I'd use it. It's a wonderful barn, actually, built the way buildings aren't built anymore." She laughed, a low unamused chuckle. "I sound like my mother. Nothing is the same as it was. Do you like working for her?"

"She pays a decent wage."

"I very much doubt that. Maybe a decent wage by the standards of 1955. How does she seem to you?"

"I couldn't really say. I haven't known her that long. Did you ask Nadine?"

Mrs. Blessing's daughter laughed again. Meredith Fox, her name was. That's what Jennifer had told him. "Nadine tells me a good deal, but only when I don't ask a direct question. When I asked how Mother was, I believe Nadine said, 'Ha!' " She looked up at the barn. "Four-by-fours instead of two-by-fours."

"You don't see that anymore," Mr. Salzano said from atop a ladder.

She nodded. "We kept horses here all through my childhood. You should have seen my mother ride. What a seat she had. You should have seen her swim, for that matter. She'd go off the dock and do the breaststroke from one end to the other and then back again. She'd swim like a fish for half an hour. Golf, too. And tennis, doubles, mostly. She stopped almost twenty years ago. Her best friend died and she was never the same."

"She seems okay to me," said Skip, thinking about the way Mrs. Blessing barked Nadine's name when she wanted her, the way she kept watch with her binoculars as though she were on the lookout for some enemy incursion down the driveway, the way she held the baby now and ran her long fingers over Faith's face. He wished he could tell all this to Mrs. Fox, who seemed so nice, how her mother sat on the porch at night and sometimes commanded him to lift Faith into her arms so that she could rock back and forth in one of the old porch rockers until Faith's lids dropped, her mouth fell open, and she breathed the slow sibilant baby breath of sleep.

"She needs to get out more, travel," Mrs. Fox said. "She can afford it. She lives in the past too much. It's not healthy."

"I guess it depends on how good the past was," Skip said, thinking of his bedroom with the bucking bronco on the quilt.

She tilted her head a bit, and Skip flushed because it occurred to him that for an older lady she was really good-looking. Her eyes were the same color as the pond, and they tilted at the corner even more than Jennifer Foster's.

"May I ask you a personal question?" she said.

"Shoot."

"Were you really in prison for armed robbery?"

"No, ma'am. I pled to a burglary charge and got less than a year in county. County jail, I mean."

"Anything else?"

"No, ma'am. I just happened one time to be in the wrong place at the wrong time."

"I can second that," Mr. Salzano called down from the top of the ladder. "Absolutely. With the wrong bunch of guys, too." He looked at Skip. "I may be dumb, Skipper, but I'm not stupid."

"Your reputation is far worse than the reality, then," Meredith Fox said seriously.

"That's sort of the way, isn't it?" Skip replied.

Mrs. Blessing's daughter took the back path to the pond then, a groundhog and its plump kits scattering in her wake. When he went to the garage to get a crowbar he saw her out in the little boat, rowing hard from one end of the pond to another. He figured the horses must keep her in better shape than most women her age, and he was glad he'd washed down the boat with the hose so she hadn't found it dusty, full of tattered webs and dead flies. He stopped for a moment to look at her, at the rise of the mountain around the valley, at the slope of the valley around the pond and the house, at the small wooden boat at its center. It was probably tough to buy a wooden boat these days. Fiberglass, aluminum, that's what they made now. He liked the wood.

"Man," he said under his breath, thinking there couldn't be greater happiness than to own a place like this.

Mrs. Fox pulled the boat onto the bare patch of lawn by the dock and went to the garage for one of the old fly-casting rods. Her arm moved back and forth as though she were drawing in the air with the line. A hairy yellow lure flew up and across, then set down solidly on the surface of the water. Skip thought he saw the dark shadow of a trout move toward it below the water. She looked toward him and smiled.

"I could dig you some night crawlers if you'd rather have an easier time of it," Skip called, walking toward her.

She shook her head. "I like fly casting. I don't particularly like catching fish. And Nadine won't clean them. Apparently she put her foot down about two things: a uniform, and cleaning fish. The uniform was almost the end of it as far as my mother was concerned."

"I'll clean fish for you if you want."

"If I catch anything I'll take you up on the offer. But I don't think I'm likely to."

Skip squinted toward the surface of the pond. At the far end a pair of green herons were hunched over the water, heads low between their folded wings, waiting for slow sunfish to edge into the warm water close to shore. One heron jabbed suddenly, hoisted a wriggling twist of silver aloft, let it slide down his frantically working craw, settled back into position. Mrs. Blessing's daughter cast out again.

"That lure's actually for big fish. Shad, maybe, or pike."

She laughed again. Skip wondered where she'd learned to laugh so easily. So far he'd never heard Mrs. Blessing laugh.

"Well, I said I wouldn't catch anything."

"Meredith," called a man's voice from the house. "Do you want to have a drink at the club before dinner?"

"Not much," she called back as a small trout broke the water and leaped into the air a foot from her moving lure. "I'm very contented at the moment."

Skip liked the sound of that. "I'd better get to work," he said. "I want to powerwash the inside of the barn before we go any further. But I can stop to clean fish. Or get you bait if you want."

"When I was a little girl I used to watch those fish jump out of the water, and I used to think they were jumping for joy," Meredith said. "And then one day when I was older I was walking around the pond and I noticed how they swam back and forth, back and forth. I suppose I finally noticed how small the pond was. And one of them jumped, and all I could think was that he was trying to escape. Except that he would die outside."

"You've got a fish on there," Skip said, watching her lure disappear.

By the next evening she and her husband were gone, the Chevy Suburban with the horse trailer pull disappearing down the long drive while the lens of the binoculars flashed in the fading light from the upstairs sleeping porch. The old barn roof was ripped off, the new shingles packed in blocks around it ready for the next day. Jennifer had put in two days with Faith and come back to the house, slightly grubby, only minutes after the Foxes' car, the roofer's truck, and Nadine's little compact had all pulled away. Rain was beginning to fall, making a pale gray haze over the pond. "I'm in love," Jennifer said, lifting Faith's slack little body from the sling on the back steps.

"Come inside," Mrs. Blessing called. "You, too, Charles."

The kitchen was at the east end of the house, and after noon Skip had noticed that it was in a kind of perpetual twilight, although when he made the coffee in the morning the old white stove and yellow cabinets were warmed by the morning light. He looked around at the clean clear countertops, the shining stainless steel sink. A platter covered with a striped cloth was the only dish in sight. Nadine was the cleanest person he'd ever known. She confirmed a suspicion he'd always had that there was some kind of link between cleanliness and meanness. He bet Jennifer Foster wasn't half as clean as her mother. Little pieces of hair were pulled loose from her ponytail now, and she had a big dirt stain on the seat of her pants.

"I wondered if you would care to join me for something to eat," Mrs. Blessing said.

"I don't want to put you to any trouble," Jennifer said.

"I probably need to give the baby a bath," Skip said, rubbing the curve of her back, warm and solid under his hand.

"I put her in the stream," Jennifer said.

"The stream? It's freezing!"

"Just her feet. She liked it. She sort of sucked in her breath, then she paddled."

"Oh, man. You should have asked me about that first."

"Excuse me," said Mrs. Blessing, leaning on the counter by the platter and folding up the cloth over it. "I thought perhaps we could picnic by the pond. There are ham sandwiches and some coleslaw. I had Nadine leave a quilt and a basket on the hall table. I suspect she thinks I'm entering my dotage."

Skip could hear the rain on the roof, a soft staccato but insistent. "It's raining," Jennifer said.

"Ah," said Mrs. Blessing, cocking her head. "I didn't notice."

"What about the side porch?" Jennifer said.

Skip wondered what the hell Mount Mason would say if it could peek in the wall of windows and see them laying the quilt on the polished wood floor, putting Faith down in one corner on a small pink blanket Mrs. Blessing had had ready, sitting with a plate of sandwiches and a pitcher of lemonade and a stack of gold-edged flowered plates so thin and fine that when one touched the other oh-so-lightly it chimed like a doorbell. Mrs. Blessing stayed in an old white wicker chair but he and Jennifer sat practically knee to knee on the quilt. Faith was sleeping on her stomach, smacking her lips from time to time.

"I've got a spare bottle left in that bag," Jennifer said with her mouth full. "She just sucked down the other three. Don't you think maybe she's ready for some real food?"

"See, that's another thing that I'm not sure about. Some of the books say four months, some say six. They're not real specific about solid food. There's a lot of stuff about breast-feeding."

"I tried, but it didn't work," said Jennifer, laughing. "Uh-oh, I shocked Mrs. Blessing. Look at her."

"I'm not sure I'm capable of being shocked at my age," Mrs. Blessing said.

"You were shocked when you first saw Faith," Skip said.

"Yes, I was. That's absolutely true. I was shocked."

"And delighted," said Jennifer. "That's the word. I picked that up from television or something when I was a little kid, and I used to use it all the time. Can you imagine what it was like in first grade when I said something was delightful? There was another word, too, I think. *Zesty,* that was it. That one I got from commercials. 'This sandwich is very zesty,' I used to say. My mother learned to speak English from American soldiers. Her big thing, when we first got here, was figuring out which words she'd learned that weren't words you were supposed to say in polite company. And getting rid of 'y'all.' I guess a lot of the guys she knew were Southern. I used to say 'y'all,' too. I remember one of my father's cousins getting a big laugh when he said we must be from South Korea."

"It must have really been bad, coming here like that," Skip said. "Mount Mason, especially. I mean, the city would have been different."

"The prejudices in cities are the same as in small towns, Charles," Mrs. Blessing said. "They are simply hidden a little better."

"It was strange, coming here," Jennifer said. "All those years I dreamed about coming to America and seeing my father and how it was going to be perfect. And then in one day I was here."

"And it was completely different than you'd expected."

Jennifer shook her head. "No. It was fantastic. I got off the plane and there was this big man, bigger than anyone I'd ever seen in my life, and he lifted me up and he held me and held me and I could feel him crying on my face and my hair. I'd never seen a man cry before, either. And he said, 'I'm never going to put you down.' He rocked me to sleep that night singing that mockingbird song, you know, 'Hush, little baby, don't say a word.' I sang it to Faith today and I could remember all the words, or at least the ones my father knew. He sang to me and when I woke up in the morning he was sleeping on the floor next to my bed."

"Whoa," said Skip. He looked over at Faith and saw that she was up on her little arms, doing what he thought of as baby push-ups, staring at all of them.

"She's awake," he said, just to have something to say, to fill a silence that seemed to fill his heart.

"She gives you that same feeling, doesn't she?" Jennifer said. "That feeling of absolute security, that everything's going to be okay." Faith's head dropped, then came up again.

"She looks like a turtle," Skip said.

"Charles, that's a dreadful thing to say," Mrs. Blessing said. "She most certainly does not."

"She doesn't really make me feel secure at all," Skip said. "She makes me feel afraid. She makes me feel afraid that something will go wrong, that she'll fall out of the crib or get some really bad disease or stop breathing or something."

"You're a pessimist."

"I guess. I guess maybe I have to be."

"I don't see why," Jennifer said, clearing the plates. "She's yours. It's been three months. She's yours."

"She really needs her shots," Skip said.

"I have the doctor coming next week," Mrs. Blessing said.

"Nothing bad will happen," Jennifer said. "She'll learn to walk and talk and we'll make up some kind of story to get her into school and she'll have this great place to live and these great people to live with. What could be bad? Right, honey?" Jennifer Foster turned with her hands full of dishes and there was Faith lying on her back, holding her feet in her hands. As if in answer to their question she arched her back and rolled back over onto her stomach.

"Faith Cuddy!" Jennifer cried. "You rolled over! You rolled over both ways, front to back and back to front." She put down the dishes and clapped her hands. "You rolled over!"

"Has she done that before, Charles?" Mrs. Blessing said.

"Not that I know of," Skip said. "Maybe she's been doing it behind my back." And Jennifer laughed, and Mrs. Blessing laughed, too, a dry laugh, out of practice. But Skip just kept thinking of Jennifer saying "Faith Cuddy." It was the first time he'd ever thought of that name. Printed crooked on the top of lined paper. Typed in at the top of a report card. Underneath a yearbook picture. Faith Cuddy. Maybe Jennifer understood better than he did. Maybe things would be all right.

"There she goes again," said Jennifer.

Nadine was more irritable on rainy days than she was the rest of the time. "I think it reminds her of home," said Jennifer, who was sitting at the kitchen table sipping tea from the heavy mugs kept for the help, waiting around with the monitor turned down low in her pocket for Faith to wake up from her nap so she could give her a bottle. "I did a report in seventh grade that said Korea has three months of the year, I think, when all it does is rain. My dad asked her once if she wanted to go back to visit. She said he was crazy."

Jennifer had a good strong voice, which was useful since Nadine had the old dryer going and the vacuum running along with the sump pump banging away. Even though the walls seemed to be vibrating, Mrs. Blessing could hear Nadine slamming doors and heaving the old Hoover violently around in the upstairs rooms. It had been raining for four straight days, since the evening they'd picnicked on the porch.

"I can't imagine she would care to go back," Mrs. Blessing said. "It would probably be entirely different than she remembers it." The last time Mrs. Blessing had gone to New York, for the funeral of Benny's mother, she had not known the place. A man in rags had lurched at the car the Cartons had sent for her and pushed a paper cup full of change toward the window, and the house where she had lived as a small girl had been pulled down for a building that looked like an aluminum jack-in-the-box. Bertram's itself had added an enormous gymnasium, like a horrible brick growth upon the old façade, and just inside the park three girls in the gray skirt and blue blazer with the familiar crest were smoking cigarettes. "At least it's tobacco they're smoking," Meredith had said wearily as she complained.

Outside the wind blew suddenly, and the screens rattled in their frames. The spillway to the pond had become choked with leaves and branches, and Skip was out, in an old pair of waders of her father's and a Barbour that Sunny had bought years ago in London, clearing out the tangle. From the kitchen window she could just make out the red John Deere cap he was wearing, and the flash of a yellow bucket. He'd been working out there most of the morning, sloshing from the lawn to the pond.

"Charles," she cried from the kitchen door, a ghost behind the thick screen as he trotted toward the garage. "Come in here!"

"That baby is really sleeping," Jennifer said.

"She's in for her long nap," Mrs. Blessing said as if it were the most natural thing in the world for the two of them to be keeping track of a baby's schedule. "I hope he has her well wrapped up. It's very chilly and damp."

"You know he does."

The workmen who were hired to put things right from time to time grumbled that, grand as it was, Blessings had been poorly sited. Or perhaps it was that it was placed in as good a spot as any when it had been a small farmhouse, two rooms up, two down, outhouse over the knoll, 150 years ago. But by the time Edwin Blessing had added on the library wing and the long porch, the guest suites and the new dining room with the stone fireplace made from the stones dug to make the foundation, the big garage on the high side and the pond on the lower lawn, the house was smack in the center of a downward flow of water in a heavy rain. It was the rainiest September in decades, pearl-gray sheets of water veiling the house and the hills, and the basement flooded.

One of Jess's boys had persuaded Mrs. Blessing, thirty years before, to put in a sump pump, and as soon as the water crept to the level of the platform for the washer and dryer the pump clicked on and began to work with a sound like someone jackhammering the concrete just below the kitchen floor. Mrs. Blessing had always found the racket soothing, as though she knew she was getting her money's worth; one of the reasons she'd been so disconcerted the night of the lightning strike was that the pump hadn't come on with all the electrical lines down. She remembered some years ago, when she had given a small open house at Christmastime and it had been unseasonably warm. Instead of drifts of snow, there had been huge washes of water across the drive, and the pump had come on, and the guests had shouted at one another across their cut-crystal cups of eggnog.

Nadine shut off the vacuum upstairs and came down, her glossy black hair still damp on her forehead and the nape of her neck. "You still here?" she said to Jennifer, who had stopped at the post office and picked up a box, two nightgowns from Pettifleur on Seventy-ninth Street.

"I'm leaving soon, Mommy."

"You here too much. You go to class now. Work."

"I only have afternoon classes two days a week this term. And I'm working nights for a month. I'll go soon."

"Nonsense. You have lunch with me," Mrs. Blessing said. "Tuna on toast."

"*Aye yi yi!*" cried Nadine. The sump pump, thumping away, had disguised the sound of Skip pounding at the back door. He stepped inside, water rolling off his borrowed jacket and onto the checkerboard linoleum. "Outside," Nadine yelled. "Outside."

"Nonsense. Come in, Charles. Hang those things up and sit down."

"Ay," Nadine muttered, pulling the string mop from the broom closet.

"That's right, Nadine. A little water never hurt anyone. Except your pants, Charles, which are soaked to the ankle, even with the waders."

"It's bad out there," he said.

"My father installed that sluiceway when I was a child. He said it was foolproof."

"It's all choked up."

"Bailing with a bucket hardly seems the best way to deal with the problem."

"The bucket was for the fish. The fish and the frogs. The pond's so far outside its banks that the lawn was all covered with trout and bass, flopping around. And about a hundred frogs. Snakes, too, but I'm not rescuing snakes. I just got everybody back in the pond with the bucket. There's a few still out there that don't look like they're going to make it. Nadine, you want two or three trout for dinner?"

"No clean fish!"

Jennifer laughed.

"Miss Smarty," Nadine said.

"That's a good idea, Nadine. Jennifer and Charles will have lunch with me. Charles can bring in some fish, and you can sauté them. There are grapes in the icebox, and potato salad. Then you can take the rest of the day off."

"Aye yi yi."

"I'm sorry, Mrs. Blessing," Jennifer said, standing and putting her cup in the sink. "My mother's right. I have to get to class. I really wanted to stay longer, but in this weather it's going to take me a while to get where I'm going." She looked at Skip. "I wanted to tell you that I saw your friend at the hospital the other day. He messed himself up pretty bad."

"Yeah?"

"I work in physical therapy part-time every once in a while. He's going to have some job learning to walk again without a limp."

"And the scars, right?"

"And the scars. Although he's the kind of guy who seems like he'd like to have a scar or two." This time it was she who colored. "Sorry. That sounded cruel."

"You're right. Not about how it sounded. You're right that he'll probably like having them. Tough guy and all that." Skip ran his hands through his hair, and a drizzle scattered around him. "I got to go, too. I got stuff over in the garage, you know. Things to do over there."

When they were both gone Mrs. Blessing settled herself at the table on the long porch and turned on the monitor. Bathtime, she thought, listening to the faint splashing sound of the water from the old faucet and the tuneless singing that rose above it. A vista of bent and flattened flowers in fuzzy daubs was faintly visible through the sheers at the windows. When she had first moved to Blessings, she had taken down the curtains, all of them, to let in the light and the sight of the outdoors. "Is this some modern invention?" her mother had said. And then slowly over the years she had ordered others and had them hung, until once again the house was veiled.

Jennifer was in some classroom smelling of chalk, its linoleum scuffed and torn, and Charles was in the bare garage apartment, which she'd been half ashamed to see when she'd gone to demand his help that night. And here she sat in solitary splendor with a tuna fish sandwich and two olives, as she had done for years and years, happily, or at least contentedly. All broken now, the happiness or contentment or resignation or whatever it was a person felt when the repeated customs of her life had become that life itself. For all around her was a shadow lunch, an imagined lunch, the one in which the aroma of butter and fresh fish filled the air, clinging slightly for a day or two to the brocade drapes, in which she listened to the two young people speak of people she did not know, things she cared nothing for, the smell of carbolic soap from the man, the smell of some lemon shampoo from the girl, the air of unimportant everyday sociability about the meal. And the child at its center, crowing and smiling and waving her arms about. They had all made her want more than she had. The curse of having young people about the house was that they were always so redolent of possibility. She turned off the little machine that brought her the sounds of life from across the way.

Nadine came in to clear the plate, muttering to herself, and wiped the table with a series of grunts and groans, and Lydia Blessing sat without moving as the gray light of the rainy day grew even grayer with dusk. She had had a pain behind one eye for the last few days, and a pain in one arm, and she rubbed the arm and pressed her fingers to the spot above her brow, and instead of just this one lunch that seemed to have taken on an importance out of all proportion to its reality, she conjured up an entire life that might have been. Once again she imagined the apartment in the building on Park Avenue, the antique Oriental blue-and-white plates on stands on the sideboard, the floral prints on the drapes, the doorman who would hail a cab when she went to the club or to meet Meredith at the symphony, the gin and tonics on a silver tray as the sun set behind the building across the way.

And suddenly she knew in her bones, the way she knew the alphabet or the Lord's Prayer or the piano fingering to "Clair de Lune," that that was a life no better than the life she had had. The great grievance she had felt for so long, the sense of being done out of something, by her mother, by her daughter, by her class, by chance, by fate: it was a Potemkin village, a stage set, a papier-mâché thing that had lost its power. She had filled her days mourning that shadow life, and it had no more meaning than the chattering of monkeys. Instead, these last few weeks, she had seen what might have been had she not felt perpetually done out of something better. From the window Blessings was almost invisible in the heavy rain, but she knew that even in this terrible chill downpour it was no longer the claustrophobic prison she had styled it for so long. It was what it had always been, a refuge. And for some reason she remembered an argument she had had with Jessie one summer, when she had been preparing to send Meredith to boarding school. "This is the right thing for a girl in her situation," she had said as she'd looked over a box of white uniform blouses.

"For God's sake, Lydia," Jess had said, her eyes dark. "Can't you for once in your life stop thinking about what's right and start considering what's good?"

She jerked upright in the chair, her hand still pressed to her head, thinking perhaps she had fallen asleep. The rain had stopped and, in the way of summer storms, had left an evening of delicately scented and colored beauty behind it. The beaten-down stems of the daisies and the coneflowers seemed to rise slowly back toward the sky, to be prepared to be warmed by the sun that had been drowned for so many days. The pounding of the sump pump had stopped, and the air was filled only with the clicking of bent-legged insects, cicadas and crickets.

Across the room was the telephone, an old rotary dial phone she had never thought to replace, and with her hands shaking she dialed and waited. "Meredith," she said, when she heard her daughter's voice, "Meredith," and in her voice was something of such unnatural unknowable shape and form that she had no idea what she would say, feared that she might be like the girl in one of her childhood fairy tales, who opens her mouth and spits out a frog.

"Mother," Meredith replied. "Are you all right? Mother? Is everything all right?"

"We've had terrible rain. The pond overflowed, and the boat floated out. How was your trip home? How is it in Virginia? How are your hollyhocks?"

"My hollyhocks?"

"Did the rain hurt them?"

"It's beautiful here, Mother. We haven't had any rain. My flowers are fine. Those pink hollyhocks I got from that catalog you sent me were a beautiful color. That true rich pink, not too pale and not too purply. Is that what you're talking about? Are you certain you're all right?"

There was a silence and then she said, "Meredith. Send me seeds. When the season is over, when everything has died back, send me seeds."

What was it she had really meant to say? It was in her mind, her heart, everywhere in her, the notion that she must say something to lift the weight of those years of resenting her self-imposed exile. That was what it had been, after all. She could have gone at any time. But she had not. Once, she remembered, she had spent a week in Paris and could not wait to come home. The "Mona Lisa" had been so much smaller than she'd expected. "Come see me," was all she said to Meredith. "Come see me soon."

The lights came on around the house, and she got out of the chair slowly, her back a little stiff. Nadine had left half a chicken on a plate in the oven, some sliced tomatoes and potato salad under plastic wrap on the counter. She pushed it all down the disposal with her fork. It was waste, but it was her waste. She walked slowly to the window that looked west. The lavender, gray, and pink striations of the sunset were mirrored in the crackle-glass surface of the pond, the fields of rye grass turned golden by the heat and shiny by the rain. As she watched, a string of lights appeared around the edge of the water. Her father had had them sunk into the banks of the pond, one every few feet, and the first time he threw the switch he had beamed like a boy, although his skin was already loose around the neck, gray and loose. Meredith had been a child then. Lyds my love had given way to Merry darling. Lydia had watched the lights come on from an Adirondack chair, her long plaid skirts eddying around her ankles. "It looks like a carnival ride," she'd said. "Exactly," Lydia's father had said. "It's brilliant, isn't it, Merry darling? We love it, don't we?" He had taken the little girl out in the boat, and the two of them had rowed from light to light—or he had rowed, and pretended she was doing so, too, as she dragged the little oar he'd had made for her through the water. At each light he told her to make a wish. A pony. A pink bicycle. A spaniel puppy. "That's too many wishes," Lydia had called across the darkening oval at the center of the ring of lights, and her father had called back, "Ah, Lyds my love, don't ever say that."

One by one over the years the lights had burned themselves out. Her father had died the year after he'd illuminated the pond. Her mother had slept her last years away in the expensive nursing home in a valley thick with wild rhododendrons ten miles from Mount Mason. "I know you," she said when Lydia drove over to see her. "I know who you are." The night before she died she had told the nurses she needed to leave. "I don't belong here," she'd said. Those were her last words, they told Lydia. The old cherry bedroom suite that had been shipped from the city apartment to the nursing home was in one of the back bedrooms now. In the narrow top drawer of the bureau she had found faded pictures of a young man she didn't recognize, a yellow baby sweater with buttons shaped like ducks, and a slim book of poetry by Sara Teasdale. "To Ethy, Forever Yours, Eddie," it said inside in faded ink in her father's beautiful handwriting.

When Sunny died, over the rise and down the hill and in the barn, she could not even bear to go through his things. The Fosters had packed up what was in his room at Blessings, and she had allowed his landlord to turn over the contents of his apartment to the Salvation Army. Jess had left her a starburst brooch and her leatherbound collection of Edith Wharton and a needlepoint bench with a floral design that she used at the piano. All around her were the possessions of the dead. The boat had floated from the center of the pond and lay at the foot of one of the willow trees, wedged into its roots so that it would be easy to get ashore in the morning. How had it happened that only it, and she, remained in this place? How had it happened that Blessings was slowly being resurrected and she with it? Charles had restored the lights around the pond without asking, and when she had first seen them lit she had felt a love for her father that she thought had been long burned out.

She cried once, briefly, two sobs that wrenched her thin chest. Then she went upstairs and slept deeply, without dreams.

Lydia Blessing had not seen Paul Benjamin for several years, since he had visited her in the hospital when she had her stroke, and she was surprised at how old he looked. His chest was concave so that his old rep tie, frayed at the edges, made a fishhook from chin to belt. She had always found him a useful doctor, a believer in the old remedies that she had never abandoned: camphor on the chest, tea with lemon and honey, salts and enemas, hot whiskey when absolutely necessary. At one time they had known each other well, and when, at age forty, he had married a younger woman, a nurse he met at the hospital, Lydia had from time to time invited them as dinner guests when she had people come for the weekends. One May evening, she remembered, he had had too much to drink and recited "Casey at the Bat" on the end of the diving board, then fallen into the pond. He had come up spouting water like a whale, and everyone had cheered except for his young wife, who turned red and pushed him into the car to go home, dripping wet. She had overdressed for the party and been out of sorts all night because of it.

"Hello, Lydia," he said as he edged himself slowly out of his car, the same sort of car she had, a Cadillac that looked as though it had been frozen in amber since the day, some years ago, when it had been manufactured. "You seem in fine fettle."

"I'm eighty, Paul. Which I believe makes you ninety."

"Ninety-one last month. I have gout. It's a ridiculous thing. Henry the Eighth had it. No wonder he killed his wives."

"My father had a classmate from Princeton who had it. I was told it was because he drank so much."

"That's an old wives' tale," Paul Benjamin said, reaching for the old black bag he'd once told her his parents gave him when he graduated from medical school. "That's what all these doctors say about everything. Anything you like is bad for you. It's a miracle we've lived this long, according to their lights. Although this young man who took over for me isn't bad. You should have had him for this, Lydia. I haven't looked at a baby in Lord knows how long."

Faith was in the living room lying on a receiving blanket on the brocade couch. Jennifer Foster bent over her while Skip sat in the wing chair in the dark corner shadowed by the awning and the porch overhang. Paul Benjamin peered down at the moon face with its fuzz of blond hair. The baby was doing what Skip loved to watch her do, coming alive bit by bit, taking in the world by inches, curling her toes around the air, moving her fingers against one another and the side of her own face, staring at the light and moving her tongue thoughtfully between her lips, tasting the air. She blew pensively through her lips. A bubble formed, then broke, and she sneezed suddenly and went still.

"Is this your baby, young lady?" the doctor said, narrowing his eyes.

"Of course it isn't her baby, Paul. Look at her. That's the Foster girl. This child is the grandchild of an old friend of mine who's visiting from the Vineyard. The baby is staying with her for several weeks while her daughter and son-in-law are in Europe, and they realized she needed her shots." Mrs. Blessing was surprised at how fluently she lied, much better than she'd done it years before, when it had been so much more important, at least to her. She realized that lying was easier than telling the truth because it had such nice smooth edges, not jagged with impossibility and inconvenience the way the truth so often was. If she were to tell Paul Benjamin the truth about Faith, he would say "What?" with a deep and solemn air of disbelief. The lie went down like honey.

"She looks healthy enough. It is a she, isn't it. Pretty little girl but her mother will need to mind the sun. She's as fair as a Swede. Take her clothes off, young lady."

All the old familiar instruments came out of the black bag, all the things that had seemed so sinister when she was a child. The pointed things for the eyes and nose. The cold and glittery stethoscope. The doctor from whom Paul Benjamin had bought his practice had let Lydia listen to her own heart once, when she was eight or nine, and she was amazed at how inexorable it sounded, like the engine of some considerable machine. Without realizing it she put her hand over her heart: still there working all these years later.

That other doctor had been named Brown, she remembered, and her father had delighted in kidding him about a patent medicine for indigestion called Dr. Brown's. Ed Blessing had loved that about Mount Mason: the simple country doctor, the simple country lawyer. It made no difference to him that Dr. Brown had been at Exeter and Yale; simple country was what he wanted, and it was what he was certain he had gotten.

"A very healthy child," said Paul Benjamin, folding his stethoscope. "I can't imagine what you thought was the matter."

"Nothing's the matter. She needed to be looked at. And the shots, too, the ones for measles and all the rest. I can't recall exactly. The shots they all get now."

"German measles, too. They used to have to send the children away when mother was expecting because the German measles were terrible for the baby in womb. Horrible things we saw— deaf, blind, retarded babies that went right to the state hospital." He nodded. "All over now, of course. I'll need the grandmother's signature on something. The state makes a martyr of us medical people now with all the forms and so forth."

"I'll send it on," said Mrs. Blessing. "She's visiting friends in the city right now. I'll be happy to sign in her stead. I have some questions she wanted answered." Mrs. Blessing put on her glasses and took a piece of paper from the top of the piano. "When should she begin solid food?"

"Four months or so. Will the grannie be keeping her that long?"

"I'm not sure. What sort of food to begin?"

"Some kind of cereal mixed with formula. Not rice. That will constipate her. How are her stools?"

"Oh, for pity's sake, they're fine. How should they be? Should she be sitting up yet?"

Dr. Benjamin put out his hands and Faith curled her fingers around his. He tugged gently and she rose into a sitting position. "Voilà," he said.

"Ah," said Mrs. Blessing. She used a finger to find the next question on the list Skip had prepared. "Vitamins?"

"Not yet. Her mother can ask for them at about a year."

"All right." Mrs. Blessing looked down the list and rolled her eyes. "Overall, how does she look to you?"

"Grand. A very nice baby, healthy and well cared for. Now, may I inoculate her so she'll stay that way?"

"Should I leave her clothes off?" said Jennifer softly.

"I just need a leg free. But I'm not sure this is right, Lydia. I could pop over when her grannie's here. I need to fill in this form with the name and so forth, date of birth, all the vitals."

"I'll send it on to you."

Paul Benjamin sighed heavily, his bowed chest rising and falling. His hands were a mess of liver spots and they shook slightly as he filled the syringe. Lydia knew they were thinking of the same thing, the night she called him after she had found Sunny in the barn.

"I cannot give a certificate that says 'natural causes,' Lydia. I cannot and I will not," he had said.

"Accident, then. Accidental death."

He had sighed then, too, she remembered, and his hands were shaking, but shaking then because of the sight of Sunny, his luminous golden hair atop the hole where his face had been, the shotgun shining atop his chest.

Paul Benjamin pinched a roll of mottled baby fat between his thumb and forefinger and plunged the needle in. Faith had been staring vacantly at the ceiling, and for just a moment her eyes were puzzled and her brow knit. Then her face went red and she screamed, gasped and lost her breath, screamed again. Without a word Skip left his chair, lifted her off the couch half-naked, and carried her away.

"Now, who was that boy, Lydia? Does he know what he's doing? Young lady, give that baby a bottle now, and tell her grandmother that she may have a fever in a day or two. You take care of her until her grannie's back. She'll be fine. This lady here is too far along in years to be saddled with an infant."

"I beg your pardon," Lydia said.

"That is not to denigrate her. She's the fittest specimen you'd want to see. When's the last time you swam the pond, Lydia?"

"Not in years."

"Is that pond still full of snapping turtles? It was then. What do you think she said when I would remind her of that?"

"I can't imagine," Jennifer Foster said, smiling.

"She said, 'No snapping turtle would come near me.' And she was right. Of course, there was that one man from someplace, Boston was it, when we were younger."

"That was entirely his own fault," Mrs. Blessing said. "A mucky-bottomed pond is not designed for standing up."

"My predecessor took care of him," Dr. Benjamin said, packing up his bag. "Not much he could do back then. Maybe today they'd put the toe on ice, send him along to the big medical center in Bessemer. Back then there was nothing."

"A snapper bit off his toe?" said Jennifer.

"It was completely his own fault," Mrs. Blessing said.

"Now, here's something that was Lydia's fault. One day she comes home from the club and she's in a temper because she'd lost in a doubles round."

"Oh, for pity's sake, Paul, this old story."

"You don't like hearing that one, do you? Who were you playing with, Jessie?"

"I always played doubles with Jess, and she always played deplorably. And laughed about it."

"That was a girl, Jessie. In any event, Lydia here comes home in a temper, hops out of the car, strips down, and jumps in the pond. And what do you think is waiting for her in the water by the dock when she swims back?"

"Oh, for pity's sake."

"Her Cadillac! In four feet of water! She'd been in such a temper she left the engine running and didn't engage the parking brake. Oh, that was a pretty feat of engineering Foster had getting that car to run again. And the upholstery smelled like fish for a year."

"Nonsense," Mrs. Blessing said.

"Put that baby down for a nap after her bottle," the doctor added. "She'll sleep awhile after this. I didn't truly hurt her. She was just aggravated at the pinch. But she may have a fever in a day or two." He looked at Jennifer. "You tell that young man. She may have a slight fever and some crankiness. It's perfectly normal."

Mrs. Blessing walked him out to his car, taking his arm as the two of them came down the steps. "Who's holding up who?" he said. "Or whom."

"Thank you, Paul. I'll send that paper by return mail when it arrives. I'd prefer it if you didn't mention this visit to anyone." He shrugged and sighed and she wondered whether he believed what she had told him after all.

"You've always been a terror, it's true," he said. "And I'm too old now to lose my license, whatever you're up to." They stood together at the car and he looked out over the pond to the line of cedar trees along the creek, and his big sad eyes, which had always reminded her of the eyes of one of the hunting dogs, filled slightly.

"This is a beautiful spot, Lydia. I remember the first time I ever came out here. I was a teenaged boy and Dr. Brown brought me along for the ride. Do you remember? It almost did me out of being a doctor for good." And suddenly she did. It was the day she and Sunny and Benny had gone along the creek on a picnic. Mrs. Foster had made them bacon sandwiches and peanut butter cookies and packed the food in a basket with a big Ball jar of lemonade.

The two boys had walked across the fields swinging the basket between them, and she had walked behind. They were all wearing Wellington boots over their bare feet, and Lydia had snuck out of the house in an old pair of Sunny's shorts. The three of them were wearing cast-off shirts with Ed Blessing's monogram on the cuffs, shirts that had gotten shabby or stained or torn at the elbow or neck. Sunny's hair shone in the light and the back of Benny's neck was sunburned. They had set out lunch at a little grassy knob that sat above the creek just around the turn from a big natural pool in which brown trout sometimes darted from beneath the dark banks to the glittering center. It was funny to her that things like this were so real and so detailed, when the things done as adults were reduced to a few gestures, a laying down of the fork here, a winning hand of bridge there.

They had all three fallen asleep on the old quilt, Lydia dozing off with the sounds of mosquitoes and Benny's hoarse breathing in her ear. And then she woke to find herself stiff and sweaty and alone, one of her Wellies tumbled over the edge into the water. She climbed down to get it, and just around the corner in the pool she could see the two boys from behind. Both of them were naked. They looked like the golden trout that had lasted in the pond only one summer because their tremulous glow had been such an easy target for predators. Lydia had stared at the shining pale flesh, her feet unsteady on the pebbles at the bottom of the steam, and then she scrambled back up the bank toward the quilt, dragging her thigh across a piece of slate so sharp that she felt nothing for a moment, saw only the puffy lips of her own ripped skin, the reds and pinks of muscle in that stop-time moment before blood rushed into the gap.

"How in heaven's name did you do this, Miss Lydia?" Mrs. Foster asked when the boys brought her home held aloft in a cat's cradle made of their thin arms. But she could scarcely remember the feeling of the stone slicing through her, could only remember that just before she scrambled up the bank Sunny had turned his head in the late-day sun coming lacy through the trees and had smiled at her with his eyes half-shut, smiled at her in a way that came to her in her dreams for years later, gloriously happy.

"It wasn't the size of that gash that scared the hell out of me," Paul Benjamin said. "It was the way you sat on the edge of that kitchen table and didn't make a sound. Without being numbed up, too. Doctor poured a shot glass of gin in that wound, and that was all."

"I still have the scar," Lydia said.

"I'd imagine so."

Lydia Blessing had never come close to remarrying. It was not so much that she covertly saw the physical side of things as the purview of the young, although she did, and found the imagined fumblings of her older friends ridiculous and demeaning. It was just that she could not imagine what it would be like to share her life. She could not imagine not being able to switch on the reading lamp next to her bed if she could not sleep at midnight, or having to ask someone else's opinion on dinner plans or weekend guests. She had had her ways from the time she was young, and she had never had to change them.

The closest she had ever come to a love affair was with Bill Stapleton, who had lived just outside of Mount Mason on an old horse farm for as long as she had been at Blessings. He had been a childhood friend of Jessie's, and she had been seated next to him at an Easter dinner just after the war was over. He was quiet and thoughtful, letting her do all the talking until she would reach one of her acerbic pitches and he would murmur, "You don't really mean that." But he had never seemed put off. He had brought Meredith a Chutes and Ladders game once, and a little hat with a feather when he took a trip to London. "That's a ridiculous gift for a little girl," she had said, but she had been secretly pleased, although she would have been more pleased if he had brought the hat for her.

"Such sad news," Jess's daughter Jeanne said when she called just as the rain was tapering off, and then she told her that Bill was dead.

That was the sort of deaths they had now: such sad news. Once there had been the unthinkable deaths, like Benny's and Sunny's, deaths mercifully obliterated by sleep so that each morning, as her mind surfaced from dreaming, she would have to accept them all over again. Then there were the deaths that changed the world, that broke it in two: her mother, her father. There had been Jess's death, which had left her feeling as though she had stiffened her spine and her shoulders for the funeral and had never again let them go. The first had been the unthinkable deaths of youth, the second the wrenching losses of middle age. Now there were the inevitable deaths of old age, which one after another prefigured her own. Such sad news.

"I'll be there by dinner," Meredith said on the phone. "Eric can't get away. But I'll get in the car right after lunch."

"There's no need," Lydia said.

And yet it was a comfort now to have her daughter on one side of her in the pew and Jeanne on the other, as though Jessie were somehow with her, too. "You drive people away, Lulu," Jess had told her after Bill married that nice woman from Philadelphia, who had been at Vassar with one of Frank Askew's daughters. "What's the saying—no man is an island. You've made an island out of yourself. Benny wouldn't have wanted that."

Thank goodness she had that photograph of Benny on the drop-leaf table. Sometimes she could no longer see his face. Jess had always liked him. When they were younger there were times when she had thought it was Jess he would marry, when she would watch the two of them making clover wreaths by the pond. She thought Sunny had thought so, too, but Jessie had made a face when she had asked once. "Benny's like a brother," Jess had said. And of course he had been like a brother to Lydia, too, until he had become like a husband.

Sunny had not wanted her to marry again. Perhaps that was what had decided her. "What's the point, Lyds?" he said one evening on the porch when she was telling him about Bill, and Bill's marriage. Or perhaps it was that trip to Paris, when she had run into Frank Askew in the lobby of the hotel. His wife had invited her to lunch, almost dared her to come, and Lydia had felt ashamed as she watched him eat, fast and loudly. Of course she had never eaten with him before; the most they had ever done was drink together, while a gaggle of complicit onlookers stood by. She'd been forty on that Paris trip, and Frank over sixty, and his dentures clicked like a piece of machinery. His wife called him "old fellow" and said he should slow down or he'd be up all night with heartburn. Later he had called her room, and she had agreed to meet him in the Tuileries and then had not gone. It made her think that she had bad judgment where men were concerned. It made her think his wife had been wiser than she'd ever credited.

The young minister eulogizing Bill was a kind of rebuke, with his pale sideburns and ruddy face. He took as his text the poem "Death Be Not Proud," and Lydia wondered if it was because he was more conversant with literature than with Scripture. Bill's two sons, surrounded by their own children, were in the front pews, along with his widow, who had been a college friend of Bill's first wife. Paul Benjamin nodded to her in the nave. "All well at home?" he murmured, and Lydia nodded. Frank Askew's daughter was on the other side of the church, and outside on the pavement she came to Lydia and embraced her, which was just the sort of thing she hated. "I knew your father," she said to Meredith, and Lydia realized with a kind of light-headedness that she no longer cared what Harriet Askew meant by that. I have outlived my sins, she thought gleefully.

"You can find a priest of a more appropriate age to bury me, Meredith," she said in the car on the way to the cemetery.

"It would probably have been difficult to find a priest Bill's age, Mother. He was ninety, after all."

"Ninety-two in September," Lydia said, adjusting her black felt hat. "And I assume there is at least one priest at St. Anselm's who is not young enough to be my great-grandchild and doesn't look as though he spends all his off-hours golfing."

The cemetery rattled her more than she would have expected. There were all those names she knew on the monuments, all the men and women who had come to the house for cocktails and played mixed doubles at the club. On a knoll in one corner she could see the edge of the square stone that marked the spot where Jess was buried between her first husband and her second, and as the car came around a curve there was the obelisk in front of her that her mother had insisted upon, with the one word at its base, BLESSING.

The plot beneath was like her house, big and empty. Her father had purchased it the same year he bought Blessings, as though to show his faith in a future in Mount Mason that even transcended mortality. There were eight spaces. Perhaps he had expected that he and his wife would have more children. Certainly he had believed that Lydia would have more than just the one. Surely he had not expected that his own two children would not want to join their parents in eternal rest. But one weekend when Sunny had come to stay, the two of them had walked around the pond, and he had flicked his cigarette into the water and said lazily, "Don't you dare put me in the ground after I'm gone, Lyds. No box for this boy." They'd had quite a lot of wine at dinner, and she'd made a face and said, "Don't be morbid," but he would not be put off. "I mean it," he said. "I can't face the dark. Toast me to a cinder and set me free as a bird. Promise."

"Sunny, are you ill? Tell me if you're ill."

"I'm just the same as always, dear heart," he'd said, and he'd kissed her on the forehead and waited almost six months to die on the dirt floor of the barn.

"I'm thinking of your uncle, Meredith," she said as the car wended its way through the shady cemetery drives.

"Are you? So was I. He told me after Grannie's funeral that he would have preferred a kneeling angel with an armful of roses as the monument. I thought he was serious."

"What a dreadful thing to say to a child. You were—what? Ten? Eleven?"

"I was sixteen when Grannie died, almost twenty when he did. He always made me feel so grown up. And loved, too. There was no one like Uncle Sunny for making you feel loved."

That was his gift, Lydia thought. If he loved you he made you feel all wrapped up in it, like ribbons or a blanket. If not, not. The minister had given a grudging little sermon about their brother Lazarus at Sunny's funeral, and she had never known why. Jess had said she thought Sunny had mocked him once about the cut of his cassock, and Lydia thought it might be the cremation that had done it. A whole carload of Sunny's friends had come from New York, several of them in light-colored suits, and gotten quite drunk at the house. "He was godfather to our daughter," one woman told her several times during the course of the afternoon. "We never considered anyone else. Even my brother. No one else." She had found one of the men curled up in Sunny's single bed, weeping with the pillow held close to his face. All she could think was that her mother would have had a fit.

"What would you say was your greatest mistake in life?" she asked Meredith in the car.

"That's an odd question," her daughter replied. "Are you thinking of Bill? Of not marrying him?"

"Goodness, no. That would have been disastrous. For him probably. No, I was simply curious."

Meredith was silent. Finally she said, "I never should have made friends with Betsy Milstone at school. She told all my secrets to the other girls. Especially the really terrible ones, like stealing bits of jewelry and cheating in math."

"You stole jewelry?"

"Mother, this happened almost fifty years ago. It's a little late for you to become exercised about it."

She was right, of course. What a soft patina the passage of time gave to everything, at least once one learned to live in the present. "That's not much of a mistake," Lydia said.

"I'm realizing that. I'm happy to say I haven't made too many terrible mistakes in my life. Quite the contrary. I've been lucky."

"Jess always said we make our own luck," Lydia said.

"I suppose there's some truth to that. Jess was always good at cutting to the heart of the matter. In any event, I guess I've lived a charmed life."

"I am happy to hear you say that," Lydia said.

A silence stretched between them. Lydia rubbed her left arm, which felt stiff and sore. Meredith came around to help her out of the car. "Are you all right?" she said, putting out her hands just as Paul Benjamin had done for the baby, and impatiently Lydia waved her away and used the door of the car to pull herself erect.

"Oh, for pity's sake, Meredith," she said. "Don't fuss at me."

"Remember man that you are dust," the young minister said at Bill's graveside. Thou, Lydia thought. Thou art dust. Why did the modern drain all the ceremony from things? And unto dust thou shalt return. She had taken the boat and the box with Sunny's ashes to the center of the pond one morning just after sunrise. The surface was a mirror. The ashes were unexpectedly heavy and they sluiced out like water, not like dust, and sank heavily except for a light penumbra that rose and held in the air. As she rowed back she had seen Meredith on the dock, wearing a straw hat, her hands crossed over her heart.

"In the air the ashes looked just like glitter," Meredith had said, and her mother had loved her as completely then as she ever had.

Lydia looked at her sidelong as they drove toward the club for the funeral lunch. Her skin was lined now by the sun but her mouth was relaxed in that way so few women of her daughter's age could manage. Meredith had arrived earlier than she expected from Virginia the day before. She and Charles and Jennifer and Faith had been out on the long lawn by the pond, sitting in the shadow of the old flowering crabapple. Nadine had called in sick and it was like being free of the dark schoolmistress, really, with cookies from the box and a thermos of sweet iced tea. The field opposite was thick with the last of the milkweed, and the pods had burst and in the breeze the white feathers carrying the seeds floated thick over them, like a summer snowstorm. The child's eyes seemed to follow them as she sat propped up against Jennifer's outstretched legs.

"I swear she's going to sit up by herself in a couple of weeks," Charles had said. "It's real early for her to be doing that, but look how strong she is."

"I still can't get over how much you've learned about babies,"

Jennifer said, handing around the tea in paper cups, which Mrs. Blessing had always loathed.

"I read. Books. Magazines. Whatever."

"My mother had an enormous set of books about child rearing that are in the house someplace," Mrs. Blessing said. "Perhaps in the back room. I will see if I can find them. Our nanny thought they were nonsense. She believed there were only three things necessary to raise a healthy child: fresh air, simple food, and quinine. I can't recall what the quinine was meant to do but we were dosed with it regularly."

"My father says his uncle said your nanny was a terror," Jennifer said.

"Dreadful. But so were the Foster boys. She would see them trying to hit down crabapples with a broom or eating tomatoes from the garden and she would come out and give them a piece of her mind. There was a time when she took the broom from one of them and hit him with it on the bottom. But she was just doing my mother's bidding. She would sit up in her sleeping porch and if she heard a disturbance she would say, 'Nanny, please take care of that.' My mother was difficult."

"Aren't they all?" said Jennifer.

"Did she use binoculars?" Charles said, squinting up at her from the blanket.

"I can't recall," Mrs. Blessing said.

"Your mother called her Nanny instead of her real name?"

"Times were different then," Mrs. Blessing said.

She could not be certain exactly when times had changed. She knew only that when Meredith had arrived down the drive and walked over to them, Charles had stood up and said to her, "This is my daughter. Her name is Faith." And Meredith had looked at the baby in his arms, who looked back with her eyelids fluttering and made a loud declarative *"Ah!"* sound. Meredith had smiled and Faith had smiled back, then kicked wildly, using both her arms and her legs. A bootie fell off, and Meredith bent to pick it up.

Mrs. Blessing looked at her old watch. "You must have been speeding on the interstate," she said.

"I was just under the limit." Meredith put the bootie back on Faith's foot herself, then patted it when she was done. "What a pretty baby!" she had said to Skip. "Aren't you lucky? How old is she?"

"Your new caretaker's not married, is he?" Meredith said in the car on the way back to Blessings when the funeral lunch was done.

"Certainly not."

"Well, I guess you can't have everything. He seems like a very good father."

"It's an unusual situation," Lydia said stiffly, and Meredith grinned.

"Mother, they're all unusual," she said, and was surprised when Lydia did not reply.

He couldn't believe he was out of baby Tylenol. Or Motrin. Or whatever. The doctor had said Faith might have a bad reaction to the inoculations, and though it was a week later he should have been ready for the fever and the restlessness. Maybe the problem wasn't the shots at all, but an ear infection, or a virus, or meningitis or pertussis or one of the other seemingly hundreds of things in the baby book that ended with the laconic sentence "May cause death." He should have been ready, but there was always so much to do, to remember, to think about, where Faith was concerned. He looked down at her flushed face and put his hand on her forehead. The feel of her hot skin reminded him of smooth stones baked by the summer sun. Hot on a warm night, the perspiration had gathered in the folds of her neck, and when he took her out to the car it ran onto his shirt like tears. He kissed the fold between her small round shoulder and the puffy bend of her elbow and could taste it, salt in his mouth. Rubbing his cheek against her damp hot one, he said, "I love you, little girl." She bobbed on his chest and made a grunting noise.

"We're going to bring this fever down," he said as he buckled her into her car seat, his words sounding loud against the cricket hum of the dark night. The lights in the house were out except for the one in the downstairs hall that stayed on always. He drove slowly down the drive.

There was an all-night drugstore in Bessemer. He'd had to wait in line behind a kid with bad skin buying Trojans and breath mints.

Skip dumped four kinds of baby medicine on the counter, for fever, for congestion, for coughs and colds just in case. The older man behind the counter rang them all up. "It's always the dads that get sent out on an emergency in the middle of the night," the man said. "It's probably nothing to worry about."

Nothing to worry about, Skip said to himself in the car, nothing to worry about. He was afraid to turn on the radio because he didn't want the sound to hurt Faith's ears, just in case it was her ears that were bothering her. Maybe the doctor would have to come back. Maybe he'd ask more questions this time about the grandmother and the traveling parents, a story that even Skip had thought sounded a little lame. As he drove back on the twisty roads over the mountain, Faith whined softly. It was October, and though the air was as warm and still as it had been all summer, the leaves were starting to fall from the black walnuts and the water in the pond to chill almost imperceptibly. The trout had slowed down, and most mornings when he came back up the cellar stairs he saw the bright yellow flash of the school bus through the trees along the road. Maybe someday it would stop at the end of the drive at Blessings. Mrs. Blessing would be eighty-one years old just before Thanksgiving, and he figured with luck she could be living here ten or even fifteen years from now. She still moved really well, although she said the arthritis in the one arm was bothering her, and her mind was still certainly as sharp as anything.

Faith snuffled in the backseat of the car. The doctor had not said a word about congestion. A fever in a few days. That's all.

Mrs. Blessing's lawyer had come in a big boxy black car. He carried a black briefcase as thick and square as a tool box. "I am trying to get that child a birth certificate, Charles," Mrs. Blessing had said when she called him into the house after the man left. It gave him hope, the notion of lawyers, made the future seem more certain. For just a moment he'd been able to see Faith with a pink book bag on her narrow back walking down the long driveway with him, hand in hand, straining to climb the steep steps of the bus, turning at the bleary window to hold up one hand as she settled in her seat. Mrs. Blessing would watch her from the sleeping porch with her binoculars. "Was that child properly dressed?" she would call down. "The thermometer says it's not much above freezing."

"It's not as simple as I had hoped," Mrs. Blessing had said after the lawyer was gone. "But I have a man working on it."

Nadine had come in then and cut off the conversation. "This crazy place," she said. "Too many people come and go."

On the drive back from the drugstore there were whirling things, in the air, on the road, so that the world seemed strange and vaguely dangerous, and he kept glancing over at the baby, who had fallen asleep pitched to one side in that boneless posture that sleep brought when she was sitting up. Moths flew into, then off, the windshield, and a raccoon trundled across the road. Skip realized that he'd once been a nocturnal animal himself, sleeping with the flat of his hand over his face to keep the sun from waking him, closing McGuire's with the guys. But always there had been the sense that he was out of place, the same sense he'd had in his aunt and uncle's house, and sleeping beside Shelly, and in Debbie and Joe's trailer. He didn't have that sense anymore.

He drove past the bar on his way down into the valley, saw that part of the neon had burned out, so that it said MCGU E's. Joe's truck was in the lot, and Shelly's mother's car, and for a moment he had that feeling of a mug cold in his fist, the beer cold in his mouth, and the smoke and the bright eyes peering out of it, saying, "Yo, man, you want to buy my brother's Camaro?" or "Yo, man, you want to buy some really good Hawaiian?" or "Yo, man, you want to crash at my place?" He remembered once when Chris's mother said that if you missed the soaps for a month or two it was no big deal because by the time you got back to them people might be divorced or have amnesia or whatever but in some way it would all be the same, you could get the drift in a day or two. And that was what it was like in McGuire's, except without the amnesia. When he got out of the county jail on a Wednesday morning he'd walked in that night and Pat, who was tending bar, had said, "Beer, Skipper?" exactly the way he'd said "Beer, Skipper?" the night Skip got busted ten months before.

"I just got out," he'd said to Pat.

"Yeah, it's cool," the bartender had replied, pulling the draft handle.

It was a boring life, and Skip had confused it with an orderly one. It turned out that Skip liked an orderly life, too, just like Mrs. Blessing. She'd changed since he'd been working at Blessings, but she still relied on rules so much that she sometimes talked in them, like fortune cookies for the well-behaved. No alcohol before four P.M. No mowing after five. Early supper on Sunday, even if it was something Nadine had left with a yellow note in the freezer: put in microwave three minutes. Gutters cleaned in spring and fall. If he was ever tempted to forget that there was still a dividing line between them, each morning he was reminded, when he gave the baby her bottle, burped her, and wound her mobile to play "Twinkle Twinkle Little Star" while he went across and up the cellar stairs to make the coffee.

"People of her generation are really into routine," Jennifer Foster had said to him. "That's why they basically like being in the hospital. The mealtimes are the same, the lights out. They like an orderly life."

Skip was not sure that Mrs. Blessing liked it, exactly, but that it was necessary to her, that somehow the smell of the coffee and the lunch on a tray and the light in the hallway were a hedge, the way the awnings were there so the upholstery would not fade. He wondered sometimes if she'd ever done anything wild in her life, and then he remembered what Jennifer had told him the doctor had said about the Cadillac in the pond. And maybe the conspiracy around the baby, too, was a piece of wildness. It had certainly made her livelier, livelier, Jennifer said, than she'd ever been before.

When he pulled into the driveway he caught the glitter of eyes in the headlights. It was only the barn cat, with something small and limp and gray in his mouth. A bird cried out at the end of the pond, something like a child's cry, something like a cat itself, and the animal raised its head suddenly, dropping its prey. The small thing lay frozen, then began to crawl toward the flower beds, disappearing into a patch of daisies and lavender at the foot of the stone foundation. But the cat sprang after it and emerged again with it in its jaws. A second cry came from across the water, but the cat wasn't fooled this time and ran off to finish killing and eating. As Skip turned the car toward his space in the garage he saw a languid angular ghost fly toward and then past him, banking over the water and then disappearing into the clouds. The heron, come to find fresh fish.

"You take out one of her old rifles and shoot those things, no one'll ever know," one of the Taylors had said. But he couldn't bring himself to do it.

A light came on upstairs when he slammed the car door, and for just a moment he saw another ghost, the white face, white hair, white gown behind the wavy glass of the hallway window. He raised a hand and the light went out. Faith was still sleeping heavily, and she sucked on the medicine dropper without opening her eyes and only flexed her fingers as he put her down in her crib. She had the funny old bear that Mrs. Blessing had brought down from upstairs, and a stuffed elephant now, that Jennifer had brought over one day, and a light summer quilt, white stitches on white cotton, slightly yellowed and smelling of camphor, that Mrs. Blessing had found somewhere in the attic. "There are some more things in the attic in the garage," she said. "Don't you go up there. I'll go up and find whatever is appropriate."

The fan blew warm air over him, not so he didn't sweat but so the sweat turned cool. The sound it made, *rr rr rr,* lulled him into a light sleep. He woke once when the baby whimpered softly, but when he got up to feel her forehead it felt cooler than it had before, and he fell quickly back into a deeper sleep. He was roused again for a moment when a big beetle flew into the fan blades and bumped around with a noise like a pebble in a bike chain. It was velvet black out when he woke for the third time, deepest night, with one of the constellations hanging low over the pond like a reflection of the string of lights that he had resurrected around it. The clock said it had been four hours since he'd given Faith the medicine, and he slipped the dropper into the side of her mouth with another dose and she swallowed lazily, a string of pink drool making a dark stain on her crib sheet. On his way back to bed he saw a long V-shaped ruffle in the pond where something was swimming smoothly, a muskrat maybe, or an otter, another one looking to pluck the trout out before Mrs. Blessing had even sent the check to the Taylors. He thought of her looking out at him, and he turned to the window that looked toward the house and saw a faint light on the first floor and wondered what was keeping her awake. He thought he saw her pass in front of one of the kitchen windows, and then he saw another silhouette, and another, and, oh, Jesus, he thought. And he got that all-slowed-down feeling again.

"Goddamnit, she should have put a phone in here," he thought, and a certain movement in the air made him realize he'd spoken aloud.

Someone else passed by the kitchen windows, and then he heard a faint click as a man stepped through the door and onto the back steps. The man ducked his head as he carried a lumpy pillowcase down the path that led to the barn, but there were things Skip knew as well as he knew the curves of the baby's face, and one was how Joe walked when he was trying to lay low.

He checked the baby once but she was snoring slightly, a bubble of saliva coming and going at the corner of her mouth, her forehead cool and dry. He put on the dirty clothes that he'd worn for the drive to the drugstore and he could smell himself but he wasn't sure if it was old sweat or rank fear or rage. He knew who else was in the house; he wasn't even surprised when he slid in the door that Joe had left unlatched and saw Chris sprawled on the brocade sofa in the living room, his bad leg up on the coffee table, his shoe propped on those old art books that were always lined up in the same order in the same place. The faces in all the pictures in silver frames looked at them stoically: Meredith in a riding habit with a blue ribbon in her fist, old Mr. Blessing holding a book as a kind of noble prop, Mrs. Blessing in the white gown with bare shoulders for what Jennifer said was her presentation to society, Mrs. Blessing's brother with his head tilted back and a big smile on his face. All of them in black-and-white on the smooth shining surfaces: it reminded him of an audience. In the dining room he could hear the soft clink of metal. Tea sets. Loving cups. Forks and spoons. He felt like the room was somehow dirty, and he realized that that was why he hadn't been permitted in in the beginning, that Mrs. Blessing had thought he was a guy like these guys. He was ashamed for himself.

"You sorry fuck," he whispered to Chris, who looked at him impassively.

"Chill, Skipper. You should have just stayed over the way and minded your own business. We'll be out of here in five. She'll get an insurance check. We'll get the cash. No one gets hurt. Everything is cool."

Ed walked softly into the living room the long way, so he wouldn't have to pass the stairs up to the second floor. "Oh, man," he said when he saw Skip.

"You help cut the alarm lines?" Skip hissed at him. Ed looked away. Skip pushed past him to the den, opened the old wooden armoire against one wall, turned the latch on the false back, and reached inside. He almost ran into Joe in the kitchen doorway, pushed past him, and went back into the living room. The gun he pointed at Chris was an old Beretta, an over-under with a stock carved with vines and birds. He'd used it on a groundhog who'd been eating the tops off the day lilies by the side of the garage. "I have no qualms about destroying pests," Mrs. Blessing had said. He'd blown the thing in half with the charge from the shotgun, and that evening turkey vultures had taken care of the rest.

"Leave all the stuff here and get out," he hissed. "You're fucking lucky I didn't call the sheriff's office from my place."

"Your place don't have a phone, asshole," said Chris. "Your place is this pathetic little skank hole and you're a pathetic little skank who thinks you're something now because you fetch and carry for some old lady who thinks she's the Virgin Mary. And you forgot who you are and who your friends are but you best not forget that nobody fucks with me." Chris got to his feet slowly, one leg stiff and straight, and looked all around the room, the piano and the tables and the pictures all shades of gray in the light from the outdoor lanterns on either side of the porch. "Place is like a damn museum," he said. He picked up an old army duffel bag from in front of the fireplace, and Skip could see that the candlesticks and the big silver bowl were gone from the middle of the mantel. The teapot from the dining room was on the floor at one edge of the Oriental carpet, and Skip picked it up in his left hand and was filled with a rage so huge that he wanted to take the teapot, with its curving handle and its engraved curlicues, and beat somebody with it until they bled. Ed was holding another pillowcase at his side, but he wouldn't look at Skip, and Chris was staring a challenge straight at him, so that Skip was the only one who was looking toward the drive, the only one who could see through the big windows and see the three black-and-whites that were coming toward the house, moving fast. Skip heard them pull into the driveway turnaround, heard the doors of the cars opening. Then the police radios started bleating, and Chris dropped the duffel and sat back down.

"You sorry-ass bastard," Chris said.

Skip didn't turn when he heard the officers coming in the back door. He was looking at the door from the living room to the dining room. Mrs. Blessing was standing there wearing some sort of long quilted robe, white and shiny so it glowed. She had taken the time to pull her hair back into a silver tail, and when Ed finally turned toward her he flinched and said, "Jesus!" like a cry, not a curse. Skip could just make out her eyes, flat and cold. She was looking him up and down, looking at the silver teapot in his one hand and the gun in the other, looking at him as if she'd never seen him before, never driven in his truck or watched him eat lunch on the lawn or held his baby. It was like all the hope and the happiness

174 · Anna Quindlen

that had been building up inside him for so long drained out of him through an opening in his guts, that were grinding like an old motor with fear and misery. Then the sheriff's men were everywhere, pushing them against the walls, leading her away, talking to her softly in the other room so she wouldn't have to see the men who had invaded her house. Loud and clear he heard her say, "The one with the gun is named Charles Cuddy. He has done some work for me around the place. He sleeps over the garage."

"It was all his idea," Chris murmured with a lazy smile, his eyes gleaming.

Skip was still holding the silver teapot. One of the sheriff's deputies, a guy named Collier who had known them all since they were kids, took it out of his hands and put it carefully on a table. Then he shook his head and said as he cuffed him, "Well, Charles, this is a helluva parole violation. So it looks like you're going back to jail."

"You lunch ready," Nadine hollered up at the window. "On the table now! One o'clock sharp."

From inside the apartment there was no answer. Nadine held a sweater close around her. From the back bedroom of the apartment Mrs. Blessing could hear her stomping her feet as though she were outside in the snow instead of in the slight cool breeze of an unseasonable Indian summer day. The shouting gave way to muttering, then the slam of the screen door, and finally no sound at all except the *tap-tap* of the old metal venetian blinds that had hung in the rooms over the garage for as long as the rooms over the garage had been there. It was a tinny melancholy sound, the sound of rooms that had been abandoned.

The blanket was thrown back on the bed as though someone had just sprung from it, and the mobile over the cradle swung in the fresh breeze from the window nearby. The fans were still on, too, although the weather had changed sharply overnight, the thick muggy air blown away and replaced by one of those clear blue-and-white days that were more spring than summer, so that, like Nadine, she wore a sweater buttoned over her blouse. Over the chest of drawers by the crib was a drawing of flowers in bright colors on which someone had written in calligraphy "Faith: Another Word for Love." A handful of zinnias in oranges and reds had been placed in a small narrow glass vase. Slowly, carefully, she opened each shallow drawer and found stacks of clean rompers and shirts and booties. There were small sachets of lavender that she recognized as belonging, once upon a time, to her own mother, and she wondered if he had found them here, discarded, forgotten. All these years, and yet when she held one to her nose and rubbed it between her thumb and forefinger, there was that faint familiar scent, the same one that came from between the stacks of stockings and white gowns in her own bureau drawers.

"I made a mistake," she had said that morning when the sheriff drove out to the house. Thinking about it now, she wondered if she had ever said those words with conviction before. Perhaps at Bertram's, when her mathematics paper had been covered with the back-slanted red scrawl of Mrs. Popper. Perhaps to Sunny on the tennis court, or dragging the oar the wrong way as they pushed and pulled across the pond when they were small. That day when she had asked Meredith about mistakes, she had been thinking of her own, but she had never had to own up to them. Meredith had not asked her the question in return, and she would not have told the truth.

"I made a terrible mistake," she had said once she managed the words.

"It was understandable, ma'am," the short thick man with the red face had said, sitting gingerly right on the edge of the sofa in the living room. "Seeing him with the gun is probably what did it. And the shock of all those guys in your house. From what we can piece together, Mr. Cuddy saw what they were doing and came over to try and get them out of the house. At least that's what one of them says, the Salzano boy. His father was apparently doing some work on your place. He's not a bad kid, a follower rather than a leader, if you know what I mean. Neither is Joe Pratt, the other one. The ringleader is a different story. He's the one I want to put away."

"Did you let Mr. Cuddy go?"

"We still have him down at the office, ma'am. On the other thing."

The other thing. That was the worst mistake she'd made. All those police cars moving slowly away until she'd seen the taillights burning at the end of the driveway, and then the one still parked in the turnaround and the dim silhouettes of the officers moving around the apartment over the garage. She'd turned on the baby monitor and heard them talking in loud voices: There's a kid in here. What? Cuddy have a kid? Not that I know of. We can't leave this kid here. She awake? Cute baby. Mrs. Blessing shivered where she sat. The sky was gray above but lightening over the pond, and as the sun slowly picked out the edges of the big mats of lavender along the stone porch foundation and the coneflowers trembling on their tall stalks behind them, another car drove in, and a woman got out. She was carrying a clipboard and a large shoulder bag, and she had the unmistakable self-important abstraction of a government worker.

"Miss!" Mrs. Blessing had called peremptorily from her back door. "Miss! My granddaughter is upstairs in the apartment." The woman had looked at her impassively. When she came down again carrying the baby, one of the officers came down behind her carrying the clipboard and a stuffed bear that had obviously come from the crib, and Mrs. Blessing thought that he must be a father himself, to think to take the bear. Her hands shook as she looked at the woman, who was twisting her head so that the small hand reaching from the folds of a blanket would release a strand of her hair. She remembered the German baby nurse, and how Meredith had tried to grab a coil of her mother's hair in bed one morning, how the woman had taken her index finger and tapped, hard, across the small knuckles. Meredith had recoiled, and the woman had done it again. "You will not like it if she grabs the tablecloth at luncheon one day," the woman had said. "This is where it all begins."

The woman with the clipboard and the sheriff's officer stood talking by the car for several minutes. Mrs. Blessing went to the door and called "Miss" again, but her voice broke on the word. "The sheriff is coming out to see you, ma'am," the sheriff's deputy had replied.

"I'm coming out there," Mrs. Blessing said, then realized that she was barefoot. Her feet were cold and stiff, and she hobbled upstairs to put on slippers, never mind her clothes. Let them talk of how they'd seen her in her housecoat. She was past caring.

From the bedroom window she had heard the car moving down the driveway, and it was too late, they were gone, taking the child who now could not be explained away, the child for whom a new story could not be fashioned out of bits and pieces of plausible lies. She had tried with the sheriff, said with her hand to her heart, "There was an infant in his room . . ." but the man had cut her off, kindly but firmly. "We've got an investigation going, ma'am. We've already talked to Mr. Cuddy about all that."

"Where is the child now?" she asked the sheriff.

"By law we have to keep her in a foster home until we figure out where she ought to go next. By the way, Mr. Cuddy said you didn't know anything about her."

Mrs. Blessing had lifted her chin and said, "Mr. Cuddy is a gentleman."

"There's been times when he's made poor choices in terms of companions, but overall I'd agree with you."

Even in the garage attic there was still a faint ineffable smell of baby. The sheriff's men had gone up there, had pulled down the stairs to the attic from the ceiling in the hallway, and she wanted to make certain that they had taken nothing with them. Dust motes danced in the sunshine, and when she got to the top she was breathing hard and her hands were gray with dirt. There was a scrabbling sound in one corner, and she heard a soft thud as the cat, who had crept up after her, sprung into the hidden space he had always coveted. He disappeared beneath the back rafters, between a bank of closed boxes labeled "Simpson's Fine Textiles" and a pair of lamps with tattered pleated shades.

"Lunch," Nadine shouted again from the back door of the house. "Getting too cold!"

There was a world here, undisturbed for decades, just as there had been that world beneath the surface of the pond: a box sent down from Newport filled with riding clothes and boots that the eleven-year-old Meredith had outgrown by the time it arrived; a box put up by Mrs. Foster of Lydia's and Sunny's summer whites grown yellow at the hems and seams; a box sent from the city by her mother of books meant to go on guests' bedside tables that had somehow never been unpacked; the boxes sent from the city filled with Lydia's party dresses laid carefully between tissue and mothballs as though sometime, magically, she would become young again and put them on and follow Benny through the ballroom of the club as he offered her a mercy dance that would turn into a mercy marriage. There were boxes of photographs and scrapbooks and dance programs and matchbooks and documents and newspaper clippings, so that if it were possible to animate possessions and papers, the attic would be filled with people, and in all their various incarnations, her father in his Princeton letter sweater and his downtown suit and what he called his "golf togs," her brother in his linen shorts and his ski sweaters and his Panama hat, her daughter in her jodhpurs and her pleated wool skirts and her going-away suit, which had somehow found its way into a box filled mostly with baby clothes. And all of Lydia's life was here, too, beautifully tailored dresses with bound seams and shoes that had been made on a wooden last of her rather narrow foot and the few boxes of stationery she hadn't burned, "Mrs. J. Bennet Carton" faded to gray.

She looked over again at the "Simpson's Fine Textiles" boxes. She had forgotten there were so many, more than twenty in all, and wondered where her father had gotten the money and why he had sent it, whether he had suspected that after he was gone her mother would cut her off somehow, or, more likely, create conditions for her support. Once she had said something to him, sitting on the Adirondack chairs by the pond, tried to thank him in some stiff and oblique way that, naturally, never mentioned money at all. He had waved his hand. "We do what we can," he had said. She had never opened a single one of the boxes after the second one. Perhaps all the rest were filled with fabric, or newspaper, or neckties. There was no point in looking now. But the possibility that they all had thousands of dollars inside made her glad that her father had used slate on the roof and that therefore it had never leaked.

She had not needed the money; something about marrying Benny Carton and moving to Blessings had made her mother love her, or at least approve of her, and without a word being spoken the money from the company, and from the investments her parents had made, began to appear in her accounts or in her name. Her mother came to visit occasionally, brought Meredith handmade clothes that were either too small or too large, went with Lydia to the club and watched from the veranda as she and her friends played golf, always finding someone or another with whom to engage in the kind of meaningless conversation that Ethel Blessing had always seemed to find easiest and most satisfying. The death of her husband had offered her a chance at a second life, one that appeared to be more suited to her talents and inclinations. She had a small circle of similarly situated female friends with whom she played cards, went shopping, and sailed on the Cunard ships to Europe. Once she went around the world with a group of them, and afterward she brought back a porcelain bisque doll in Chinese costume for Meredith, who was then nearly thirteen, and an enormous rope of black pearls for Lydia, which had lived ever after in a safety-deposit box. All she had said about the trip was that the food was decent, but that Singapore had been too hot and had the most peculiar smell. It was right after that trip that her mind had begun to fail. From time to time when Lydia had visited her in the nursing home where she had spent her largely insensible final years, she had seemed to think she was still aboard, and would occasionally ask where Lydia had joined the cruise. "Hong Kong," she always said, and once her mother had said fiercely, "You oughtn't to have missed Bangkok."

Here was the Chinese doll, its red robes faded and crushed, in a box of dolls. There was the one that said "Mama," which sounded like kittens mewing, and the one that looked like a Gibson girl with a pompadour and a parasol attached by a wire to her right hand. The Raggedy Andy was folded in upon himself near the bottom. The Raggedy Ann had been taken off to Virginia by Meredith when she was first married, in a truck filled with castoffs from Blessings that had furnished the farm, and Lydia had assumed that it was to be given someday to Meredith's children, her grand-children, who might wear Frank Askew's ruddy hair into the next generation. She had thought Jess was ridiculous about the notion of grandchildren, working out the due dates on her fingers, keep-ing a bag packed so she could go off at a moment's notice to help with bottles and diaper changes, choking the top of her old piano with photographs of newborns and toddlers. But even Lydia had had plans for some of the things in these boxes, the small smocked dresses with the matching bloomers, the soft white cot-ton undershirts—vests, the baby nurse had called them. Her plans had evaporated as Meredith grew older, and then they had re-turned with the little girl who had just been carried down her drive by policemen like evidence of a crime. As she looked around her she thought that surely there must be a way to make things as they had been, to persuade the sheriff that the baby was best off here, to make Charles understand that, as the sheriff had said, ap-pearances had deceived her.

There were footsteps on the stairs below and Nadine's head poked through the entrance to the attic. "Every day, lunch at one. Every day. Two o'clock now. No lunch."

"I will have lunch later, Nadine."

"Dinnertime soon. No lunch." She looked around. "Dirty up here."

"Go away, Nadine."

"I say, no good, no good, listen to me. You don't listen. She don't listen. She sit home, cry and cry. Hah!"

"Go away, Nadine. Tell Jennifer that she may come to see me when she wants to. Tell her it was a mistake."

"Hah! You eat lunch."

"Go away."

The box labeled "Lydia's things" had her old books, Kate

Douglas Wiggins and a clothbound copy of *The Secret Garden* and a leatherbound edition of *Heidi* that she had been given one Christmas. Another said simply "Sunny" and contained several tweed jackets and a flat cap that she remembered her brother had worn in the autumn, his hair curling around the edges. The jackets smelled of him, of some sort of lemon stuff he'd gotten when he went to Oxford one year. She lifted one out and mothballs rained down into the rest of the box. There at the bottom was another suit, a linen one, stained and crumpled, and a hat the color of mown hay that Sunny had liked to wear with it. Lydia recognized them. She stared down into the shadowed depths of the old box and remembered her brother wearing both suit and hat as he had disappeared toward the barn that last day, with the shotgun somehow jaunty under his arm. The night before they had sat together on the banks of the pond, the lightning bugs flickering around them with their ceaseless unknowable signaling, the trout leaping joyfully, the ice making faint tapping sounds in their glasses. The dark fell softly so that soon all she could see were his cool light eyes and the white collar of his shirt, and for a long time there was silence and then a sound that she thought was a chuckle. When she turned to him she had seen the tears glistening silver on his face. He was past forty then, but he was as unlined as a child, and as unashamed as one, too, as he wept and looked out over the deeper black of the water set in the black of the lawn.

"What is it, Sunny?" she had said softly.

"Ah, Lydie," he'd replied with a great gallant sniff, "my own true love is gone."

"You never told me about any of that," she'd said.

"No," he said simply, as though he never would.

The hat and the suit had been like his hair and his skin and all the rest of him, pale golden. She lifted up both and wondered how the hat had not been damaged. Perhaps he had taken it off first; it had lain on the barn floor to one side of his body. She remembered that she had felt herself wondering, inconsequentially, whether he had been wearing it even as she had felt herself breathing hard and felt herself screaming, screaming, until Mr. Foster had come running from the garage, carrying a gun himself. "My brother has had an accident," she cried, and the older man had looked, then held her back while she twisted in the twilight, so that it must have looked as if they were dancing, even embracing, the hat a light blur beside them, like the moon.

She had never known exactly what had happened to the clothes Sunny was wearing that day. She had never thought that the Fosters might have saved them, perhaps been afraid to throw them away. The back of the suit was grimy on one shoulder but largely untouched, and the front was stiff with blood, as though someone had bundled it up still damp and pushed it here into the box that said "Sunny" on it. The jacket hung low on one side, and with shaking hands she found his billfold in one breast pocket, and wondered that she had not noticed at the time that it was missing. She was trembling now, and faint, and her arm hurt so, and she went over to an old chair, its spindles cracked and awry as a spider's legs, and sat down. The black leather was still supple and shiny, and inside there was some money: two twenty-dollar bills and six singles. Business cards from the advertising agency: "Sumner E. Blessing, assistant vice president." A card from the Continental Club with a phone number written on the back in the old way: "Clearview 7, 8579." There was no license; Sunny had learned to drive one summer in the Fosters' truck, driven it into an old oak across the road, and never tried again. "I can't imagine going anywhere that's not accessible by train, taxi, or limousine," he liked to say.

That was all there was until she reached into the recess behind the business cards. There was a flimsy square of paper there, and a photograph. The photograph was folded so that only two thirds of it appeared, a very old photograph, black-and-white with a stippled margin, of Sunny and Benny by the split-rail fence around the far field. They were squinting into the bright summer sunlight, and Sunny had his arm around Benny, and his head cocked slightly toward him, as though he was waiting for him to say something.

There was a deep fold in the picture, but even before she turned it slowly in her hand, Lydia knew what had been left out. She flattened it on her lap, smoothing it with her fingers gently, as though she could make the fold go away, and there on Sunny's other side she stood, her brother's other arm around her shoulders. But the picture had been divided for so long that when she unfolded it it broke in two, and there were the two boys together, and the other piece pinwheeled to the dusty floor.

The folds were deep in the paper put away with the picture, too. It was the paper, thin as tissue, that the boys had used to send letters home from the war. In Benny's familiar, almost illegible handwriting it said, "Greetings, pal. Don't worry. Everything stays the same. Ben and Sun to the end, just like in Newport. You know."

She sat there until the wind had died down, so that the tap of the metal blinds came only occasionally, as though someone was asking to come inside. "Lunch now," Nadine shouted again. "Lunch now or I go." But she was not hungry as she turned the picture over in her hands and wondered whether Sunny had meant her to find the wallet after he was dead, and whether, in some circuitous fashion that had taken her her entire life to unravel, she had killed him when she had saved herself.

They were coming at eleven, the sheriff had told him. The man owned an insurance agency in Loganville, twenty miles north. His wife was a seventh-grade English teacher. Their daughter was a sophomore at the state university. They were coming at eleven to Mrs. Blessing's house. It had taken almost a week to iron things out. The meeting at Blessings, that was the sheriff's idea, to spare them all the scent of disinfected corridors and the stares of people wearing laminated ID tags and maybe even a couple of local reporters who got wind of the story. But Skip thought it might also be poetic justice, Mrs. Blessing having to see what she'd done where she'd done it. And that girl, too. They were coming at eleven.

"Tell them I'll give them a car seat," Skip said. "They need to put her in a car seat. Tell them that's the law."

They were coming at eleven and Skip started to drive at nine-thirty in the morning, right after the social worker, her mouth tight, had handed Faith back to him. She'd been with a foster mother somewhere out on one of the farms for five days, and she was wearing a dress that left her little legs bare from foot to thigh. She kicked and kicked as though she liked it, and the skirt of the dress, which was yellow with rocking horses printed on it in blue and pink, flew up over her face, and she sneezed and beat the air with her fists. She smelled like talc. Talc was bad for babies.

"Support her head," the social worker said as she handed her over.

"I've been supporting her head since the day she was born," Skip said.

That had done it, just pushed him past the point of standing the whole thing. He'd given her two ounces of formula in the front seat with the door open so they both wouldn't be stifled by the dead air in the truck, making certain that her bib was on tight so if she spit up, the dress wouldn't get stained. She stared at him as she sucked hard on the nipple, and curled her hand as she always did around the one he was holding the bottle with, raising and lowering her fingers slowly. Halfway through the bottle her lids began to lower. Her lashes looked so long, and her fingers, too, and for a moment it was like he was seeing her again for the first time, lifting her from the box into the light and knowing in his gut that she was his.

He drove for nearly thirty miles with her asleep next to him in her car seat. When he'd gone to get his truck, Mrs. Blessing had come out of the back door, tall and dark and faceless against the golden light from inside the kitchen. He'd gone upstairs to the apartment and pitched his things into the old duffel bag that his dad had had in the army, and he'd stopped to figure out what he should take and then taken nothing because he didn't need anything, nothing at all.

When he got to the truck she was standing by it, stooped slightly, one hand to her heart. Jennifer was right; she looked older now, smaller maybe, diminished, but instead of feeling bad he thought it served her right. He bet he looked older, too.

"Charles, I've spoken to my lawyer, and he says there is some possibility that you could fight these people for—"

"He's full of shit," he said, throwing the duffel in the back without looking at her, using the crude language intentionally. If she thought he was one of those guys, he'd be one of those guys. "Fight them for six months while she stays with another set of strangers and at the end they win. She has a mother. The mother always wins. That's the way it is."

"You were as good a mother to that child as any woman I've ever seen. I told the sheriff so."

He looked her in the eye and he thought she moved back a bit when she saw what he looked like. "Well, that didn't make a whole lot of difference when you called the cops on me like a common criminal. That didn't make a whole lot of difference when you let them think that I was the kind of person who would live here and take care of your place and make the goddamned coffee and then sneak over and cut the wires for the alarm and steal the silver out of the dining room. You knew me. You knew me. You knew me better than anybody has ever known me. You knew what kind of person I was. And one look and you passed judgment on me like I was an entirely different person from what you knew."

"I made a mistake," she said.

"You sure did," he said, and he got in the truck and drove down the drive without looking in the rearview mirror.

They'd gone over the truck, after they'd hauled him in with Chris and Ed and Joe. They'd gone through the glove compartment and the tool box bolted to the flatbed. He could tell they'd gone through his drawers upstairs, and the other rooms, and then they'd found something worth looking for, sleeping soundly, her fever down. He hoped they'd fed her before they carried her off, so that she hadn't wailed all the way to town.

They'd left him in a windowless room at the police station, the cuffs tight and a cramp growing in his shoulder where the angle of his arm pulled on the joint. There was no clock and he couldn't see his watch. There was no night turning to gray dawn and blue day, no feedings to figure the time by. He'd felt like he was going crazy. The sheriff had finally come in and unlocked the cuffs, his arms falling hard to his sides.

"By rights I ought to get your side of the story, but let me tell you what your buddies say," he'd said.

"They're no buddies of mine."

Ed and Joe had told the truth, for once, had just thrown down on Chris and said that Skip hadn't been part of it, that he'd tried to get them to leave, and leave the stuff. The sheriff said he'd asked Chris about what happened, and he'd asked for a cigarette. "You guys saw who had the gun," Chris had said, leaning back in his chair.

"He's a damn liar," Skip said.

"Thanks for the news flash. Now I got another problem I need to discuss with you." And from his breast pocket he took out a flyer and laid it gently on the table in front of Skip, so gently that Skip thought it might be a warrant, or a photograph of something awful, something the sheriff thought would shock him out of his seat.

POSSIBLE HOMICIDE INVESTIGATION, it said at the top, and then it told a story in the way the cops always did, like a science experiment instead of something about human beings. A white female, age nineteen, had been brought to the hospital with postpartum bleeding at the end of June. Investigation found no trace of an infant. White female uncooperative. Officers investigating the whereabouts of the infant or its remains.

"Ah, hell," Skip said, and put his head down on the table.

"You want a cigarette?" the sheriff said.

"I don't smoke."

"I bet you never figured that, that she'd get caught and they'd think she killed it. The only reason she hasn't been arrested is because they got no body. I talked to the girl's mother this morning. We're about halfway between the university and her house. She asked her daughter if she'd ever been in a place named Mount Mason and she broke down."

"She's mine. She's mine." Skip kept his head down on the table and he cried until he couldn't cry anymore and the sheriff sat by silently.

"You know Mrs. Liggett that lives up on Thatcher Street?" the older man finally said. "She used to be the nurse at the high school, maybe before your time. She is a hard case, and I say that knowing she and my wife have been friends since they were girls together. She came and took that baby away and she said to me when she called from the hospital, someone has taken very good care of that little girl. She's clean, she's well nourished, and she's got a pleasant disposition." And at those words Skip wept again, thinking of Faith smiling at Mrs. Liggett, who was a hard case. It had been a long time since he cried, and he did it the way he did everything to which he was unaccustomed, in fits and starts but with conviction.

"This child has to go back to her mother. You know it and I know it. There's no two ways about that. But I can cut you a break when the time comes so you get to play a part."

He'd given Skip a copy of the flyer, and when he came out of the station, blinking in the noon sun, feeling dirty in last night's pants and an old "Don't Do Drugs" T-shirt one of the officers had found in a box of castoffs for when they pulled homeless people in, Jennifer was sitting in the lot in her little blue car, reading the paper. Her eyes were red and there were two empty cardboard coffee cups on the console.

"I drank your coffee. I'm really sorry," she said.

"My stomach couldn't take it anyway."

"There's got to be a way to get her back."

"You're an optimist."

"One of us has to be. Get in. My dad wants to talk to you."

There was an apartment over the auto body shop that no one ever wanted to rent because Mr. Foster opened for business at seven A.M., and the banging and clanging and yelling at one another went on all day and sometimes into the evening, and he rented only to nonsmokers and people who didn't have pets and who went to church. But Skip got up early anyhow, and the noises were companionable even when he was done for the day, and he didn't mind the smell of motor oil or the view of the township road stretching off between flat cornfields because at least it didn't remind him of the smell of mown grass and freshly laundered baby shirts and the sight of the pond reflecting back the spiky swell of the pine-covered hills. There was the smell of coffee in the morning, from the Mr. Coffee that Craig Foster kept on the file cabinet, and that was bad sometimes, struggling up from sleep, like a dream of a life that disappeared as he set eyes on the unfamiliar acoustical tile ceiling above his head.

"I hear you're a good mechanic," Mr. Foster had said.

"You're going to get in trouble with your wife," Skip replied.

Mr. Foster had shrugged. "You have to know how to take Nadine. You have to see where she came from and what she went through. You think there's bad places around here? That's nothing compared with where she lived. All these little tin shacks with no toilets, kids all naked and running wild, the soldiers carrying on. Men of a certain age, they give her the heebie-jeebies. Like your age, you know? She doesn't mean anything, really. You just have to know her, know what her life was like."

Nadine never came to the garage. Maybe it was because all the guys who worked there were men around Skip's age. When Jennifer visited there was a strange silence. "I think she's working on something with her lawyer," she said to Skip.

"I don't want to hear it," Skip said, bending over an engine.

When he went into town to pick up two special-order parts at the post office, he'd stared into each stroller on the street. He'd run into Chris's mom taking a plastic garbage bag into the Laundromat. Her nurse's aide's uniform made a rustling sound as she fidgeted. "Well, Skipper, that damn boy managed to get himself into trouble again," she said, as though being arrested for breaking and entering were like a tornado or a hole in the field that you caught your foot in, one of those things that just happened to a person because of timing and bad luck.

"He should have been locked up a long time ago," said one of the other mechanics in Craig Foster's garage, whose sister had gone out with Chris a couple of times.

He was a nice guy, a guy named Fred who'd been two years behind them in high school, and he'd tuned up Skip's truck so it was humming as he drove along the interstate with the baby drooling on her dress. He'd never put her in a dress; it seemed foolish, all that fabric eddying around her working feet and legs. He glanced over. She looked like he supposed a baby should look for a special occasion, meeting the mother who'd dumped her in a box on his doorstep in some sad-sack flannel shirt.

He saw a playground from the highway and took the exit and sat

her car seat near the swings, where she could see the two little boys whose mother was pushing them, her left hand on the back of one, her right hand on the back of the other. Faith's eyes went up and down as the swings did, and her smile went on and off, on and off, like a blinking neon sign. She hooted at the boys, and they imitated the sound right back at her, and she did it again, more loudly.

"What I wouldn't give for a girl," their mother said to Skip as the boys tried to grab at each other across the empty air between them.

"You'll make those boys feel bad," he called back.

"Not them. Nothing makes them feel bad." She shook her head. "There's only sixteen months between them. Tell your wife not to push it."

He got back on the highway, with Faith making loud bird noises, her head moving from window to windshield as though she were looking for something. He kept thinking he could just drive on, drive and drive until he got somewhere flat and stale and safe, Nebraska, maybe, or Kansas. He'd never been to either place, never been anywhere, really, but somehow they sounded like places where you could get a little apartment and tell people your wife had died and take your daughter to school without much fuss or many questions. A rest stop flew by, then an exit, then another. He figured there were times in everybody's life when they thought, just for a moment, that they could be different than they were. He'd had one of those times years ago, when he'd won that middle-school science prize with some experiment about fruit flies. He'd seen the ribbon on his little arrangement of corrugated cardboard and old Ball jars, and that night lying in bed he'd imagined a future: "Nice job, Skip—ever think about medical school?" "Yo, Skip, man, can I copy your homework?" "Skip, come on over to my house and study." Maybe there was a way he could have made that happen; he still didn't know. He taped the ribbon to the wall over the card table he used as a desk, and then, when his aunt and uncle painted his room one summer, it had disappeared. That was all right, too, because seeing it just reminded him that it was kind of a fluke. Like Faith had been, a burst of something incandescent in a long stretch of gray days.

He pulled into the next rest stop and laid his head on the wheel. She was slumped forward, too, so that the two of them were in the same position of surrender. She raised her head and gnawed on her fist, got her thumb into her mouth and sucked on it loudly. He bought a doughnut and a soda and fed her again, stroking her hand with his index finger. He smiled and smiled at her, and she smiled back, so that the nipple fell from her mouth.

He thought about begging those people to let him keep her, explaining how he had gotten up in the middle of the night to feed her all those weeks, so dopey that in the morning he could only be sure he'd done it by seeing the empty bottle on the nightstand; how he'd stuck out his tongue and razzed her so she smiled, then chuckled, then laughed; how he'd coaxed her pathetic little fuzz of hair into a kind of curl on top of her head with a bit of baby oil on his finger; how he'd made a little tent of netting over her so she could lie on the grass and watch the clouds and the birds go by overhead and not get eaten alive by mosquitoes. And he knew what they'd say if he asked. When all this had started he would have said that it was because he didn't have enough—enough family, enough money, enough of a life. He would have thought that if he'd been able to offer Blessings instead of the garage behind Blessings, it would have made a difference. But listening to Jennifer talk about her father, watching Mrs. Blessing and Mrs. Fox with their strong profiles bowed over bowls of soup at the table near the window, he'd figured out that sometimes it all came down to blood.

There were two ways to get out of the rest area, one that led to the highway running west, to Nebraska or Kansas, and one that led east, back the way he'd just come. He went east. It was a kind of circular thing: to be the kind of person who would have taken Faith in, he had to be the kind of person who would take her back. He drove with a buzzing sound in his head, careful to keep just a little above the speed limit. There were two dead deer along the shoulder, and an RV having a tire changed by a man who didn't look like he knew what he was doing while a clutch of heavyset women circled him like disconcerted pigeons. There was the playground where he'd stopped, filled now with day-care kids with name tags on colored paper hung around their necks with cord. There was a Best Western where he could check in and play with the baby on the bed for another hour or two while the sheriff put his license-plate number out over the state police radio. He kept on driving. Faith was asleep.

He drove past the exit you took to the Boatwright place and saw a heavy woman in red shorts hanging laundry on a droopy line. It seemed like there was a raccoon in a cage on the front porch, sitting on top of the washing machine. He drove past the exit for McGuire's and could see the parking lot half full even though it wasn't even lunchtime. Someone had painted the side of the garage next to McGuire's with the words "Real Men Love Jesus." Off the other side of the highway he could see the peak of Foster's auto body behind a stand of elms. The Wal-Mart loomed off the highway, and then the trees closed in, and he was getting off on Rolling Hills Road, his shoulders stiff from holding on to the wheel so tightly. The fields were striped yellow, brown, and faint purple with high grasses, and a pair of hawks rose through thin clear air. He turned in and reflexively thought that the grass needed to be cut at Blessings. The cat had left a dead squirrel splayed in the doorway to the basement, and he wondered who was making the coffee now that he was gone.

There were three cars in the driveway, the sheriff's car between the big sedan that belonged to Lester Patton, Mrs. Blessing's lawyer, and a blue Toyota he had never seen before. The Toyota had a bumper sticker that said WE BRAKE FOR ANIMALS and an infant car seat in the back. He wondered what they thought he was going to do with his. From the back of the house he could see Nadine peering through the window, wiping her hands on a striped dish towel, and even though it had been only a week he felt that he was coming back here after a long time away, the way he felt whenever he drove by the elementary school, as though a ghost of himself lived there still even though he was long gone.

Nadine stood at the back door and he was waiting, just waiting for her to say something. He could hear her voice, crowing, "Big trouble for you." But she just stood there with her arms crossed, her head to one side. Faith was still asleep, a dead weight against his shoulder, her red lower lip thrust out as though she were annoyed at her own dreams. When he moved past Nadine she looked down and her eyebrows came up and she said, "Pretty baby," but without rancor.

The living room was full. Mrs. Blessing was in the wing chair. She struggled to her feet, said "Charles," half questioning, but he would not look at her, remembering the crowded darkness of the room the last time they were there together, the accusation in her eyes. Her lawyer was on the sofa with its back to the room; the sheriff stood in the corner with big circles of perspiration on his khaki shirt. On the brocade sofa, shadows cast on their faces by the awning outside the window, were the other three, a woman with soft brown hair and glasses and dangling silver earrings, a man in a green polo shirt with the words "Lucky Dog" over his heart and a hairline with pale points over both his temples, and between them the girl. Skip knew she was nineteen and that her name was Paula Benichek. What he needed to know he could see in an instant, the light brown hair that had surely once been blond, the small pointed chin with a kind of soft knob at the end, the narrow upper and full lower lip. She looked as much like Faith as an adult can look like a small child, and so, while the girl's mother raised her hands to him, her fingers splayed and trembling, while the daughter sat with her arms crossed and her face truculent, it was into the lap of the younger woman that he placed the baby, angling her so that the young woman's lap made a natural cradle. Faith blinked, closed her eyes for a moment, then opened them and made the shouting sound she'd made to the boys in the playground.

From his pocket Skip took a letter and laid it next to the young woman, who was staring at Faith with a broken terrified expression in her eyes. He'd written the letter the night before on some lined yellow paper, not thinking, just doing, the way he always did when he had to get a dead thing off the drive or clear the septic lines. "6 a.m.," it started out, "4 ounces formula Isomil no iron (constipates her). Back to sleep two hours. 9:30 a.m. 4 ounces. Up until 12." He wasn't willing to give too much, but for Faith's sake he wanted them to know her schedule, and that she'd had her first set of shots. The other stuff they'd have to find out themselves: how she kept her fist next to her one cheek when she slept, how she blinked so hard in the sunlight and then sneezed and sneezed and smiled as though she loved sneezing, how she raised her feet to the ceiling and tried to grab on to them with a little furrow in her forehead.

"Son, we'd like to thank you," the girl's father said, standing and putting out his hand, but Skip could only put his palms up as though he were pushing him away.

"Sir, I appreciate that, but there's nothing you could say right now that I want to hear. I just think you should know that she's— that she's—" But he couldn't push any more words past the harsh twist in his throat, and he just put his head down and shook it over and over. The door slammed in the kitchen.

"Don't let them do this!" Jennifer Foster cried from the doorway. "Don't let them do this to her!"

"Not your business," Nadine said.

"This is the way it is, Jennifer," Skip said. "This is the way things go."

"Bull. This is wrong. You know this is wrong. You've done everything for her and now that the hard part's done, they show up and want to take her back?"

All faces were turned to him, even Nadine's, peeking furtively around the corner from the kitchen. "There wasn't a hard part," he said wearily, taking the diaper bag off his shoulder and putting it down on the floor. "It was all good." He turned and walked back through the kitchen without a word, drove down the drive in his car and turned toward McGuire's. He lowered the windows on Rolling Hills Road so he could get the smell of talcum powder out of the car, but it was still there when he went into the bar, bought a six-pack, drove up on a back mountain road, and drank it all down. Sitting behind the wheel, he fell into the deep unsatisfying sleep of the thoroughly drunk. When he woke up there were drifts of leaves in yellow and orange on his windshield, and it was morning.

Again the sound came, and again, and she turned slowly in bed, stiff and bone weary but not at all sleepy, reaching for the book on her bedside table. There was a small brass light clipped to the headboard that Meredith had given her for Christmas two years before. "It's the one I have so I can read in bed without keeping Eric up," she'd said as Lydia had turned it over in her hands in the way she had of looking at gifts before she was certain that she really liked them.

"I don't know why you two don't have your own rooms. A lot of marriages have been saved by a little privacy," she'd said, frowning at the fixture.

"She's not going anywhere," Eric had said, putting his hand over his wife's, and Lydia had felt a throb of what she believed to be strong disapproval but was really envy.

She had read this Agatha Christie perhaps a dozen times in her lifetime. She had it in hardcover, an edition published during the war. She was certain because on the back jacket it said in big red letters "Buy War Bonds. Be a true soldier of democracy." Her books, her photographs, and her winter clothes: those were the first things her mother had had the maids pack up and send out to Blessings once she was there, the necessary provisions for the extended exile of a young lady of a certain class.

She liked to reread the Christie books and the other mysteries that filled the pickled pine shelves in the old den because they had a certain fine inevitable immutable order. The lovers had a misunderstanding; the wrong person was suspected, and an innocent killed to cover up the crime. But in the end Poirot or Miss Marple, that silly old woman, would have the brainstorm that Mrs. Blessing herself had had twenty pages before, and all would end as it should, the lovers reunited, the guilty party brought to justice, Miss Marple's knitting complete and Poirot's mustaches waxed. They were foolish books signifying nothing, but they had the appeal of scales played on the piano or multiplication tables recited aloud, a perfect predictability that she had learned unconsciously to love.

Her life had once been in tumult, and that was how she had shoehorned it back into a manageable shape, by the imposition of rigid order. And then Charles had come, and the baby, and then the baby was gone, and Sunny's wallet found, and all the order had gone, so that in the mornings she now woke in the silver-gray hours on the leading edge of dawn to nothing more than the faintly sweet odor of autumn air and the occasional sharp reminder that a skunk had been frightened by something in the far fields. There was no odor of coffee in her house until hours after she awoke, when the shape of her day and her mind had already gone awry because of its absence. One day she had crept down in her gown and robe to try to do it herself and discovered that she did not even know how to use the grinder. Pulling herself along the balustrade to retire, defeated, to bed to wait for the sound of Nadine playing her discordant matins on pot and pan, she saw in the mist that hung over the valley a blue heron poised at the end of her pond, thin and pale and still as she was. His beak flashed and shattered the reflection of the trees upon the mirrored surface and he came up with a rainbow trout speared and struggling.

"Go!" she had hissed from the landing window. "Go away. Scat!" The enormous bird turned his head slowly, almost mechanically toward the sound, and in measured movements gulped down the fish.

Now it was too dark for her to see anything, but the faint strips of silver coming and going beneath the scudding clouds showed her where the center of the pond lay. Perhaps it was the heron that made the sound that repeated itself over and over again. It did not sound like a birdsong, but, then, she had never heard a heron make a sound; she thought of them as ghostly mute birds that dropped down and ate and disappeared like smoke. She imagined that one of them was there now, plundering the pond, and she wished she could throw the lights around its rim and catch him out, as though that would satisfy something in her that was itching inside. But someone had turned the pond lights out, and she was ashamed to say that over the years she had forgotten where the switch was.

"What do we do if he doesn't show up?" that fidgety man in the golf shirt had said as he sat in her living room.

"He'll show up," the sheriff said.

"He's very late," the woman said, looking yet again at her watch.

"So are all of you," Mrs. Blessing had said fiercely, and all heads in the room had turned toward her, and the girl had started to sniffle and wheeze and finally sob harshly. Her mother had patted her back but the girl had pushed her away with a sharp roll of her shoulder and buried her face in her hands. "She has asthma," the mother had said, burrowing in her purse. It occurred to Mrs. Blessing that the noise she kept hearing from outside was like the noise that girl had made, a kind of ragged and breathless crying.

She had not offered them refreshment, not tea or a cold drink, though the parents certainly acted as if they could use one. She had hated having them in her house. "People I have never met in my life," she had said to Lester Patton. "You had some pretty dicey characters here when you were younger, Lydia," he'd replied, sipping halfheartedly at Nadine's dreadful coffee. "People we knew," she said. "That's completely different."

But they both knew that that was not what she had objected to. They had destroyed that sense of order that she found inside these old books and these four walls. They destroyed it because she should have thought their presence perfectly proper, because if someone had said to her in springtime, just seven months ago, when the shoots of the daffodils were shafts from the soil around the back door, Now, Lydia, suppose a young man, unmarried, inexperienced with children, was to discover an infant lying by his back door, and was to keep that infant and try to raise her as his own, and suppose the mother was to come forward and claim her, what ought to be done? She knew what she would have answered.

And yet today she knew it should not be so. She had called Lester Patton off the golf course, where he was playing a creditable nine holes for the first time in a month, and astonished him by saying, as she seemed destined to say these days, "I have made a terrible mistake." And she had asked him to find a way for Charles to keep the baby, asked him to offer the girl money, have her charged with abandonment, have an action for custody brought under her own name. "She still thinks the name Blessing opens any door," he'd told the other men in his foursome as he cleaned his cleats and changed his clothes. But Lester Patton, wisely, had begun by talking to Skip, and when he arrived at Blessings from Foster's garage he took a gin and tonic, the glass slick in his hands, and told her that Skip thought the child should be returned. "He thinks the baby belongs with her mother."

"The baby belongs to the person who loves her most," Mrs. Blessing replied.

"The law assumes that that person is the one who gave birth to the baby."

"Then the law is an ass."

She lay in bed and turned a page and found that she could not attend to what the vicar had found when he paid an unexpected call on the lady from London renting a cottage. There was another cry from the back edge of the pond, like a tormented wild thing calling, like her own voice crying so many years ago, "My brother has had an accident." On the bedside table was one of the old albums, so old that the pictures were held in place with black brackets and the photos themselves were black-and-white, now faded to gray and yellow. And in so many of them it was as though a tissue scrim were lifted, the same sort of tissue that covered all the invitations to parties, debuts, weddings. She could see clearly now: the way Sunny's shoulder touched Benny's in the foyer of the Carton house. The way they looked at Lydia in her dance dress, fond brothers both. The way they looked at each other over Lydia's bent head. The emotional code hidden beneath the social one.

Maybe that was what her mother was trying to hide, and not just for her own sake but for Lydia's, too: not the pregnancy by a married man, but the marriage to the boy who was really in love with Lydia's brother instead. Up in the garage attic her first thought had been that her union with Benny had been a sham, and then she had been shamed by the hypocrisy of her outrage, since the sham had not seemed so egregious when she was the sole perpetrator. It was like a French farce, in one door and out the other. And where just a few years ago she would have been disgusted and bitter, now she was merely sad at the dumb show.

She tried to imagine a world in which the two of them sat by the pond, she and Sunny, and she told her secrets and he told his. But it was not the world in which the two of them had grown up, and grown older. Perhaps he had known about her and Frank Askew. Perhaps everyone had known. But order was maintained by silence.

Looking at that young woman sitting in the living room bookended by her uncomprehending parents, waiting for her fate to find her, the notion that that thought was simply a relic of her youth fell away. She wondered if it would always be so, and if the coda of that silence was always regret, so that she would give anything now to cry out to Sunny, in the same ragged voice as the cry that kept sounding in the dark night, "Tell me the secrets of your heart." But if she had said that, she knew what his reply would be, could almost hear him all these years after she'd found him on the floor of the barn sprawled amid the blood and hay, hear him drawl, "Lydie, love, don't be so dramatic."

So much had come back to her after she found the wallet. She remembered one night seventy years ago when she had lain in bed in the narrow room at the end of the hallway with the blue walls and the white counterpane that had been hers until her marriage.

A truck had driven into the driveway with the tearing sound of tires and gears coming to a sudden halt, a door had slammed, and she had heard her father's low voice and another man, higher, distraught, finally crying, "You keep your goddamned boy away from my son!" She remembered how many times Sunny had come home bruised or with broken bones, and how the family legend had grown about how accident-prone he was. "I don't mind the taste of blood so much," he said one morning after a split lip, and she had shuddered, knowing and not knowing both at the same time.

The little light cast a circle of gold on the pages of the old book, its margins set wide and the edges deckled in the fashion of long ago. She had called Meredith to tell her what had happened, about the burglary and Charles and the baby. "That's dreadful," Meredith had said. "He seemed like such a nice man. So good with that baby, too, in the way so few men are. My goodness, Mother, you have had a time of it." Something about the way in which Meredith had said that last sentence reminded Lydia of something. She realized that it was exactly the sort of remark she herself might have made to cut off a certain sort of conversation. Perhaps the next time Meredith came she would sit with her by the pond, sit in the old Adirondack chairs and say, my dear, tell me what you know and what you suspect and what you fear. And I will tell you what is true and what is not.

But on the phone she had said only, "I am still not myself."

Her arm hurt, and she shifted the book from one hand to the other, and the sound outside was louder. She pushed back the covers. She had turned ten pages without reading one, she thought as she put the book down on her bedside table, beside the ugly cut-crystal water carafe. It had been so like her mother to think that it would be grand for every room to have one and to ship them from the city, but to save on the cost by buying something square and graceless. The right instincts, the wrong execution. Lydia sighed. How deep the training of a lifetime, that she could still note something so mean and unimportant.

She opened the front door and the breeze blew back against her, warm for an October night. The clouds had blown away and there was a full moon throwing a great blocky house shadow across the grass and turning the surface of the water into a mirror reflecting the willow trees. She pulled on her father's old shooting jacket, tied a scarf around her hair against the wind, and walked slowly across the grass in her house slippers until she was standing by the little boat and could hear the cry echoing off the mountains. It was human, she was certain of it now, and when she considered that that wretched girl, who hadn't even had a tissue to mop her streaming nose, might have brought the baby back yet again, she was filled not with the disapproval she ought to have felt but with happiness that things might be as they had been, the occasional picnic, the well-groomed lawn, her coffee made, her days fuller.

"Jennifer," she would say, "find Charles and tell him I have a surprise for him."

She picked her way around the ragged edges of the pond, a few frogs unafraid of early frost leaping from beneath her feet in terror, but the more she followed the sound the farther away it seemed. The fat grass carp moved darkly just beneath the surface, their backs breaking the water, and she could hear the whispery night noises that came from nocturnal animals crouched low and moving through the high grasses in the fields.

By the time she had gotten to the far end of the pond, there was a roaring sound in her ears, like the inside of the old pink conch her mother had used for a doorstop on the long screened porch, and she could no longer be certain from which direction the crying came. There were the two old Adirondack chairs in the spot where the spring came in, so that her father could sit when he was tired from fly casting. "Lyds," he would say, patting the one beside him, "come keep an old boy company." Those chairs had been in this same spot for nearly eighty years; one set would rot, their nails giving way, the slats bowing, and be replaced by another that was exactly the same, and it would no more occur to her to change this arrangement than it had occurred to her that she could leave Blessings whenever she wanted to and start fresh. She dropped into one of the chairs heavily.

Overhead the moon was a bright silver disk. "Like a new dime," Sunny had said one night when they were floating in the little boat. "The moon is so much better than the sun." She had never again known anyone who would think to say such a thing. The moon is so much better than the sun. She wished she could climb into the boat now and feel the almost imperceptible landlocked tide of the Blessings pond. She had loved it so as a child, the little village steeped in deep green: the trout glowing like stained glass with their colored scales, the turtles floating spread-eagled in the shelter of the plants, the carp pulling weed free and munching like cows, the curious goggle-eyed bass. All of them were there now yet she could see nothing but black and silver reflections, hear nothing but that inchoate cry, feel nothing but an ache in her heart. She would rest and then she would find the child and all would be well again. She would arrange things so they would be as they had been. She tilted her head back to the new dime above her, her eyes dazzled. It was better than the sun because you could stare it in the face. A fish broke the surface, a bat swooped low by the dock, and an hour later the loon that had been crying insistently all night from the fen behind her flew low over the chair where she sat, but she could no longer see him.

Meredith Fox had been sitting in one of the old Adirondack chairs when Skip came down the driveway. She was so still, so settled, that he wondered for a moment if she'd been in that exact same spot ever since the funeral. Well, not a funeral exactly, the way he thought of a funeral. There had been no hearse, and no limousine, and no cemetery, just Meredith and her husband in the old Cadillac. A parade of dark sedans had pulled up to the old stone church, and from the cars had emerged a parade of small wizened women in black suits, women who had borne some ineffable resemblance to Mrs. Blessing herself. He had heard them murmuring to Meredith on the sidewalk afterward, parsing family trees: this one was the sister of a boy who had gone to school with Meredith's father, that one had been at someplace called Bertram's a year ahead of Mrs. Blessing. Afterward they had come to the house for sandwiches and iced tea. He had not gone to the lunch. It didn't feel right. But Mrs. Fox had called him at work after the lunch and asked him to come over.

"You," said Nadine, coming out of the kitchen door to stand on the back steps as he parked the truck.

"Yep," he said.

"She out there," she said, pointing, wiping her hands on a faded dish towel. He supposed Mrs. Fox was the *she* around Blessings now.

Coming at her head-on down the lawn he could see all the ways in which Meredith Fox was like her mother, not so much the facial features, which were softer, less sharp, but the upright posture, the way she laid her hands on the armrests of the chair, the set of her squared shoulders. She smiled at him, squinting against the sun, and rose to shake his hand.

"Sit," she said, not in that familiar peremptory way but as though they had known each other a long time.

"This is where Nadine found her," Meredith said, looking out over the pond. "I can only imagine the scene. Nadine says she called Dr. Benjamin right away, but I'm assuming she yelled at her for a while to get her to get up."

"People say it was a stroke."

Meredith shrugged and smoothed her hair back from the deep V at the center of her forehead. "I suppose. It doesn't really mean much to me, one way or another. She was eighty years old, and she'd outlived everyone she loved. Her father, her brother, her best friend. She still had all her faculties. I never had to try to discuss a retirement home with her. Actually I never would have dared to try to discuss a retirement home with her. And she seemed happier these last few months than she had been in ages."

"I feel really bad. I was so mad about what happened, the police and Faith and all the other stuff. I wouldn't talk to her the last time I saw her. I blamed her for everything."

"I used to do that, too, but I got over it," Meredith said. "Don't torture yourself. You brought her a lot of happiness. And she probably understood how you felt better than you did yourself. No one understood righteous indignation better than Mother. She was in a temper the entire time I knew her. If it wasn't a broken storm window, it was a blown fuse in the garage. And of course she was always outraged that a person painted the house, and then twenty years later you had to paint it again. I couldn't get over how you persuaded her to fix the roof of the barn."

"I didn't have to do much."

"She liked you."

"I don't know. I think she liked keeping the place up."

"No, she liked you. You got her out of herself for the first time in years. Since her friend Jess died, I think. She liked you, and she liked Nadine's daughter. Is it all over town, what she did for that girl?"

"Pretty much."

"She was furious that Nadine wanted to keep her here in Mount Mason. She said the girl wanted to be a doctor, and that her mother was standing in her way, trying to keep her prisoner here in town. I suppose one of the primary obstacles was money. So Mother left Jennifer the money to go to medical school. Mother told me about it last year. I couldn't figure out whether it was a gesture designed to provide a better life for that young woman, or whether she just wanted to spite Nadine."

"I think maybe it was a little bit of both. She sure succeeded on the Nadine front."

"Nadine cried at the funeral. Sometimes it's difficult to figure people out, isn't it." She sighed. "I'm so sorry about your baby," she added, patting Skip's hand.

"I'm so sorry about your mother."

"She was sorry about you, too, about what happened. She called to tell me and I've never heard her so regretful. And my mother scarcely ever expressed regret. I'm still not certain why she seemed to have gotten such a kick out of that baby. I've never known her to show the slightest affinity for babies."

"I think it just made a change, you know? She sort of liked the drama. We had to keep it a secret, from Nadine, and I think she liked that. And from you, too, for as long as we could. Sorry about that."

"It's all right. Of course you didn't succeed on either count. Nadine knew almost from the beginning. She used to call me all the time. She said she knew about the baby in the beginning because when you carried her around strapped to your chest you looked just like she'd looked when she carried Jennifer around her village when Jennifer was born. I suppose it wasn't popular to get pregnant by an American soldier, so she tried to hide her child in the beginning, until apparently she decided she just didn't give a damn."

"Whoa. Whoa. We thought we'd fooled her the whole time. Jennifer did, too. Whoa. That is so strange."

"No, she knew. And she heard you on the baby monitor one day when my mother left it on by her bed. Some people like to keep secrets. My mother was one of them. Speaking of which, did Mr. Patton call you?"

Skip shook his head. Mrs. Fox smiled. "Well, then, here's a nice surprise. She left you a life interest in the garage."

"The garage?"

"I know, it's crazy, isn't it? She left you all its contents and the right to live there for the rest of your life. She had Lester Patton work out the language a couple of weeks ago." She looked over at him with her eyebrows raised. "I have to admit, it's going to make it good and hard to sell this place."

"You're not going to keep it?"

"For what?"

"For you. For the family."

Meredith Fox looked back over the pond. "The family is gone. I'm the last," she said.

"I'm sorry. I didn't know that. I remember now that she told us you didn't have any children."

"I'm sure she did," she said with a tight smile, and then he saw her mother in her face, and in her eyes, blue marbles with a rim of steel gray. Then she shrugged and grinned and that look was gone. "My husband and I had dogs and horses and it seemed to be enough. And we have a place in Virginia that is perfectly situated for both the dogs and the horses. I don't want to live here. It doesn't feel right to me. I remember my grandfather with this place. The whole enterprise had an air of unreality, and of failure, somehow. He bought cows. What in the world did he know about cows? Or the corn he had somebody plant one summer? I was only a child when he died, and I went away to school when I was young. I don't think I spent more than a month at a time here after that. I can't imagine who will want a place this large. There are eight bedrooms, and the furnace must be fifty years old. Maybe someone who wants to open a bed-and-breakfast, who will be haunted by my mother for putting samplers and stencils in the kitchen. Maybe someone like my grandfather, who wants to come out from the city on weekends and play gentleman farmer. Or a big family that likes privacy. I suppose I would like someone to be happy here."

"I was happy here."

"That's wonderful. And still will be, I hope."

"I don't think I'm going to want to live in the garage for the rest of my life."

"Don't forget its contents. You're the heir to a rider mower, twenty shovels, a rototiller, a Cadillac, and about fifty boxes of junk that are in the attic."

"I can have the Cadillac?"

She laughed then, a deep belly laugh of the sort that he'd never heard from Mrs. Blessing and didn't imagine anyone ever had, that made him think that her father must have been a different sort of man than he looked in the picture of him in his uniform in the living room, with his soft mouth and weak chin. "No wonder she liked you," she said. "The car is yours. The mower, too. If you're amenable, we'll pay you to clean out the garage and work out a lump sum for your life share in the rental."

"You can just have it."

"Oh, no. Mother would haunt me forever. She'll haunt me in any event, but it would be a double haunting if I took your garage away from you."

Meredith cared about the old house more than she thought she did, as Skip had discovered people often do. There had been a box of linen baby clothes, as creased as Mrs. Blessing's face had been, and a tattered collection of old children's picture books that he had carried over to the big house from the garage. She had put labels on those boxes so they would be sent to her home in Virginia, and packed up with them most of the photographs from the living room and the chenille spread that had been on Mrs. Blessing's bed. When she wasn't sitting by the pond he had seen her through the windows of the house, moving from room to room with a pad of paper and a sheet of stickers, putting a yellow circle on a dresser here, a chair there, so that the movers could ship some things to her and send the others to the auction house in New York City she had told him about. Midday Jennifer had come with a big bag, and he had seen the light on in the side porch and known that the two of them were having lunch together, talking across the table as each of them had once done with Mrs. Blessing. There was an oil painting over the fireplace in the library of dark and tangled trees hanging low over swampy ground beneath a threatening yellow sky. Mrs. Blessing had left that to Jennifer, along with the small desk at which she had always sat to do her correspondence and enough certificates of deposit to pay for college and medical school.

"So you're finally going away to college," Skip said when Jennifer came out to put the big painting in its gilt frame into the back of her little car.

She shook her head. "Not until next year. I'll finish this year at the community college, then probably transfer to State and finish my pre-med credits. I'll be around. I'll buy you lunch. I guess everyone figures I can afford it now. Is everyone talking about me?"

"Yep."

"I'm used to it. Besides, I think that was the point, to stir the pot."

"I think the point was to let you do what you want." Skip thought for a moment. "And probably to stir the pot, too."

"So can I take you to lunch?"

"Maybe," Skip said.

"It would be weird without her," Jennifer said, and almost as fast as a baby's smile she had started to sob. Skip put his arms around her and patted her shoulder and that reminded her, too, so that for a moment she cried harder. When she pulled back she was smiling. "I guess when we say 'her' now we mean both *hers,* don't we?"

"I guess so," he said.

"Do you miss her?"

"Which one?"

Jennifer Foster wiped her eyes. "It was a stupid question, anyway. Never ask a question that you already know the answer to."

"How are your parents taking all this?" Skip said.

"What did I just say? Never ask a question that you already know the answer to."

Did he miss her? That wasn't how it felt, not like something fine and fond, edged in gold like those plates Mrs. Blessing had that made the high ringing sound. Sometimes the sound of the car engine, or the dying drone of the crickets beneath the deepening carpet of leaves, or just the no-sleep buzz in his brain, lulled him into a sense that nothing had changed. Morning meant grinding coffee and filling bottles. Noon meant the flash of binoculars from the big house and the long nap in the crib over the garage. One benefit of an ordered life was that the order took on a life of its own, so that he could almost imagine things remained the same, governed not by happenstance or even fate but by the regular movement of the hands of his old alarm clock.

But there were also the mornings when he woke up in the apartment over Foster's garage to the sensation of confusion, the sensation that he had imagined something so terrible that it could not be true. And then the swaddling of sleep was swept aside, and there was a sharp ugly thing that took shape in seconds under his breastbone, so that he felt all the time as though he'd been stabbed. No food would pass it, and it was all he could do to breathe. There were pale blue shadows beneath his eyes, and his walk had become stooped without his knowing it. He was not even certain which loss he was feeling, or whether it was the two together that made him feel as though he were swimming through sludge in his sleep, dreaming through the daylight hours, half-alive.

He hadn't imagined, over those long slow satisfying summer

days, that he would ever thank God that he wouldn't be coming to Blessings ever again. But he felt it now, coming down the drive, making the turn, taking the steps into the apartment, looking out over the curled confetti of browned black walnut leaves on the grass by the pond. Someone needed to rake those, but it wouldn't be him. All he had left to do was to go through the things in the garage attic and decide what he wanted to keep. "The garage and its contents." He figured it would wind up meaning mainly the tools and the car and that old upholstered chair that had gotten to know the contours of his body.

But once he got into the attic he realized he was heir to a treasure trove of old suits, broken chairs, water-stained books, and dozens of boxes. He was going to have to go through everything and decide what Mrs. Fox might want to keep, what could be given away, and what was still good enough to be sold in New York. The apartment already had the dusty air of a place where no one lives. Before he'd even arrived someone had put the crib away and left the small folded blankets on the chest of drawers in the back bedroom. He could picture Nadine banging around and shaking her head, her black hair bouncing with indignation. "You don't want to be anywhere near my house," Craig Foster had said grimly. Skip was working long hours and Craig was working them, too, working every night until eight or nine, trying to keep from stepping in between two stubborn pissed-off women set at odds by a third, now dead.

Skip put pieces of masking tape on the few things he thought he could get down the stairs of the garage and up the stairs to the apartment over Foster's auto body shop. Maybe he could rent one of those storage places for the long oak table that would be good in a kitchen, if he ever had a kitchen. The boxes by the window he figured he would bring down for Mrs. Fox. He could see by the few that were opened that they were filled with old things that ought to stay with her, family photographs and knickknacks and some clothes that looked as though they'd been folded away in another lifetime.

The big stack of sealed boxes were in shadow against one of

the long sloping windowless walls. They had those old-fashioned mailing labels, pretty really, with curved corners and frames of red faded now to pink. "Simpson's Fine Textiles," the labels said in script. He took a box cutter and split the center join of one. There was a thick bolt of some pale purple material with gold flowers. The next box had white fabric with pin dots of pale blue. Then there was dark green velvet, and some stuff that he'd seen before but didn't know the name of with streaks all through it like water had run up and down the length. He picked that up and looked beneath.

"Holy shit," he said aloud.

There were seventeen boxes, and when he was done going through them all he found that he had seventeen bolts of assorted fabrics and what seemed, on first count, to be something in the neighborhood of seventy thousand dollars in old twenty-dollar bills. The strange thing was that only two of the boxes had been opened before, and none of them appeared to have been touched. He went downstairs and had a soda and a tuna sandwich he'd brought from the lunch place on Main Street, counted again, ate a package of Sno Balls, counted again, and changed the oil in the rider mower.

"Holy shit," he said, sitting in the mower with one foot on the garage floor to steady him. It occurred to him that Mrs. Blessing would have been appalled at how much swearing she'd occasioned, and then that maybe she would have been amused without ever admitting it. "What the hell was she thinking?"

He sounded just like Jennifer's father. Skip had taken the old Cadillac to Craig Foster's garage first thing in the morning, figuring he could work on the Caddy during his lunch hour, maybe trade in his truck. "I still can't figure out what she was thinking," Craig had said, first thing, when Skip drove in. "I never would have believed it in a million years."

"That she left me the Cadillac?"

"You know what I'm talking about. I never would have believed it." He'd said it at least twenty times during the course of the first workday after the will was filed for probate.

"How come?" Skip had said.

"How come? How come? Do you know how much money she left that child? Do you know what it costs to go to a private college and a medical school? That's a hell of a lot of money. Excuse my French, but that's a whole hell of a lot of money. You seem to have gotten on with the woman better than anyone except Jenny. What the hell do you think she was thinking?"

Craig Foster was a deacon of the Presbyterian church, a man who drank lemonade at picnics and called women "ma'am" and once fired a guy who hung a girlie calendar in his car-repair shop, even though car-repair shops were more or less the official home of girlie calendars. He'd said *hell* more in that day than in the last five years put together.

"I think she really liked Jennifer."

"I like you. I gave you a job and a place to live at a decent rent. I didn't give you a small fortune."

"Maybe she didn't think it was a small fortune. She had a lot of money."

"Son, excuse me, but the woman was as tight as a tick, as my grannie used to say. The reason I didn't work on that car of hers is because the one time I did, I charged her a hundred forty-four dollars for a battery, which as you know is the cost to me. She said I was gouging her. Now she's left the girl enough to buy a battery company, except that she can't spend it on anything except her education. You know what people in town are saying about that? They're saying Nadine exerted undue influence. Undue influence."

And at that Skip had started to laugh. He laughed and laughed and couldn't stop, and when he'd try to get ahold of himself he would have a mental picture of Mrs. Blessing sitting straight as a stick in the wing chair and Nadine fuming and the two of them talking to each other as though they'd been the leading edge of a full-fledged family feud for fifty years. Every time Mr. Foster repeated the words *undue influence* he would start to laugh some more, until he found tears running down his face. He was glad Mr. Foster was there because he knew that if he had been alone he would have finally given way, and his broken heart would have spilled out, down his face, into his scarred and greasy hands, where he would have had to really look at it for the first time. He couldn't stand to do that yet, couldn't stand to glance at a baby in the grocery or see one on the television or remember for even an instant how Faith had smelled and the way she wrapped her little fingers around his big one as he fed her. He'd had a lifetime of little bad things, but a big bad one felt entirely different, worse than he could let himself feel all at once. And he'd had two big bad things right on top of each other, because when he thought of Faith he thought of that old woman, too, and the way she held her head up in a way that had convinced him, just for a while, that dignity was not only possible but simple. He'd loved them both.

So as he'd wiped the tears from his face, pretending they were the laughing kind, making half-moons of streaky black in old motor oil beneath his eyes, he said only, "I still don't know why, but I really liked that old lady."

"Well, I get your point, but I can't imagine what she was thinking. It's a small fortune, any way you look at it."

"I think she liked people to be able to do what they wanted to do," he'd finally told Mr. Foster at the garage.

"Well, that just isn't the way the world works," Craig Foster had said.

This isn't the way the world works, Skip thought to himself as he got off the rider mower, went back upstairs, and looked into the boxes again. That much money didn't look real somehow, the way money in the movies never did, or that trick money they'd sold in the five-and-dime when they were kids, that you were supposed to leave on the sidewalk and jerk away when someone bent to pick it up. Maybe that was why he kept leaving and coming back, because he was waiting for the jerking-away part. Dusk was slowly coming down on the back end of the property, the automatic outdoor light had snapped itself on, and the edges of everything in the attic were blurred, so that the opened boxes looked like they contained nothing but gray shadows, their promise evaporating with the light. The only thing still clear in the room was an old straw hat that sat atop a bureau, so pale gold it almost seemed alight in the gloom, like the little boat on the surface of the pond that he could see from the attic dormer, Mrs. Fox sitting in it in the center of the pond with the oars splayed on either side.

He heard a sound, the sound of a car door slamming, and Mrs. Fox's head came up slowly, as though she'd been sitting in the boat thinking and been brought back to life by the sharp noise. When he got to the foot of the apartment steps there was a figure he didn't recognize at first, her back to the day's last light outside, and then he saw that it was that girl. That bitch, that witch, that things-so-bad-I-can't-put-them-into-words girl, that girl Paula, that he swore he would never call a mother in his mind. Paula Benichek, pulling at a strand of hair along her face and looking down at her shoes, then up at him, then down again. His heart swelled and then dropped again as he saw her empty arms.

"I remember those steps outside," she said.

He felt foolish being kind to her, but he couldn't figure any other way to be, and he couldn't figure anything she could possibly be there for except for kindness. He'd built her up into something so bad over the last few days, and then she was just a girl, aimless, quiet, a little lost. He showed her the room in which he had slept with Faith, and the wagon hookup to the mower in which he'd laid her down, and the front pack in which she'd slept while he mowed the lawn. It wasn't much to show, really, and it made him realize how little of the baby's life had been lived with him. He had a book that said they couldn't even tell the difference between you and other people before eight months. That's what he told the girl now, and as he said it he felt himself becoming invisible in the child's life, like the dawn mist on the pond that burned off by full morning.

She was wearing silver hoop earrings and she played with them nervously, as though she had come for something but it was not what he was giving her. She had a small nose with a bump on the bridge, and her eyes were a little far apart, and she was growing out one of those ill-considered hair colorings he was always surprised girls undertook, so that she had pale brown roots and slightly reddish ends. He wondered if Mrs. Blessing had noticed that. She wouldn't have liked that much. Her nails were bitten, too.

"I never actually had the chance to say thank you," she finally said, sitting in the chair in his living room, looking out over the pond, its outlines soft in the light of a half-moon.

"Anybody would have done the same."

"I still can't believe I really did it. It was such a stupid thing to do. It just seemed at the time—like, I don't know, like we could undo what was done."

"I guess not," he said.

"My mother is so into her. She's thinking of working part-time so she can be home with her more. And I'm staying home and just taking a couple of classes for a year or two. Or whatever. I'm not sure yet."

"What about her father?"

She made a small disdainful pained sound. "Don't ask," she said. "Jerk."

"Asshole."

"It'll be okay. She's a really good baby. Everybody said so." He couldn't believe he was being so nice, and then he realized that that, too, was his only choice. This was Faith's mother. This was Faith's future. He felt a shiver through his shoulders.

The girl didn't notice. She was picking at a cuticle. Mrs. Blessing wouldn't have liked that, either. "It's just a lot of work, you know," she finally said. "I don't think my friends really get that. Like, you can't just get in the car and go to the mall. There's the car seat, and the diaper bag, and then you have to bring the stroller. You can't just go wherever you want, you know? Yeah, I guess you do know. I guess I sound incredibly stupid and selfish saying all this stuff to you, of all people."

"You'll get used to it. It's only been a couple of weeks."

"I guess. My mother keeps bugging me about names. I think I'm going to call her Samantha."

"That's one of those soap-opera names."

"Well, what did you call her?"

"They didn't tell you that? Faith. Her name is Faith."

"I never even heard of anyone named Faith."

"That's her name," he said, and his voice was harder now.

He walked her back downstairs. Upstairs in the closet was the box, and the flannel shirt, and the barrette, and a T-shirt that said "Daddy's Girl" that Jennifer had gotten at the mall, and a dried piece of clover Faith had pulled from the lawn with her fist, and six disposable cameras full of pictures. And he realized that he wasn't going to give any of it away. It was little enough for him to have. Soon the smell would wash out of his shirts, the feel evaporate from his hands. And it would be all he would have left. Maybe from the beginning he'd always known that. Maybe every picture was a way of saying *click click,* bye bye. I will love you forever.

Outside she turned, a little breathless, and said, "I didn't really come to unload all my problems on you. I just wanted to tell you that I'll come by and see you sometimes and bring her with me. Like visitation, you know, maybe once or twice a month. You guys could hang out. She could play with you. I could even leave her with you so I wouldn't be in the way."

"You'll be all right."

"So can I bring her by soon? Just for a visit?"

He shook his head. "I don't think that's a good idea. It might confuse her. Kids need to understand who's who, you know?"

"But if I were around here anyway?"

He shook his head. "I won't be here much longer."

"What are you going to do?"

"I'm not a hundred percent sure, but I think I'm going to buy myself a little house somewhere." And as he said it he knew that it was true. He had money. He would buy himself a house. Maybe he'd start a business. Landscaping. That would be good. He could do what he'd done here, mow and prune and trim and keep things alive and thriving. Cuddy Landscaping. No tree too tall. No lawn too wide.

"What?" he said to Paula Benichek, and in his head he heard a voice say, "Charles, the phrase is 'pardon me?'"

"I said, where are you going to buy a house? Like in California someplace? Or Florida? A lot of my friends want to move to Florida."

He shook his head. "Somewhere around here. I like it here."

She looked sullen when she got in the car, as though things hadn't turned out the way she wanted. Maybe she was one of those girls who always looked that way. Skip had known a lot of them. He hoped Faith didn't turn out to be one. A year ago he would have taken the turned-down set of this girl's mouth, her ragged nails and narrowed eyes, as an omen, a prediction of the future, sure as Boatwrights begat more Boatwrights. But look at Jennifer Foster, or Meredith Fox. Look at Skip Cuddy, who'd managed to do for four months with a baby he found in a box what his father, as far as he knew, hadn't managed in his whole life. Most people turned out the way you would expect. But not all. Not by a long shot.

"Just look at her, you know?" he said, leaning in the car window. "Look at her like she's not yours, like you've never seen her before. She does all these amazing things. And they change all the time. I mean, watching her just move her arms and legs is one of the coolest things you can do."

She shrugged. "So if you cared about her so much, why did you give her up?"

"I didn't give her up. You gave her up. I gave her back."

I n the late afternoon of November 2 Meredith Fox sat on the front porch of the big house at Blessings. She had asked Skip to leave the two rockers on either side of the front door, and she used her heel to push herself back and forth in one of them now, in a rhythm that still, after all these years, she found disproportionately soothing. The rocker creaked monotonously. The black walnut trees had dropped all their leaves, and the oak trees were following. The yellow and gold mums around the pathways were browning slightly now.

When the real estate agent arrived Meredith would have to go inside the house, but she would not do so until then. She had been inside empty houses in the past. She had walked through the big house near the water in Newport after her Carton grandparents had died within six months of each other. There was a weight to the emptiness of rooms in which you had once lived that was more fearsome than anything she had ever encountered in life, not because they were haunted, as she had joked with Skip Cuddy, but because they were not. The conversations, the quarrels, the long fraught silences, the tears: they had disappeared utterly and completely. A cemetery was a place intended to be still. It was here, where once there had been life, that death was felt most profoundly.

She remembered that once she had asked her mother why she had stopped her nightly circuit around the pond, down the back drive, to the barn and through the fields. And when she heard herself mention the barn and saw the set of her mother's chin she had understood, and had said softly, "It's been more than ten years, Mother. I doubt very much that Uncle Sunny would haunt you."

"I don't believe in ghosts," her mother had replied, with both a chill and a tremor in her voice.

Now she knew what her mother had meant. The dead deserted you; there were ghosts only among the living. Meredith was a knowing person, had always been. As a child she had been so well behaved that adults often forgot she was in the next room, and in this way she had known a good many things that she realized later in life her mother had assumed were a mystery to her. She had known that the parents of some of her friends at school were disdainful of her Blessing relations and she had known that the parents of her few friends in Mount Mason were awestruck by them. She had heard her uncle called a pansy in various conversations, and her mother a recluse. Mrs. Foster had let her slip upstairs to the attic above the garage when her mother was in a temper, and it was there, in a box filled with silk and satin dresses with long narrow skirts, that she had found her parents' marriage license and later worked out that her mother must have already been pregnant when the two of them had married before her father went overseas. Her husband said there was a secret at the heart of every family. In his it had been that there was no money, that the enormous house in Winnetka in which he'd grown up had nine bedrooms and five of them had not a stick of furniture within. If someone wandered into one of those rooms at a party his mother had always explained that she had been unable to stand the wallpaper, the dust skirt, the bed, and the dresser one moment more and had ordered the room redecorated. "I don't think she fooled a soul," he'd said to Meredith with a laugh.

She supposed she'd always known that part of her secret was her parents' marriage, that it was a ghost in the house. "Nana, do you think my mother and father loved each other very very much?" she had asked her grandmother Carton one day, and the woman's eyes had filled and she had taken her onto her lap, although she was really too big to sit there any longer.

"Has your mother ever married again? Does she go into town and dine with men? Has she had anyone come to the house to stay?"

When she shook her head her grandmother's scent, a perfume called Arpege that Meredith wore herself now on special occasions, had risen faintly around them, like a memory.

"Well, then, my love, you have your answer, don't you?"

There was the lesson of her life: fidelity was all. She had realized later that it was not really the answer to her question, that her grandmother had made certain that she did not answer it directly, but addressed only a larger, apparently more important theme. Her mother had been the most faithful of daughters, wives, sisters, frozen in the amber of this beautiful hidden forgotten place.

"One of the girls at school asked why my name is Carton and your name is Blessing," she had said at lunch one day with her mother's friend Jess and two of her daughters. Chicken salad, iced tea, pound cake. Her mother's company lunch. Fidelity.

"I am amazed at the way in which people think they can comment on one another's business," her mother had replied.

"Oh, Lydia, for heaven's sake," Jess had said. "What sort of an answer is that? Here's the truth, Merry: this house has been called Blessings and your mother has been Lydia Blessing for so many years that a place like Mount Mason simply can't master the change. And it's not just her. There are still shopkeepers in town who call me Jessie Thornton, and I haven't been Jessie Thornton in fifteen years. And I would bet you if my house were called Thorntons I'd never get called anything else. Tell your friend at school that your mother has taken up permanent residence in a place where absolutely nothing ever changes."

"She's not really my friend," Meredith had said.

"I would imagine not," her mother had replied.

Oh, yes, there were ghosts in the house then: the ghost of her grandmother's palpable disdain for her grandfather, the ghost of her grandfather's prep-school bonhomie, the nameless faceless spirits of her father and the marriage and Uncle Sunny's moods and her mother's disapproval. She remembered when the guests had come and gone, and the ghosts of their whisperings and their grunts and moans. It had been a peculiar place to be a child.

"Marry that man!" Jess had said the Friday after the Thanksgiving she had brought Eric home, when he was out shooting clays by the creek with Jess's husband and sons.

"That's a hasty judgment," her mother had said coolly.

"Oh, Lydie, for pity's sake. Have you looked at her face when she's looking at him?"

"Oh, that." How had she known exactly what her mother meant in just those two words? Was it because she remembered the date on that marriage license, the counting of the months on her fingers, the effort of trying to imagine Lydia Blessing trapped into doing something that, perhaps, she had not wanted to do, or compelled to do something messy and undignified? Meredith's face had pinked up hotly beneath her auburn hair, mainly because, on the warmish November night when they'd arrived, she and Eric had done the deed, as the girls at college called it, on the back bank of the pond on an old blanket. He had wanted to go to the hayloft of the barn. "Not there," Meredith had told him.

Sometimes she thought her marriage had saved her. There were no ghosts within it, and great peace, and passion, too. She had not meant it to be childless, but she did not mourn the children she had never had, perhaps because, almost without knowing it, she had spent so much time mourning the mother she had never had, and the father, too.

When she had come to stay at her mother's house, when her mother had had that first stroke, she had gone looking for something to read in one of the back bedrooms and found an old set of books called *The Mother's Encyclopedia*. She had pulled them out at random, sitting on the window seat by the shelves, reading homely admonitions about cereal and fresh air and high shoes. Three books in, she had found one section heavily underlined in pencil, a part of "Mother's Job" entitled "Can Love Be Compelled?" She could almost remember the words, could surely remember the sense: "for the mother, poor girl, is frightened at herself for not wanting the baby; she feels that she is a criminal and no one else was ever like her; perhaps she has even wished that it might die, and here it is now, rosy and sweet, kicking its heels and making funny amiable noises at her."

So there it was, the ghost of her mother and herself, the enforced mother, the unwanted child. The sadness she had felt after that day had prepared her for the sadness she felt now, as though she had lost something by inches. After the funeral she had arranged for all the books in that room to be sent to a used-book store in New York.

The real estate agent's car came slowly down the drive. It was a nice car, nicer than Meredith's, which was designed for dragging horse trailers and edging up a snowy drive. They always had nice cars, real estate agents, in the same way the prettiest house in town was always turned into the funeral home. The pond was illuminated now, and the windows so clear that the glare was terrible when the car lights struck it. Skip and Nadine had worked for a week together to leave the place like this. Even the garage was empty now. Eric had helped Skip with the logistics of having a great deal of cash and no knowledge of where to put it or invest it. It was more difficult than you might imagine, to bank that much money in old bills without someone making a fuss.

"They act as though the poor boy has discovered the Lindbergh ransom," her husband had said, walking around the pond with her, holding her hand.

That was another thing she had known: that the money was there. She had known that that boy was a nice boy, but never more so than when he had come to her and told her, like a confession, about all those boxes filled with bills in the attic. "I assume that's what she wanted you to have," she'd said. "That, and the Cadillac." Meredith had found those boxes herself when she was a child, found them on one of those days when Mrs. Foster had let her go up into the attic. But of course it wouldn't do to say anything to her mother, because then there would be questions and accusations and Mrs. Foster would get into trouble and so would she. Meredith had discovered, when she married, that she was wealthy, and, after her grandparents died, that she was rich. Now, of course, she was richer still. She wondered what would happen to all the money when she was gone, the last of the Blessings, the last of the Cartons. Perhaps she would leave some of it to Bertram's, or the hospital in Mount Mason.

The real estate agent was carrying a clipboard and a leather briefcase with gold initials monogrammed on the flap. Her mother had always hated conspicuous monograms. "What sort of person needs to be reminded of his own name?" she always said. She'd tolerate initials embroidered on the cuffs of men's shirts, and the monogram on her linens that was white on white. But gilt? Never.

"Gorgeous," said the real estate agent, a blonde with the eyes and coloring of a brunette. "Absolutely gorgeous. A postcard."

"It is," Meredith said, and meant it. The white house, the striped awnings, the brown barn, the silvery water, the green hills. Everyone who'd ever visited Blessings had felt it was a place apart, including her. When she had scattered her mother's ashes from the little boat in the middle of the pond, she had expected them to glitter in the air the way Sunny's had. But night had fallen by the time she had finally steeled herself to open the box, and the ashes were almost invisible against the darkness as they floated on the surface of the pond, then slowly fell through the water. There had been a heron on the far bank, its blue-gray blending into the lowering night sky, and it had reached out its great strong wings, bent its head toward the earth, and then swept away into the dark. She had raised her head to look at it, and when she had looked back down, the surface of the pond was undisturbed.

"There's no substitute for these mature plantings," said the real estate agent, scanning the rows of chrysanthemums.

"Do you think we should take down the sign at the end of the driveway?" Meredith said to the woman as she opened the front door.

"Why?"

"Well, I'm assuming the place won't be called Blessings anymore."

"No," the woman said. "Leave it where it is. People love the idea of a place with a name."

ABOUT THE AUTHOR

ANNA QUINDLEN is the author of three bestselling novels, *Object Lessons, One True Thing,* and *Black and Blue.* Her *New York Times* column "Public & Private" won a Pulitzer Prize in 1992, and a selection of those columns was published as *Thinking Out Loud.* She is also the author of a collection of her "Life in the 30's" columns, *Living Out Loud;* a book for the Library of Contemporary Thought, *How Reading Changed My Life;* the bestselling *A Short Guide to a Happy Life;* and two children's books, *The Tree That Came to Stay* and *Happily Ever After.* She is currently a columnist for *Newsweek* and lives with her husband and children in New York City.

ABOUT THE TYPE

This book was set in Bembo, a typeface based on an old-style Roman face that was used for Cardinal Bembo's tract *De Aetna* in 1495. Bembo was cut by Francisco Griffo in the early sixteenth century. The Lanston Monotype Company of Philadelphia brought the well-proportioned letterforms of Bembo to the United States in the 1930s.